HER
MOTHER'S
GRAVE

Books featuring Detective Josie Quinn

Vanishing Girls
The Girl with No Name
Her Mother's Grave
Her Final Confession
The Bones She Buried
Her Silent Cry
Cold Heart Creek
Find Her Alive

Books featuring Claire Fletcher and Detective Parks

Finding Claire Fletcher
Losing Leah Holloway

Books featuring Jocelyn Rush

Hold Still
Cold Blooded

Other books by Lisa Regan

Kill For You

HER MOTHER'S GRAVE

LISA REGAN

GRAND CENTRAL
PUBLISHING

New York Boston

Grand Central Publishing
Hachette Book Group
1290 Avenue of the Americas, New York, NY 10104
grandcentralpublishing.com
twitter.com/grandcentralpub

Originally published by Bookouture in 2018.
Bookouture, an imprint of StoryFire Ltd., Carmelite House, 50 Victoria Embankment, London EC4Y 0DZ

First Grand Central Publishing Edition: November 2020

Grand Central Publishing is a division of Hachette Book Group, Inc. The Grand Central Publishing name and logo is a trademark of Hachette Book Group, Inc.

The publisher is not responsible for websites (or their content) that are not owned by the publisher.

The Hachette Speakers Bureau provides a wide range of authors for speaking events. To find out more, go to www.hachettespeakersbureau.com or call (866) 376-6591.

Library of Congress Control Number: 2020935809

ISBN: 978-1-5387-0124-9 (Trade paperback)

Printed in the United States of America

LSC-C

10 9 8 7 6 5 4 3 2 1

For my brother, Andrew Brock,
for showing me you can always rewrite your own story!

PROLOGUE

She started the fire in the nursery. Her lips curved into a smile as amber flames licked the walls and spread throughout the room, consuming the perfectly matching furniture and the carpet from which she'd spent so many hours scrubbing invisible marks. The gossamer crib canopy she painstakingly arranged every day went up in a satisfying whoosh. *Don't wake the babies. Don't go in there till the children are up. Don't, don't, don't.* This'll teach her.

As the air thickened and began burning her nose and throat, she backed out of the room. Tendrils of thick, black smoke slipped around the edges of the door, coating the ceiling and chasing her out into the hallway. She used her forearm to cover her mouth as she ran. Soon the flames would rage through the house, burning up every fancy thing that spiteful, snobby bitch owned. It was going to be wonderful.

She fled downstairs, stopping to hold a match to the heavy drapes and valances that adorned each window in the living and dining rooms until the taste of fire in her throat became unbearable. She made her way to the kitchen, intending to leave through the back door before she was caught. She was never supposed to set foot in the house again after they'd accused her of stealing.

She was halfway there when a glimpse of something in the family room stopped her dead in her tracks. A frisson of excitement spiraled inside her. Here was something even more destructive than fire, a way to bring down that bitch for good. The grin spread further across her face as she darted into the room, hands outstretched.

CHAPTER 1

PRESENT DAY

Six-month-old Harris Quinn giggled from his high chair as the small plastic pot of pureed baby peas hit the kitchen floor with a splat, covering Josie's sneakers with drab green mush. Startled, Josie took one look at his little food-covered face and laughed too; it was impossible to get mad at him. Plucking a paper towel from above the sink, she bent to clean the mess from the floor, muttering "Rookie mistake" to Harris, who banged his palms against the tray in delight. Throwing things on the floor and watching Josie pick them up was his new favorite game.

Dumping the clump of paper towels into the garbage can, she turned back to see Harris's pea-covered little fists pressed into his eyes for just a moment. Josie looked at the clock on Misty's microwave. "Time for a nap, little man," she told him.

She looked around her for any further traces of food on the floor or walls of Misty Derossi's immaculate home. It wasn't often that she asked Josie to look after her son, but every once in a while, if Harris's grandmother wasn't available, she would get the call. Josie looked forward to these rare visits and didn't want to jeopardize her status as one of Harris's trusted babysitters by leaving a mess for his mother.

Grabbing a cloth from the sink, she cleaned Harris's face and hands as he squirmed and wailed in protest. "All done," she announced as she unfastened the straps of the high chair and lifted him out of it, marveling at how big he had grown in such a short amount of time. She could still remember the first time she had held him, pinned against her chest after rescuing him from the deathly cold currents of the Susquehanna River. He had only been a few days old then, tiny, frail, and lucky to be alive. Now he was chunky and solid, his blond locks growing thicker each day, with a real personality beginning to emerge.

Now that Harris was older, Josie enjoyed making him giggle, watching him spread his meals across his rosy cheeks, cleaning him up and then falling asleep together in the rocking chair that Josie had bought for Misty. It was one of only a handful of modern pieces of furniture in the house, and completely out of place in the sitting room, which looked as though it had been torn from the pages of *Victorian Homes* magazine.

Harris rested his head on Josie's shoulder as she settled there now, using her feet to gently rock the chair back and forth. From the cloth pocket beside her, Josie pulled out one of Harris's pacifiers, which he reached for greedily. Shifting him a little lower so that his cheek rested on her chest, Josie stroked his hair until he slipped into a deep sleep. There was nothing quite like this feeling, she thought as she began to doze off herself.

The digitized beat of her cell phone broke into the silence, and Josie's eyes snapped open, alert and searching. The sound was muffled and coming from the other side of the room, where her jacket was slung over the back of the couch. If it was important, whoever it was would call back. Looking down at Harris, she was relieved to find him undisturbed, his pacifier teetering just on the edge of his bottom lip, about to fall. A pool of dribble fanned across her T-shirt below his head. Josie smiled, running her hand up and down his back and nudging the chair into a gentle rocking motion. The phone stopped ringing, and she closed her eyes again. If it was a true emergency, Lieutenant Noah Fraley and Detective Gretchen Palmer knew where to find her.

She had just drifted back into a warm drowsiness when her phone rang again. This time, Harris stirred. Josie tucked the pacifier back into his mouth as quickly as she could, and he sucked loudly for a moment before crinkling his brow in preparation for what she suspected would be an unhappy howl. She held her breath in anticipation, but his features smoothed and he let out a little sigh instead. Silently, Josie cursed her phone, knowing there was no way to get them both across the room to her jacket without waking him. Not that it mattered—a moment later she heard the front door open and close, and Misty's voice called out, "I'm home!"

Harris stirred again, eyes scrunching, pressing his face into Josie's chest as Misty's voice drifted in from the hallway. "Josie? You in the living room?"

Harris lifted his head, his blue eyes bleary with sleep as he searched the room for his mother. She appeared in the doorway, a huge smile lighting her face at the sight of him. One side of her mouth still drooped, like an invisible finger was drawing it downward, but she had regained a lot more function since the assault she'd survived the day Harris was born. Clapping her hands together, Misty crossed the room and scooped him off Josie's body, cooing and smoothing his wayward locks down. "Hi, baby," she murmured to him. "Did you have a good nap?"

Josie stretched and adjusted her T-shirt. She looked up at Misty. "How did it go?"

Grinning, Misty pointed to her top front teeth. "Got my permanent implant. Feels great. I'm so glad to be done with it."

When she'd had one of her top front teeth knocked out during the attack, she'd been given a temporary crown in the hospital, but it had taken a few months for her to save up the money to have it permanently repaired. Josie had been helping her when she could, but Misty used all the funds Josie gave her for Harris's needs first. Before Harris came along, Misty made a lucrative living dancing at the local strip club, which had enabled her to purchase and furnish her lavish home. She had used her savings for an in vitro procedure to get pregnant with Harris and decided not to return to stripping once she gave birth—even if she wanted to, the injuries she'd sustained placed dancing again firmly outside the realm of possibility.

Josie stood and moved over to the couch, riffling through her pockets to find her cell phone. "Looks good," she told Misty.

Misty shifted Harris from one hip to the other. He rested his head on Misty's shoulder, the pacifier bobbing in his mouth. "Did he eat?"

"Some fruit puffs and a bit of mashed peas. He was more interested in seeing how it looked on the floor."

Misty laughed. "Oh yeah, that's his new thing. No worries. I'll see if he'll take a bottle."

Josie pulled up her missed calls. Both from the same number. Not one she recognized.

"Thank you again," Misty said, although she had thanked Josie about a dozen times before she left for the dentist. "If Mrs. Quinn wasn't so sick, she would have watched him. Some kind of stomach bug."

Josie pulled on her jacket and walked over, patting Harris's back. "No problem. We don't want him catching whatever's going around. You can call me. We're finally finishing up all the paperwork for the district attorney on our last big case, so things are slow."

"That drug dealer, right? Lloyd Todd?"

"More like a kingpin," Josie said.

"Hard to believe he had such a big operation," Misty remarked.

Lloyd Todd had been considered a pillar of the community in the small city of Denton. His general contracting company was one of the busiest and most well-known, but as Josie and her team had found out in the last two months, it had been mostly a front for a large drug-dealing operation. Todd had had nearly two dozen young men and a couple of young women working for him as mules and low-level dealers. He'd been supplying about eighty percent of the city's illegal drugs to needy customers. It was no surprise to Josie that the number of overdoses had gone down sharply after his arrest. Of course, they'd go back up once Todd's customers found their fixes elsewhere.

"It was a shocker," Josie agreed.

Misty followed her through the labyrinth of lavish rooms until they reached the front door. Once on the front porch, Misty said, "Want to stay for lunch?"

It wasn't the first time she had asked Josie to stay a little longer, but while Josie would love to spend more time with the baby, she wasn't sure her relationship with Misty was quite ready for a girls' lunch. It had taken them a long time to reach the civil place they found themselves in now. Several years earlier, when Josie's marriage to her late husband, Ray Quinn, fell apart, he had started an affair with Misty. Ray had cared deeply about Misty, and his dying wish had been for Josie to respect his choice. It was a difficult task, even on her best day. It had taken the assault on Misty and the birth of Ray's son to finally bring the two women together. Still, Josie knew she could be abrasive, even when she tried not to be, and she was afraid the fragile relationship she had developed with Misty would be ruined if they spent more time together. "I have to work," she lied.

Misty's mouth sagged with disappointment, the partial paralysis of her face making the expression even more acute.

Josie felt a prickle of guilt. "Maybe next time."

Misty's gaze dropped to the wooden floorboards. "You always say that. Listen, I know we haven't always gotten along, but I want you to know that I—"

The ring of Josie's cell phone interrupted Misty's speech before it had started. Both women stared down at Josie's jacket pocket. Fishing the phone out, Josie gave Misty a sheepish smile and glanced at the screen. It was the same number as earlier. Desperate to avoid the topic of their reconciliation, Josie quickly swiped answer and pressed the phone to her ear.

"Quinn," she said.

A man's voice answered. "Josie Quinn?"

"Yes. Who is this?"

"I—I—you can call me Roger."

"I can 'call you' Roger? Who is this?"

Hesitation. Then, "I'm calling about your ad. You know, on craigslist?"

A sinking sensation swept through Josie's stomach. She glanced up at Misty, who was looking at her with puzzled concern. Josie stepped off the porch, using her free hand to mimic bringing a phone receiver to her ear and mouthed, "Call if you need anything."

She turned away from Misty and strode to her car, turning her attention back to Roger. "My craigslist ad? Which one was that?"

"Which one?" Roger asked, and again Josie heard more hesitation in his voice. "You don't—do I have the right number?"

"You called me, Roger."

More dead air. Then Roger said, "You don't sound like you're looking for fun."

"Being pranked through craigslist isn't my idea of a good time, Roger."

But Roger had hung up. Josie glanced back toward Misty's house, but she'd gone inside with the baby. With a sigh, Josie got into her Ford Escape and started the engine. She used the internet app on her phone to pull up Denton's craigslist site. It took a couple of minutes of browsing to find the ad. This time it was under Casual Encounters. It had been posted three hours earlier. *Kinky girl seeks playmate—Woman seeking man.*

Dread froze her finger over the screen. She didn't want to read it, didn't want to know what it said, but she had to look. Better to do it now, in the privacy of her vehicle, than to do it at the police station with her lieutenant and detective reading over her shoulder. The first time it happened, her face had taken fifteen minutes to recover from the flush that had reddened her cheeks. She took a deep breath, held it, and pressed the link to the ad.

Looking for some kinky fun. Hot girl early thirties seeking afternoon delight. A tongue so skilled I will never leave you unsatisfied. Always clean, always discreet. Call to hook up.

Below that was Josie's name and cell phone number.

She let out the breath she'd been holding and tossed the phone onto the passenger seat as though it had burned her hand. A movement in one of the windows of Misty's house caught her attention. It was likely Misty peeking from behind the curtain, wondering why Josie was still sitting curbside. Josie pulled away and headed to the police station. It was her day off, but this couldn't wait.

CHAPTER 2

The calls had started just after Lloyd Todd's arrest a month earlier. They were always the result of a craigslist ad that gave her name and cell phone number, some so disgusting and graphic she could barely get through reading them. She'd changed her number three times already. Whoever was writing the ads managed to get hold of her new number each time. She'd tried to figure out how—in fact her entire staff had come under suspicion—but she still couldn't track it. She'd gone to the cell phone store, even gone so far as to bring in the store associates for interrogation, but that lead had fallen flat pretty quickly. Even if someone at the cell phone store was giving out her new number each time she changed it, she had no way of proving it. She'd switched cell carriers after the last ad, but it was now obvious that hadn't worked.

Josie wove through the streets of downtown Denton. Her city was roughly twenty-five square miles, many of those miles spanning the untamed mountains of central Pennsylvania, with their one-lane winding roads, dense woods, and rural residences spread out far and wide. The population was edging over thirty thousand, and it increased when the college was in session, providing plenty of conflict and crime to keep Josie's team of fifty-five pretty busy. She arrived at the police station in only ten minutes, parked in the chief's spot in the municipal parking lot, and went in the front door. Her desk sergeant nodded to her. "Is Lieutenant Fraley here?" she asked him.

He pointed to the ceiling. "Upstairs finishing the paperwork on the Todd case."

"Great," Josie said.

She took the steps two at a time and found Noah at his desk, staring at his computer screen, a gnawed pen hanging from his mouth and his thick brown hair in disarray. Without moving his head, his eyes tracked her. "I hate paperwork," he mumbled, pulling the pen from his mouth. "Did I mention that?"

Josie perched on the edge of his desk. "You might have," she said.

He tossed the pen onto his desk, used his mouse to close out the programs on his computer, and turned his attention to her. Brow furrowed, he said, "What's going on?"

She held up her cell phone. "I got another one."

He glanced at the phone, then stood up, nodding toward her office where they could speak in private. Noah closed the door behind him and already had his notepad out by the time Josie rounded her desk. She plopped into her chair, pulled up the ad on her phone, and read it aloud to him as his pen flew across the page and his face grew increasingly stern. She told him about the call from Roger and rattled off the phone number.

"I'll flag this as prohibited and fax another warrant over to the craigslist offices," Noah said.

Josie sighed. "And that will get us nowhere, just like the last three times."

"But we need to build a case. When we find out who's doing this, we need to have everything in order to be able to put them away."

"We know who's doing it. Lloyd Todd and his legion of assholes."

"Fine, then we need to be prepared to put those assholes away."

"Like we did when they slashed the tires of all the cars in the police lot? Or when they egged the downstairs windows? They're angry because we arrested their boss and took away their drugs, and now they're all unemployed and in withdrawal. They're blowing off steam."

"Directed specifically at you," Noah pointed out.

"Because I'm the one who gets the job of going on TV every time something big or bad happens in this town."

"Yeah," Noah said, smiling. "I know that's your favorite."

She glared at him.

"You should hire a press liaison," he suggested.

Josie rolled her eyes. "We can't afford a press liaison. Just get today's ad taken down, would you?"

"Fine, but I'm faxing over a warrant as well."

"So you can get dummy email addresses and IP addresses that don't help us find the person who's doing this? Knowing the person posted the ads from an IP address somewhere in the city of Denton doesn't exactly narrow it down. Who knew these idiots were so tech-savvy?"

"Last time we narrowed it down to the Starbucks near the college," Noah pointed out.

"Yes," Josie said. "Someone piggybacking on their wifi. We have no idea if that person was even in the store, or if they were in a car or across the street. There was no way to tell from the video footage inside the cafe whether it was one of the patrons. Everyone in that place is on a damn computer or a phone."

"It's still worth looking into," Noah said. "We might catch a break. This is getting serious. I think these craigslist ads rise to a higher level than pranks, Boss."

"Noah."

He stared at her, and she knew what was coming. "Don't even say it," she said.

"Boss, let me put a detail on you. Just until we catch these punks."

"I don't need a detail," Josie said. "Not for this. This is dumb high school shit."

"You've got men calling you for sex."

"Men who think I'm someone I'm not. Believe me, I'm not worried about the Rogers of the world. That guy couldn't even handle a phone call with me. I doubt he's going to try to track me down."

"I'm not worried about Roger," Noah said. His eyes bored into her. "I'm worried about the jerk placing the ads. Are you certain this is coming from Lloyd Todd's camp?"

"Well, I've put a lot of people away as Chief of Police. It could be anyone, but it started after we arrested Todd, after I'd given at least three press conferences. If his lackeys are looking for someone to direct their rage toward, I would be that person. But listen, this is just a nuisance. It hasn't risen to the level of putting a detail on me."

He opened his mouth to speak again, but Josie stopped him with a raised palm. "I'm not ruling out the possibility of a detail—although I can certainly take care of myself—but not now, okay? Right now, I have to go back to the phone store and get my number changed. Again."

He knew her well enough by now not to push her. "Fine," he said. "I'll get to work on this. Text me with your new number."

CHAPTER 3

The Spur Mobile store was completely empty, for which Josie sent up a prayer of thanks. Even more annoying than calls from unwitting men looking for sexual encounters was waiting in line to have her number changed. The disinterested kid behind the counter pulled a pair of headphones from his ears as she approached the counter. He didn't ask many questions, even when he pulled up her account and saw how many times she'd changed numbers in the past month. A half hour later she was all set. Outside in her vehicle, she texted her most important contacts with the new number. Putting a call through to her grandmother, Lisette, she breathed a sigh of relief when it went straight to voicemail; she didn't feel like explaining the craigslist situation, especially not to her grandmother.

Her phone buzzed in her hand just as she was putting it back in her pocket—a return message from Trinity Payne. *A new number again already? WTH is going on?*

Trinity was the only reporter that Josie would consider a friend, and even that was a stretch. Trinity had shot to stardom in the national news market straight out of college, only to fall from grace after a source fed her a bad story. She had been doing penance reporting for her hometown television station two years ago when Josie cracked a big missing girls case that had made them both famous. Trinity had been an indispensable ally during the fallout from that case, and since then, an excellent source of information on just about everything under the sun. Josie kept in contact with her for that very reason.

None of your business, Josie texted back.

Did you think about what I said? My producers would love it if I did a story on you. Small-city chief cracks big cases. It would go national.

Trinity had been after a profile of Josie ever since she solved a string of murders that ran the length of the East Coast. *No way,* Josie texted back.

It only took a moment for Trinity to answer. *Some other time, then. I'll be in town in a couple of weeks for a retrospective piece on the missing girls case. We'll do lunch. What about the Lloyd Todd arrest? That would make a great story for a national news magazine. How about an exclusive?*

Josie shook her head, chuckling. Trinity was nothing if not persistent. Josie didn't bother to respond. She was sure that Trinity would get what she wanted eventually. She decided to wait it out until she needed a favor from her, and then she'd use the Lloyd Todd story as leverage.

A loud growl emanated from Josie's stomach as she got back into her car. She should have taken Misty up on her offer of lunch—so much for a relaxing day off! In her mind, she catalogued what waited in her fridge at home, and headed off in the direction of the nearest drive-thru.

She had just polished off a burger when her phone rang. A glance at the screen showed it was Noah calling. Pulling over, she abandoned the bag of fries on the passenger seat and swiped a greasy finger over the answer icon. "What've you got?" she said.

"It's not about the ads—or Todd's crew."

She could tell by the slight strain in his voice that whatever he was calling about was serious. "What is it?"

"Some kids found human remains behind the Moss Gardens Trailer Park. You know it?"

She knew it all right. "Yes," she said, surprised by the steadiness of her voice. A stillness overtook her. Movement felt impossible. "What kind of human remains?"

"Skeletal. Old. Gretchen's over there now. Dr. Feist is on her way."

"I'll meet you there," Josie said. Forcing her limbs out of their momentary paralysis, she put her vehicle in drive, the smell of the French fries suddenly nauseating. Pulling back into traffic, Josie headed toward the trailer park she hadn't visited since she was fourteen years old, the trailer park she used to call home.

CHAPTER 4

JOSIE – SIX YEARS OLD

"Hey, JoJo, want to play a game?"

Josie heard her mother's words drifting down the dark hallway of the trailer, slithering under the door to her bedroom. The red crayon she clutched in her right hand froze, hovering over the coloring book her mother had given her earlier that day. She hardly ever gave Josie presents, so Josie had taken it and run off to her bedroom, closing the door and spreading out on the floor with all of her crayons before her mother could think about taking it back. She had already colored four full pages.

"JoJo," came the voice again. "Mommy wants to play a game."

Josie stared at the half-colored flower beneath her hand. Her mother rarely wanted to play games. "Coming," she called back.

She stuffed her crayons back into their box, closed her coloring book, and snatched up her small stuffed dog, Wolfie. Racing into the living room, she found her mother sprawled across the lumpy brown couch. Across from her, the television played a newscast on mute. Dust motes floated in the late-afternoon sun that streamed through the windows. "JoJo," her mother said in a sing-song voice. "Come closer."

Josie took a step forward. "What kind of game are we going to play, Mommy?"

Soft laughter carried through the air. "The kind where we see how fast you can get me a beer from the fridge."

"Oh." Josie knew from experience it was only seven steps from where she stood to the fridge. Her mother always put her beer cans on the bottom shelf so Josie could reach them easily. Sometimes her mother counted off the seconds as Josie raced back and forth to the fridge, but not today. As she handed her mother a beer, she saw the belt loose around her upper arm, and on the couch beside her, a blackened spoon, a lighter, and a needle. Josie never asked what these things were for, but they made her feel funny inside. She was staring at the small dark scab in the crook of her mother's elbow when the trailer door burst open behind her.

Wolfie fell from her grasp as she turned to see a man standing in the doorway.

CHAPTER 5

Moss Gardens sat on top of a hill behind the city park, a collection of about two dozen trailer homes spread far enough apart that if you screamed, your neighbors might not hear you. Josie knew this to be true.

When she had lived there, the entrance was marked by a large boulder by the side of the road with the words MOSS GARDENS emblazoned on it in black calligraphy. Today, the boulder was overshadowed by a wrought-iron archway that announced the name of the park in large, ornate letters. Beyond it, Josie saw that the drab brown trailers of her youth had all either been replaced or refurbished. The park held none of the dreariness she remembered. Almost all the trailers were brightly painted and well kept; some even had potted plants outside. She knew it was meant to feel welcoming, but knowing what she did about the place made the vibrant colors and homey touches seem garish and unnerving.

She passed the lot where her childhood home had once been. The trailer she'd lived in with her parents had long since been removed—or torn down—and now the nearest resident was using the space for extra parking. A few pipes that poked from the yellowed grass were the only sign that anyone had once resided there.

Toward the back of the park was a wooded valley that lay between the trailer park and one of Denton's working-class neighborhoods. There was no marked path, but Josie remembered a shoulder-width break in the brush where the local kids trampled the tall weeds to cut through. At the very back of the park, beyond the last row of trailers, was a paved one-lane road that ran alongside the edge of the woodland. Josie spotted Noah's department-issue SUV parked in one of the driveways. Two patrol cars sat in the middle of the road, their front ends facing the old path like arrows. As she pulled past, Josie saw the metal gate with a No Entry sign across the opening. She remembered the day the gate and sign were installed. It was shortly after her father had walked down that very path and put a bullet in his head.

Unfortunately for the landowner, a No Entry sign in Denton was generally considered to be an invitation to explore, and Josie and her late husband, Ray, had spent the majority of their childhood in those very woods. They should have felt afraid in the dark, dangerous woodland, but compared to their respective homes, the forest had offered a sacred and much needed respite. It wasn't cold, but Josie felt a chill envelop her as she parked behind the medical examiner's small white pickup truck and got out of her vehicle.

Josie was relieved to see that news of the discovery hadn't spread, and no nosy neighbors lolled about the perimeter of the scene, craning their necks for something to gossip about. Only Noah and some of Josie's other officers stood along the road—Hiller next to his patrol car, Wright guarding the gate. They nodded to her as she approached Noah, who leaned up against the other patrol car, his notepad and pen in hand.

"What've you got?" Josie asked.

Noah pointed to the backseat of the cruiser. "Couple of kids playing in the woods found some bones."

Josie peered through the window into the backseat of the cruiser, where the faces of two young boys stared back at her. They couldn't be older than ten or eleven, twelve at the most. They both had dark eyes and brown hair—one short and spiked, the other nearly covering his eyes. Both were covered in mud.

"Gretchen went to get their mom," Noah said. "Apparently their dad is no longer in the picture."

"They're brothers?"

Noah nodded.

"Who called it in?"

"One of the neighbors. Barbara Rhodes. She watches the boys while their mom works at the Denton Diner. She let them play in the woods. When she called them in for dinner, one of them was carrying what we think is a jawbone. She called 911."

Josie looked back at the boys. The long-haired boy stared back at her, chin jutted forward in defiance. His eyes, wide with fear, told another story. Beside him, his brother chewed on his fingernails. "Where's the jawbone now?" she asked.

"Gretchen took it into evidence," he replied. "The evidence response team is down there now with Dr. Feist processing the scene."

"The neighbor?"

He gestured toward the last row of trailers. "Third one from the left, number twenty-seven. The white one. I took her statement and sent her back home. The fewer people out here, the better."

Josie nodded, glad they didn't have to contend with a crowd of onlookers—at least not yet. The sound of a car drew their attention. Gretchen's Chevy Cruze turned a corner and pulled up behind Josie's vehicle. Before the car even came to a stop, a woman dressed in black jeans and a polo shirt with a matching black apron leapt out of the passenger's side and ran toward Josie and Noah. The long-haired boy pressed a hand against the window of the cruiser, and Josie reached back and opened the door. The boys tumbled out in a pile of gangly limbs and raced toward their mother. She swept them up in a tight hug, kissing both their heads and then studying their faces one by one. The younger, short-haired boy looked relieved. His brother did not. Josie, Noah, and Gretchen met the three of them in the middle of the road.

Gretchen introduced the woman. "This is Maureen Price, the boys' mother. I explained to her that we can't talk to her boys without her permission."

Maureen squeezed the long-haired boy's shoulder. "This is Kyle, my oldest. He's twelve, and this is Troy. He's eleven." She smiled tightly. "Irish twins," she explained.

Up close, Josie could see Maureen was quite young, probably not even thirty-five. There was something familiar about her round face and clear blue eyes. Her chestnut-colored hair was pulled back into a tight bun. Josie wondered if she'd gone to Denton East High School. She would have been a few years ahead of Josie and Ray.

"Chief Quinn," Josie said, extending a hand. "This is Lieutenant Fraley. Why don't you boys tell us what happened?"

Maureen looked down at their two heads, their thin bodies wedged against hers. "I thought I told you two to stay out of those woods."

"Aww, Mom," Troy said. "It's boring at Mrs. Rhodes's house."

"What were you guys doing in there?" Noah asked.

"Playing," Kyle answered. His eyes were still wide and wary.

Troy jumped away from his mom and mimicked holding a rifle, spinning around and squinting one eye as though he were looking through the sights. "We were playing war!"

"War?" Gretchen asked.

Maureen rolled her eyes and tried to gather Troy back to her side. "They've been watching the military channel. They're obsessed."

Noah raised a brow. "The military channel?"

Troy said, "We wanted to make foxholes. Like in the World Wars."

Josie glanced at his older brother, but he said nothing. "Where did you get the shovels?" she asked.

"Mrs. Rhodes," Troy said.

Finally, Kyle spoke. "We borrowed her gardening shovels. She said it was okay."

Maureen chewed her bottom lip. "Boys, really. You shouldn't be bothering Mrs. Rhodes with stuff like that. Why can't you just play video games till I get home?"

Josie said, "How many foxholes did you dig?"

"Three," answered Troy. "We stopped when we found the, you know, bones."

"How far down?" Josie asked, looking directly at Kyle.

The older boy shrugged. "When we stand in them, they come up to about here." He pointed to his solar plexus. So, a few feet down.

"Which one of you decided to bring one of the bones home?" Noah asked.

From the flush of young Troy's face, Josie knew it had been him. Neither boy answered. Maureen gave them each a stern look. "Boys, you answer the policeman."

"You're not in any trouble," Gretchen told them. "We're just trying to put together exactly what happened."

Troy looked to his brother, but Kyle's gaze had dropped to the asphalt. With a sigh, he said, "It was my idea. I didn't think Mrs. Rhodes would believe us. But as soon as I showed her, she called 911 and told us to stay away from the woods."

"Did one of you show Detective Palmer where the body was when she got here?" Josie asked.

Both boys nodded, and haltingly, Kyle raised a hand.

"Lieutenant Fraley tells me the piece of the skeleton you brought back was a jaw bone," Josie said. "Tell me, was it loose already? Separated from the skull? Or did you break it off?"

The two boys looked at one another. The older brother chewed on the nail of one of his index fingers.

"It's okay either way," Josie told them. "Even if you broke it off, you won't be in trouble. We just need to know so that we can tell what happened to these bones before, and after, you uncovered them. You understand?"

Young Troy nodded. "You want to make sure the killer didn't do it!" he exclaimed.

His mother swatted his shoulder. "Troy!"

"It's okay," Josie said. "We don't actually know what happened, but it helps us to figure it out if we know all the details."

"We snapped it off," Kyle said, his tone flat. He looked at his feet. "Sorry."

Gretchen smiled at them. "It's fine," she assured them. "Thank you for telling the truth."

She pulled a business card out and gave it to Maureen. Addressing the boys, she said, "If you think of anything else that might be important, you can give me a call. You will have to stay out of those woods though, at least until we're finished gathering evidence, okay?"

"That means no more foxholes," Maureen told her children pointedly. She grabbed Troy by his collar and pushed him along, toward their trailer. Josie guessed it was the one next to Mrs. Rhodes's trailer with two bicycles propped against its side.

Once the three of them were inside the trailer, Gretchen clapped her hands together and looked at Noah and Josie. "Let's go see what Dr. Feist has unearthed."

CHAPTER 6

Josie hoisted herself over the gate and walked into the woods. Behind her, Gretchen and Noah followed, twigs snapping beneath their feet. The path was exactly as Josie remembered it, leading them deep into the trees before disappearing where the forest grew too dense. Josie stopped and turned back to Gretchen. "Which way?"

Gretchen pointed to the left and Josie felt goosebumps erupt all over her body; the woods were nearly three miles long and yet she knew, almost instinctively, that they were heading toward the one section she dreaded revisiting the most. Wordlessly, Josie gestured for Gretchen to take the lead, and Noah fell in behind her. They picked their way through brush, weaving through the thick trunks of red maples and northern oaks to a giant Norway maple tree encircled with a strip of yellow crime-scene tape.

Josie felt her stomach sink as she stopped abruptly, and Noah's chest bumped into her back. "Boss?" he said.

It was hard to say how she knew, how her body remembered, but it did. She had only been six when her father had shot himself beneath this tree. She wouldn't have known which tree it was had her mother not insisted on marching her through the woods to look at it whenever she was feeling particularly cruel.

Josie heard her mother's voice like a whisper soughing through the leaves over her head. "This is where your precious daddy came to die."

Noah's hand slid under Josie's elbow, a gentle nudge. His voice was softer this time, meant only for her to hear. "Boss, you okay?"

Josie gave her head a shake. "Fine," she mumbled.

Tearing her eyes from the tree, she counted up the three foxholes the Price boys had dug in a half circle around the base of the tree. The evidence response team moved around in white Tyvek suits with clipboards, cameras, and evidence flags, documenting everything.

"Those don't look like foxholes," Josie said.

"They were dug by kids, Boss," Gretchen pointed out.

The holes were sloppily dug, and the larger of the three, more of a rectangular shape, had been cordoned off with string and evidence flags. The voice of the county medical examiner, Dr. Anya Feist, floated out from inside the hole. "Chief? That you?"

"I'm here," Josie called. "What've you got down there?"

Dr. Feist's head shot up, a white evidence cap holding her silver-gold hair away from her face. A camera hung round her neck. "I'll let you know. You just stay over there. I don't need any more people traipsing around this hole. With all the rain we've had, the soil is pretty soft as is. I've just got to excavate without this damn thing collapsing on me." She held up her gloved hands—in one was what looked like a paint brush, and in the other was a small trowel. "My assistant is on his way. He's done this kind of work before. He'll help. What I need you folks to do is keep everyone away from here. And to answer your question, Chief, there's not much I can tell you until I get these bones back to the lab."

"You won't even hazard a guess as to how long the body has been there?" Josie asked.

Dr. Feist rolled her eyes but said, "Nothing but bones, a body buried this deep, unembalmed? My best guess is it's been here at least eight years, probably longer. Could even be thirty or forty years. All I can tell you is the skull has a hell of a fracture."

Josie felt Noah's eyes on her. She could practically hear his thoughts. Two years ago, Denton's famous missing girls case had unearthed dozens of remains buried in a wooded area on a mountaintop and led to the discovery of two serial killers who had been operating in the area for decades. This scene felt like déjà vu.

"It's not related to the missing girls case," she said. "We don't even know it's a woman."

He gave her a weak half-smile. "You can read my mind now?"

Josie managed her own wan smile. "I'm getting better at it." She motioned around them. "We're at least fifteen miles away from the mountain where those girls' bodies were found. This is something else."

Noah frowned. "We have no matching open missing persons files, Boss. None that would be old enough to be this decomposed."

"I know that," Josie said. She knew exactly how many missing persons cases there were in her city at that exact moment—and in the county. She even knew their names. Noah was right. The oldest open missing persons case they had was from three years ago, and that young man was a habitual drug user and had been deemed a runaway. She took a careful step forward, her shirt brushing the crime-scene tape, and peered over the edge of the hole where Dr. Feist was painstakingly carving dirt away from a skull. "Then it's someone who hasn't been reported missing. One way or another, we'll find out."

CHAPTER 7

JOSIE – SIX YEARS OLD

Josie's heart skipped several beats until she realized it was just her daddy standing in the doorway. She ran to him, but he didn't scoop her up and spin her around like he normally did. Instead, he placed a hand on top of her head and stared past her toward where her mother lay on the sofa. Josie turned to see a smile curve across her mother's lips as her eyes fluttered open and closed. "Shit," her mother said. "I thought you had to work."

"I do," he said. "But I wanted to see—" he broke off. His hand moved to Josie's shoulder, and he pushed her back toward the hallway, his eyes never leaving the sofa. Josie watched her parents stare at one another for a tense moment, and a strange shaky feeling started in her legs. The room felt full of something—something bad, but Josie didn't know what.

"Go to your room, JoJo," her daddy said. "Now."

CHAPTER 8

The next morning, Josie, Noah, and Gretchen stood around a sheet-covered metal examination table in the Denton City Morgue. The drab, windowless room was situated in the basement of Denton Memorial Hospital, an ancient brick building on top of a hill that overlooked most of the city. Josie could never get used to the smell—a putrid combination of chemicals and decay. Beside her, Noah looked pale, almost green, while Gretchen, completely unaffected, looked almost bored. Josie remembered that Gretchen had seen a lifetime of autopsies during her tenure as a homicide detective with the Philadelphia Police Department before coming to Denton.

Josie elbowed Noah lightly.

"I'm fine," he mumbled from the side of his mouth.

Dr. Feist breezed in from the small office she shared with her assistant just off the main autopsy room. Her hair was tied back in a loose ponytail, and she now wore dark-blue scrubs. "I've already recorded my initial findings," she told them with a smile. "So, I'll allow questions."

Carefully, she removed the sheet. The bones seemed small and insubstantial lined up in a perfect body shape across the examination table. The dirt had all been brushed away from the bones, which now looked off-white. The four of them stood around the table sharing a moment of silence for the stranger who had been murdered and forgotten for so long that only the thin, yellowing framework remained.

Josie knew before Dr. Feist even spoke that they were looking at the remains of a young woman; she had seen more than her share of female skeletons while concluding the case that had made her chief.

"I believe we are looking at female remains," Dr. Feist announced. "I'd estimate the height to be about five foot two, five foot three." She pointed to the mandible, which had been separated from the skull. "The chin is rounded, where men tend to have more squared-off chins." She pointed to the forehead. "The frontal bone is smooth and vertical. The mastoid process"—Dr. Feist's finger moved to a small, conical bone behind the jaw, where the girl's ear would have been—"which is this bone here that kind of protrudes where certain neck muscles attach to it. As you can see, it's small. In men, it is very pronounced."

Gretchen scribbled on her notepad. Josie stepped forward and pointed to the pelvic bone. "The pelvis gives it away."

Dr. Feist smiled, her eyes alight, looking at Josie as though she were a prized pupil. "Yes, it does. Why is that, Chief?"

Josie pointed to the pelvic girdle. "This opening here is broader and rounder—so women can give birth. Also, here, this angle—" she pointed to the bottom center of the pelvic bone.

"The pubic arch," Dr. Feist put in.

"Right. This angle where the two sides meet is more obtuse in females. Greater than ninety degrees."

Noah said, "For childbirth as well?"

Both Josie and the doctor nodded.

"How old was she?" Gretchen asked, pen poised over her notepad.

"Between sixteen and nineteen years old," Dr. Feist replied.

"That's quite specific," Noah remarked.

"Well, the growth plates—or lack thereof—make it pretty easy to determine," Dr. Feist said. "The long bones in the body have three parts: the diaphysis—that's the shaft—the metaphysis, which is the part where it widens and flares at the end, and then the epiphysis, which is basically the end cap of the bone or the growth plate. In children, there is a gap between the epiphysis and the metaphysis."

Gretchen, busy sketching on her notepad, said, "You mean there's a space between the growth plate and the knobby end of the bone."

Dr. Feist's head bobbed from side to side. "Basically, yeah. As you get older, your growth plates and the 'knobby end,' as you call it, fuse together. The growth plates fuse at pretty predictable ages. For example, the epiphysis of the femur at the proximal end—that's where the femur goes into the hip socket—fuses between ages fifteen and nineteen, give or take six months on each end."

One of her gloved fingers ran up the length of the girl's right femur, stopping at the hip socket and pointing to the very top where the bone inserted into the pelvis. "It's fused, which means she could have been as young as fifteen, fifteen and a half, and as old as nineteen or nineteen and a half."

"But you said sixteen," Josie pointed out.

"I'm estimating, of course," Dr. Feist responded. "But the distal radius fuses at around sixteen, and hers are fused." Her gloved finger found the long bone of the arm on the thumb side of the girl's right hand. Touching the flared part where the radius met the intricate bones of the hand, Dr. Feist said, "No space. The epiphysis has fused to the metaphysis."

"When does the last growth plate fuse?" Gretchen asked.

"The medial aspect of the clavicle fuses by age thirty at the latest," Dr. Feist answered. "However, we don't see epiphyseal fusion of either the medial or lateral aspect of the clavicle until age nineteen, and this young lady doesn't have it."

Josie leaned in and peered at the girl's collarbones.

Noah ran a hand through his thick brown hair. "I'm trying to remember my college anatomy class."

"The lateral is the part that goes into the shoulder," Gretchen said. "The medial attaches to the sternum."

"Show-off," Noah muttered.

Gretchen kept her head down, her pen sketching the skeleton at a furious pace.

"That's correct," Dr. Feist said. "More or less." She pointed to the gap between the epiphysis and the metaphysis on each end of the collarbones. "If she were nineteen or older, these growth plates would be fused."

"So, this is a teenage girl," Josie said, acid in her stomach fizzing.

"Yes," Dr. Feist agreed. "It's possible to estimate a year on either side of the range—perhaps fifteen to twenty—but I believe you're looking at a sixteen- to nineteen-year-old female. Oh, and this teenage girl gave birth at least once."

Josie could see by Dr. Feist's raised brow and amused smile that she enjoyed tossing out that little surprise. Hands on her hips, Josie matched the doctor's expression and said, "Just how can you tell that this girl gave birth?"

Dr. Feist beckoned them all closer to the table. They gathered round, and she pointed to one of the flat planes of pelvic bone, where Josie could make out a smattering of small holes roughly the size of shotgun pellets. "It's called parturition scarring, or pitting," Dr. Feist said.

"Par-nutrition?" Noah said.

"Parturition," Dr. Feist corrected slowly. "Childbirth. When a woman gives birth, her pubic bones separate to allow the baby to fit through, and sometimes the ligaments attached to the bones tear and leave these small scars. It's not always one hundred percent accurate, but in a girl this young, I'd say these are from her having given birth."

Josie frowned. "No way to tell how old she was when she had her baby—or anything about the baby?"

"I'm sorry, Chief, but no. All I can tell you is that she had a baby before she died."

"Maybe someone killed her and took her baby," Gretchen suggested.

Dr. Feist shrugged. "I can't speculate on why she was murdered or what happened to her child—but she was definitely murdered. You can see the fracture better now that she's cleaned up."

She moved around to the head of the table and reached up, adjusting the large, circular lamp that hung from the ceiling so that its beams shone directly onto the girl's skull. Josie shuffled closer to Dr. Feist, and Noah and Gretchen followed, craning their necks to see the top of the skull. "See these," Dr. Feist said, pointing to faint squiggly lines running down the center of the skull from front to back and then across the front from temple to temple. "These are called sutures. They're openings where the skull plates fit together. These are normal, and you can see they're still partially open, which is also normal for a teenager. Most of the skull's sutures close well into adulthood." She pointed out other sutures in the back of the skull and above where the ears would be. Then she pointed to a large depression on the top of the skull, on what would have been the girl's left side, about midway from the front of her head to the back. Jagged cracks extended from where the bone had caved slightly. "This is not normal," Dr. Feist said.

Noah gave a low whistle. "What could have caused that?" he asked.

Dr. Feist shrugged. She used her thumb and index finger to frame the size of the fracture. "A hammer maybe? The blunt side, not the sharp edge. It's big enough that whatever she was hit with would have been blunt, but we're still talking about something relatively small."

"A baseball bat?" Gretchen asked.

Dr. Feist frowned. "Maybe, but it's more likely something smaller and heavier."

"Tire iron?" Josie offered.

The doctor nodded. "That's more likely. Whoever hit her used a great deal of force. It's hard to say from just bones, but I'm not sure the struggle—if there was one—lasted long. She doesn't have any other fractures. Of course, she may have sustained bruising or lacerations, but we'll never know that now."

"How about the angle?" Josie asked. "What would you say? Someone taller than her? Shorter? Same height?"

Dr. Feist held up a finger. "I estimate her to be about five foot three. I would say she was killed by someone about the same height, but using an overhead strike." She motioned to Gretchen, who was about her height. Gretchen moved closer, and Dr. Feist approached her from the side, slightly to her rear, both arms raised high over her head as though she was clutching something in them. She brought her invisible weapon down on Gretchen's head, stopping before she made contact. "If it was someone taller than her, or if she had been kneeling, I would expect the fracture to be more depressed, because there would be more follow-through with the strike."

"All right," Gretchen said. "So we suspect she was struck over the head by someone close to her own height, and then she was buried in the woods."

"And we suspect whoever killed her was a woman," Josie said.

"How do you figure that?" asked Noah.

Josie said, "How many men do you know who are five foot three?"

"Not many, but they exist," Noah countered.

"I'm aware," Josie answered. "But if I had to make an educated guess in this instance, I would say we are more likely looking for a female assailant." Josie turned back to the doctor. "No way to tell if she was killed there in the woods, or if she was killed elsewhere and then moved to the grave?"

"I'm afraid not."

Noah turned his gaze to Dr. Feist. "No way to tell if she was sexually assaulted?"

Dr. Feist gave him a tight smile. "There's no way to tell a lot of things. This poor girl has been buried for a long time."

She walked over to a table along the wall and picked up a brown bag, which she emptied out onto the exam table near the skeleton's feet. Dirty scraps of fabric came first, and then a larger garment. It was dirt-covered and faded, and some of it had disintegrated, but Josie could see that it was a windbreaker—dark blue with squares of what used to be bright yellow, teal, and pink on the shoulders and where the pockets were. There was only one sleeve left, and as Dr. Feist held the garment up, Josie could see several swaths of fabric missing from the back, the collar, and the waist—worn away by time and the earth's erosion.

"This is what's left of her clothing," the doctor said.

Gretchen raised a brow. "No chance there are any identifying items in her jacket pockets?"

Dr. Feist laughed and placed the jacket carefully onto the countertop. "The insides of the pockets are gone. Decomposed. The rest," she waved at the scrap pile, "is just buttons, a shoe sole, and what are probably scraps of leather."

Josie stepped forward and looked down at the sad collection of items: a rusted zipper, a couple of blackened grommets from shoes requiring laces, a few small scraps of leather, the tiny folded nickel clasps of a bra, and a grimy rubber shoe sole deteriorating around the edges. Josie looked from the pile to the jacket and then pointed to the jacket. "What material is that made from?"

"My guess is nylon."

"Looks like something from the 1980s," Gretchen said. "Windbreakers were all the rage back then, especially the style with the blocks of bright colors."

Josie nodded. "How long does nylon take to decompose in the ground?"

Noah pulled out his phone, his fingers working fast over the screen. A moment later, he said, "Thirty to forty years."

"Seems about right," Dr. Feist said. "The challenge in a case like this is figuring out how long the body has been in the ground. Usually the items we find along with the bones—if any—are the most helpful in trying to pin down a time frame. I was going to have a friend of mine from the college's Archeology Department consult, but thirty to forty years would be a place to start."

"That's all fine and good," Josie said. "But you know as well as I do that we don't have any missing teenage girls in the entire county going back that far."

Dr. Feist grinned and raised a finger in the air. "Oh, I may be able to narrow it down for you."

Josie, Noah, and Gretchen stared at her. Gretchen's busy pen finally stilled in anticipation.

"Wait till you see this," Dr. Feist said as she returned to the head of the table and grasped the sides of the skull with both hands. She lifted it away from the lower jaw bone and held it under the overhead light so they could see inside what would have been the roof of the girl's mouth. All three police officers leaned in.

"Holy shit," Noah said. "Are those fangs?"

Behind the two front teeth were two additional, conical teeth that came to points.

"Supernumerary teeth," Dr. Feist explained.

"Extra teeth?" Josie asked.

"Yeah, pretty much. The condition is called hyperdontia. It's an inherited defect. Extremely rare. Something a dentist in a city this small would remember, especially given the fact that her supernumerary teeth actually looked like fangs. I did a little research. Supernumerary teeth can appear anywhere in the dental arch. Not all patients present with extra teeth that look so fanglike. Trust me, this girl would have been memorable to look at."

Josie met Noah's eyes, and then Gretchen's. "Well," she said. "Start tracking down dentists who were practicing in the city thirty to forty years ago."

CHAPTER 9

A week passed, and every night Josie dreamed of the tall maple tree in the woods behind the trailer that was her childhood home. Sometimes her father was there, a hole in the top of his head, a macabre smile on his face. He beckoned her. "Come," he said. "I have to show you something." Each time, Josie was too afraid to get close to him. Sometimes Ray, her ex-husband, was there—only it was Ray at nine years old, crashing through the woods behind her, telling her not to get any closer. She woke sweaty and thrashing in her king-sized bed, her limbs twisted in the sheets.

Today was no different. Her eyes snapped open, her heaving chest and gasping breaths slowing gradually in the warmth of the sunlight streaming through her bedroom windows. She sat up, pulling her sweat-soaked T-shirt away from her skin, and looked around the room, taking in the high ceilings, the large windows, and the walls painted a soothing cream color. It was her favorite room in the house, open and airy in a way she usually found comforting, but still she shivered as the sweat on her body dried, leaving her clammy. She would have just enough time to shower and stop for coffee before reporting to work.

Twenty minutes later she was locking her front door, her mind on the performance evaluations and equipment requisitions waiting on her desk at the station, when her cell phone rang. It was Noah.

"What've you got?" Josie answered.

Noah's laughter filtered through the phone line. "You're getting better at the small talk, Boss. I'm fine, thank you."

Josie smiled as she made her way from her stoop to where her Escape waited in the driveway. "I'm glad to hear that, Fraley," she said. "I'd really love a latte from Komorrah's Koffee. Maybe you could make your way over there before I get to the station. How's that for small talk?"

"The latte is already on your desk," he responded, making Josie smile.

"You may need a raise," she joked. "Now, what've you got?"

"I've got a preliminary ID on our mystery girl. We didn't get any hits in Denton, so Gretchen expanded the search area. We tracked down a dentist in Bellewood who inherited his father's practice about ten years back. His dad practiced for decades before he retired. Apparently, his dad repeatedly mentioned the patient with hyperdontia he treated in the late '70s, early '80s, because the condition was so rare. Gretchen is over there now getting the chart so Dr. Feist can see if they're a match."

Josie stood beside her Escape, feeling a tingle of excitement. An ID in a week. It was a good start. "That's great," she said, fishing her key fob out of her jacket pocket.

"Yeah, we lucked out with her having those fangs."

"Extra teeth," Josie corrected. Ever since she'd seen them, she couldn't help but wonder what the poor girl had been through because of them; kids could be exceptionally cruel.

"Sorry," Noah said. "Supernumerary teeth. Anyway, we might have never tracked down her identity if it weren't for them."

Josie lifted her shoulder and used it to keep the phone pressed against her ear as she reached for the handle of her Escape. On the underside of the door handle, her fingers sank into something cold and mushy. "What's her name?" she asked.

The smell reached her nose the moment she took her hand away from the door handle—foul and stomach-clenching. She held her fingers up in front of her face, the brown color confirming her guess. "Shit," she muttered.

"What's that?"

"Nothing. Her name?"

"Belinda Rose. Date of birth October 15, 1966."

Josie felt the color drain from her face, the clamminess of the early morning returning and coating her skin like a greasy film. In that moment, she wasn't sure what made her feel queasier—the excrement covering her fingers or hearing the name from Noah's lips.

She held her hand away from herself, looking around, realizing she'd have to go back inside to clean up. But her legs felt heavy and stuck in place, and her lungs were filled with lead.

"Boss?"

"That's not possible," Josie croaked.

"What's not possible?"

"Belinda Rose can't be dead—she can't have been dead for over thirty years."

"Oh yeah? Why is that?"

"Because Belinda Rose is my mother's name, and as far as I know, she's still alive."

CHAPTER 10

JOSIE – SIX YEARS OLD

The trailer only seemed too small when her mother was angry. When she got really worked up, her fury filled the whole place like thick clouds of steam from a hot shower. Her rages were inescapable, even when Josie hid beneath the kitchen table and watched her feet stalk back and forth, back and forth. It was never good when she started pacing.

"I don't know who he thinks he is," her mother growled, spittle flying from her mouth. The refrigerator door opened and slammed closed, and Josie heard the snap of a beer can opening. She clutched her threadbare Wolfie to her chest, shrinking back as far as she could, out of reach from her mother's hands, which she knew would thrust under the table and drag her out eventually.

But they didn't come. Josie's eyelids grew so heavy she could barely keep them open. She stifled a yawn and tried to ignore the cold that seeped from the tiles into her nightgown. It was late. She knew because it was dark outside.

"That bastard," she heard her mother mutter, her feet suddenly moving again across the kitchen.

Josie tried to tune out the sound, listening hard for the sound of her daddy's truck outside. She wished he would come home. Next, she heard the sound of kitchen drawers being torn from their homes and silverware clattering to the floor. Then her mother's voice again, thick and slurred this time, talking though no one else was there. "You're not going to get away with this. Goddamn you. I'll destroy everything you love. Everything."

Then suddenly—terrifyingly—her mother's face appeared in the tiny space beneath the table. She smiled at Josie, and Josie got that sick feeling in her stomach she always got when her mother did bad things. She reached out a hand to Josie.

"You come here now, girl."

CHAPTER 11

Josie went inside and got cleaned up without making a mess anywhere. But even after she had scrubbed her hand several times and assured herself the excrement hadn't gotten on any of her clothes, the smell still lingered deep in her nostrils. She'd ended the call with Noah abruptly, but he was on his way to her house, and that knowledge settled her agitation a little. She went into one of her spare bedrooms, where she kept her laptop on a small desk in the corner of the room. She pulled out the chair, sat, and booted it up.

She'd had a security camera installed in her driveway a month earlier, after she'd found all four of her tires slashed—just a week after all the department vehicles at the station house had suffered the same fate. Replacement tires for her Escape had cost her a small fortune, and she wouldn't let the vandal get away with it a second time.

She queued up the footage from the moment she'd pulled in the night before, and then fast-forwarded until she saw a figure slink into the driveway. Josie looked at the time stamp: 3:12 in the morning, when she had been fast asleep. The person wore baggy pants and a hoodie pulled down low over their face. She couldn't tell if it was a man or woman, but based on the height—she guessed about six feet—Josie thought it was probably a man.

She watched the hooded figure reach into a paper bag, come out with a handful of dark matter, and push it up under the door handles of Josie's car. So she would have to clean all four handles.

"Great," she muttered to herself.

When the figure was done, Josie could see him peeling off latex gloves, shoving them into the paper bag, and then jogging off down the street, bag in hand. Resetting the footage to when the figure first appeared, Josie leaned back in her chair and sighed. At three in the morning, none of her neighbors would have been up. Even if they were and had seen the guy, it was unlikely they'd seen anything more than what Josie had caught on camera.

Noah arrived ten minutes later. She let him in, and they reviewed the footage together. Josie saved it to a flash drive and handed it to him. "I want a report filed. By you. No one else."

Noah sighed. "You're documenting this, but you're not letting me do anything about it."

Josie gave him a dismissive look as she stood. "There's nothing to be done. These are little teenage pricks doing pranks. I don't need a detail."

He knew better than to start that argument with her again. Instead, he took the flash drive from her and dropped it into his pocket. "The craigslist ad is a dead end. You were right. All we can get from the IP address is that it was somewhere here in Denton—this time near the mall. Probably someone piggybacking off the free wifi of one of the stores, or something like that."

"Figures," Josie said.

Noah didn't move from the doorway. His gaze made her face feel hot. She put her hands on her hips. "What?" she said.

"We need to talk about Belinda Rose—and your mother."

CHAPTER 12

JOSIE – SIX YEARS OLD

The hospital was big and bright, with endless tiled hallways and ugly blue curtains for walls. Behind every curtain Josie could hear hushed voices and sometimes cries of pain. Nurses dressed in periwinkle scrubs rushed up and down the halls and in and out of the curtains. After a long, agonizing wait while her whole head throbbed, one of them stopped by her cubicle, snapped on a pair of latex gloves, and prepared a smelly, folded piece of gauze to clean the wound on the side of Josie's face.

"This is gonna sting, hon," the nurse told Josie. She beckoned for another nurse to hold Josie to the bed before pressing the wet pad against her jawline.

It felt like her skin was ripping open and they were setting it on fire. The more she squirmed against their big hands, the harder they pressed her against the plastic mattress. The nurse holding her head loosened her grip for a moment to check the wound, and Josie looked down at her blood-soaked nightgown. Her heart did cartwheels in her chest. Had she died?

No, she thought. She hadn't died.

She hadn't died because Needle had shown up just at the moment her mother's knife had sliced down the side of her face. Needle wasn't his real name. Josie didn't know what he was really called, only that he came to the trailer when her daddy was at work, and he always brought sharp, dangerous needles. He wasn't a nice man, but when he'd walked in that night, he had looked scared, and that terrified Josie more than her mother's white fury, and more than any blade.

It was Needle who'd pried the knife away from Josie's mother. It was Needle who'd insisted that Josie needed to go to the hospital, scooping her off the floor and carrying her to the car. Josie couldn't remember if he had come with them, but she definitely hadn't seen him at the hospital. Needle was gone.

She couldn't be dead if Needle had made her mother stop. But the blood. There was so much blood. She struggled against the nurses, fighting for her life.

"Josie, honey, you have to hold still." Her mother's voice came from somewhere beside her.

"I'm sorry, hon. I know it hurts. We're almost done," said one of the nurses.

She wanted her daddy.

Finally, they stopped. Her breath came in heavy gasps. Gently, one of the nurses turned her onto her back. "I'm real sorry, hon," the nurse said, a pained smile directed down at Josie. The big light behind the nurse's head burned Josie's eyes.

The other nurse turned to her mother. "She's gonna need stitches. You wanna tell us what happened?"

CHAPTER 13

Josie watched Noah circle her Ford Escape, leaning over to get a good look at the shit caked under her door handles. He wrinkled his nose, snapped some photos with his phone, and turned to her. "Want to send a sample to the lab? See if it's human?"

Her stomach turned. "No," she answered. "I'm not spending department money on a bad joke."

"How long is the backlash to Lloyd Todd's arrest going to last?" Noah asked.

"Hard to say. Hopefully not much longer. We'll take your car. I want to get back to the station before my latte gets cold."

Noah smiled. "And leave this crap caked under the handles all day? I don't think so. I'll clean this up for you while you tell me about your mom."

Josie stood in her driveway, arms crossed over her chest, while Noah moved in and out of her house gathering latex gloves, paper towels, surface cleaner, and a plastic bag. He went to work on the driver's door first, talking as he cleaned. "So your mom's name was Belinda Rose."

Josie didn't answer.

Once he got all the sludge out from under the handle using paper towels, he sprayed it with disinfectant and used more paper towels to wipe away the remnants, depositing all the dirty towels into the plastic bag. The smell wafted over to where Josie stood. Her nose wrinkled, but Noah seemed unaffected.

"Used to dealing with crap, are you?" she asked.

He smiled. "Don't change the subject."

"It's just that the smell at the morgue turns you green in seconds, but you're practically face-deep over there, and it's not bothering you at all."

"There could be more than one Belinda Rose," he pointed out, moving to the next handle.

"With the same birthday?"

"I thought your maiden name was Matson, not Rose," Noah said.

"It was. Matson was my dad's last name. My parents never got married."

"Where's your mother now?"

Josie's chin dropped to her chest. She didn't like talking about her mother; she'd been actively trying not to think about the woman for the past sixteen years. Her mother had taken enough from her. She didn't deserve any more of Josie's time or mental energy. "I don't know," she said. "I haven't seen her since I was fourteen. She left."

Noah turned and looked at her, one brow raised. "You never tried to find her?"

Josie's hands found the lapels of her jacket and tugged them closer together. Her eyes drifted away from Noah. "She's not the kind of person you go looking for."

"How tall is she?" he asked, and Josie knew he was thinking of their post-autopsy meeting with Dr. Feist.

She sighed. "Tall enough to have hit this girl over the head with a hammer or tire iron. Probably about five four."

"Do you have a picture of her? We could work from that."

"No, I don't."

"That bad, huh?"

You have no idea, Josie said silently. Out loud, she told him, "She destroyed every picture there was of her in the house before she left."

At the time, Josie had thought it was exactly in keeping with the kind of spiteful, vengeful monster her mother had always been—mostly because the only photos Josie had of her mother also had her father in them. Josie remembered coming home to find the whole trailer smelling of smoke, and finding the last slivers of photographs in a pile of ashes in the stainless-steel kitchen sink. Belinda hadn't left Josie a single photo of her father. Back then, Josie figured her mother was just trying to hurt her, like she always did, but now she wondered if there was a more sinister reason for destroying the photos. It sure didn't make Josie's job of tracking her down any easier.

"What about your dad?" Noah asked. "Would he have any?"

"He passed away when I was six."

She waited for more questions, and her body went loose with relief when they didn't come. Instead, moving to the other side of the car and starting on the handles there, Noah said, "I'm sorry to hear that. Well, look, we can talk more about your mom later if it turns out we need to find her. Right now, I think the first order of business is to confirm the dental records. We'll have a look at the chart Gretchen's pulling and go from there."

CHAPTER 14

JOSIE – SIX YEARS OLD

Josie's mother paced the cramped curtained area. One hand pressed against her heart while the other clutched a tissue, dabbing at the tears that fell freely from worried eyes. Josie stared at her, shocked and confused to see her mother cry for the very first time.

"I was sleeping," she explained. "I woke up to go to the bathroom and went in to check on JoJo. She wasn't in her bed, so I searched the trailer. Didn't find her. The back door was unlocked, so I got a flashlight and went looking for her. I found her lying on the ground in the woods, covered in blood." A wail tore from her throat. "My baby. My little baby. She was just co-co-covered in it."

Josie glanced at the two nurses watching her mother cry, their faces unreadable.

"She must have fallen," Josie's mother went on. "I mean, it was dark and those woods are filled with trash and glass, all kinds of things children can hurt themselves on."

"Did you ask her what happened?" one of the nurses asked in the same kind of voice Josie's kindergarten teacher used when the students didn't put all their stuff into their cubbyholes.

"Of-of course I did," Josie's mother said. "She told me she fell. That's how I know she fell."

The two nurses exchanged a skeptical look. Then one of them said, "The doctor will be in soon."

They left, one of them tossing a concerned look over her shoulder at Josie before disappearing through the curtain.

Seconds later, Josie's chin was gripped tightly in her mother's hand, fingers squeezing against the bone and pulling at the skin around her wound. Her eyes watered with the pain. "Mo-mommy," she gasped.

Her mother's blue eyes were almost black with fury. When she spoke in an angry whisper, spittle sprayed across Josie's nose. "You don't say one fucking word, you got that?"

"You told lies." Josie squeaked through the part of her mouth that was still mobile.

Her mother's fingers tightened, making Josie feel like her face would tear apart.

"I told you to shut up. Not one word. What I say is what happened, you got that? If you tell one person—just one person— what happened, you're going into the closet. Forever. And Daddy and Gram won't be able to save you. You understand that?"

Fear set her entire body into a quiver, and she felt a hot wetness spread down her legs and through her nightdress. She whispered, "I promise." At last, her mother let go, moving to the other side of the room to peek through the curtain. Hugging herself, Josie wished she had thought to bring Wolfie. Then she remembered—the last time she saw him he had been lying just out of reach in a puddle of her blood on the kitchen floor.

CHAPTER 15

Noah had done a good job cleaning up Josie's door handles, but she was still convinced that the smell clung to her. Standing beside him in the morgue, she sniffed the air but could only smell the chemical odor of death that saturated Dr. Feist's small basement empire. They had stopped for coffee on the way, but now Josie held her full paper cup in one hand, feeling too queasy to drink it.

Dr. Feist breezed into the room with Gretchen in tow and headed over to the ancient x-ray viewer that hung on the wall. Dr. Feist snapped it on, and the fluorescent lights inside flickered to life. She took two films from Gretchen and hung them side by side. It didn't take an expert to see that the dental x-rays Dr. Feist had taken during Belinda Rose's autopsy were a perfect match to the ones that Gretchen had retrieved from the dentist. Josie's heart skipped painfully in her chest; if Belinda Rose had been buried in the woods for over thirty years, who the hell was the woman who called herself Josie's mother?

"Well," Dr. Feist said, turning back to the officers. "Now you've got your victim's identity. Guess you just have to find her killer."

"How old was she when those x-rays were taken?" Josie asked Gretchen.

Gretchen put her reading glasses on and riffled through the thin file she had brought with her. "Looks like the last exam was done when she was fourteen years old."

"What else is in that file?" Josie asked.

Gretchen shuffled more pages around, frowning.

"What is it?" Noah asked.

"Looks like she was a ward of the state," Gretchen said. "There's a notation here. She lived in a group foster home in Bellewood."

Bellewood, the county seat, was forty miles away from Denton. Josie crossed the room and peered over Gretchen's shoulder, studying the address. "That place was torn down when I was in high school. There's a strip mall there now. Is there a contact listed? Someone had to bring her to her dental appointments, sign off on treatment and stuff."

Gretchen turned a page. "Maggie Smith."

"Let's find her. If she's still alive. We'll write up some warrants and see if we can get this girl's file from Child Services," Josie instructed.

Noah stepped forward. "I'll run Belinda's name through the databases." He glanced at Josie. "We think someone might have been using her identity after she was killed."

CHAPTER 16

JOSIE – SIX YEARS OLD

It seemed like an eternity before the doctor came. He was young—he looked young like her daddy—and he asked a lot of questions. Her mother answered them all with the same sad, tear-stained face she used when she talked to the nurses.

"What about Josie's father?" he asked. "Where was he when all this happened?"

"He works overnight at the gas station out by the interstate."

"Have you called him?"

Josie's mother gave a wavering smile. "For a little cut? No, I didn't want to bother him."

The doctor raised an eyebrow and walked to the bed where Josie lay. Gently, he lifted Josie's hair and leaned in, studying the side of her face. He frowned at Josie's mother. "This is not a little cut, Ms. Rose. I'm afraid your daughter is going to require several stitches."

Josie's heart did a somersault. Tears threatened, and she concentrated as hard as she could on holding them back. The doctor's palm was warm on her shoulder. When she looked up at him, he smiled. "I'm going to give you some medicine so they won't hurt, okay, sweetie?"

She nodded, not sure whether to believe him or not.

The doctor looked at Josie's mother again. "I think Josie's father should be here. Why don't you go call him?"

Alone with Josie, the doctor called in another nurse, and they asked her a lot of questions: Did her mommy hurt her? How did she get the cut? What was she doing in the woods, and was there another person there who hurt her? And last of all, was she scared of her mommy? Josie knew better than to tell the truth. She kept mumbling, "I fell," again and again like a broken toy. At first the lie was hard, but the more she said it, the easier it became, until it was as normal as breathing and her body didn't know she was lying anymore.

The doctors and nurses insisted on checking her limbs and torso for injuries as well, and they asked more questions until Josie could barely keep her eyes open. By the time the doctor started the stitches, Josie didn't even care what they were or whether they would hurt. She just wanted to go to sleep. She didn't have to be held down. No one had to tell her to hold still. She just turned on her side and closed her eyes. The doctor was right. She felt the needle he gave her to make her face numb, but that was it. She didn't feel a thing.

Her daddy came while the doctor was hard at work on her cheek. She knew he was there because she could hear him fighting with her mother outside the curtain. She only heard some of the words he said. "You…your fault…sick…leaving…never see… police…abuse…custody…hate you."

CHAPTER 17

Josie sat behind her desk at the station house, laptop open before her. Gretchen was off writing warrants to get the Department of Human Services foster care file on Belinda Rose. Noah was getting more coffee. Josie opened up the first of several databases to enter in Belinda Rose's information, but her hands froze over the keyboard. Her scalp prickled. Once she started down this road, there would be no turning back. She had hoped to leave her mother firmly in her past, but that was impossible now. The Denton Police Department had a murder to solve. They needed to know who the girl buried in the woods had been. Since Josie's mother had clearly stolen the girl's identity sometime after her death, there was little choice but to track her down, or at least find a connection between the two women.

The door to her office swung open, and Noah stepped through, a steaming mug of coffee in one hand. She nearly lunged for it. He laughed. "Whoa! Feeling a little tired, are you?"

Curling both palms around the mug, she sat back down in her chair and sipped it. "Looking for a distraction," she said. "Close the door."

The sounds of her officers moving about in the bullpen outside receded as Noah clicked the door shut. He sat in the chair across from her and raised a brow. "What's going on, Boss?"

"I'm trying to figure out a way to solve this murder without actually having to get back in contact with my mother."

"Not sure that's possible," Noah said. "You know we have to follow all the leads, and if your mother was using this girl's identity—not that long after the murder—that makes her a significant person of interest. I mean, Belinda Rose doesn't show up on any of our missing persons lists, so how would your mother have known so soon after her death that she could use her identity?"

Josie put her mug down on the desk and traced the rim of it with her index finger, keeping her eyes on the steam rising from inside the mug instead of on Noah. "I understand what you're saying."

He waited a beat. Then he asked, "You have no interest in finding out who your mom really was?"

Josie met his eyes. Her fingers reached up and pulled her black hair down over the long scar on the right side of her face. She swallowed once to quell the dryness in her throat. "Oh, I know who she really was."

But I don't know if I want the rest of the world to know, she added silently.

"Boss," Noah said.

"Yeah."

"You know who you are too. Don't forget that."

It was exactly what she needed to hear, delivered perfectly.

"Thank you," she said.

Noah leaned forward, pulled a rolled-up bunch of papers out of his back pocket, smoothed it out, and pushed it across her desk. "I already did a search using the name Belinda Rose with the October 15, 1966 birthdate to look for a last known address."

Josie snapped her laptop closed and looked at the report. As her eyes roved over the addresses associated with Belinda Rose, Noah stood and moved around the desk next to her. He pointed to the first address, which Josie recognized immediately. "This was the foster home run by Maggie Smith," he said. "We're still trying to track her down. I've got Lamay running some searches. He'll have something for us soon—as long as she's still alive."

Noah's fingers continued moving down the list. "The next address was an apartment in Fairfield. The real Belinda Rose would have been eighteen when she lived there."

"That's almost an hour away from Bellewood, in Lenore County," Josie said. "I wonder if she actually lived there, or if she was already dead by then. It might have been my mother living in that apartment under her name."

"I'm sure we'll be able to make a better guess as to when she died once we have the DHS file and once we talk with Smith," Noah said.

"Look at this," Josie said. She pointed below the Fairfield address. "She had a bunch of apartments throughout Alcott and Lenore Counties before she came to the trailer park—all of them at least forty miles away from Bellewood, if not more. Well before my mother came to the trailer park. I don't think this is the real Belinda Rose." Josie remembered vividly how often and how abruptly her mother came and went, abandoning her for months at a time and then returning when she least expected it like a tornado tearing through her life, destroying everything.

"Okay, so we know it was your mom who lived in the trailer park," Noah said. "And you think these half-dozen apartments before that were probably her too. Should I have someone go out to these buildings and talk to landlords?"

Josie leaned back in her chair and took another swig of coffee. "I'm not sure it's worth it," she said. "That was over thirty years ago. Some of these places might not even be standing anymore."

"Nosy neighbors?" Noah suggested.

"Make some inquiries," Josie instructed. "You never know."

"Is there anyone still living in the trailer park who would remember her?"

"I doubt it," Josie said. "But you can send someone over to ask around."

There is someone, she thought to herself, *though he isn't at the trailer park anymore.* Josie didn't even know if he was still alive; she hadn't thought about Dexter McMann in sixteen years, had put that entire episode out of her mind, just as she tried to do with everything else connected to her mother. She doubted he would know more than she did anyway. She didn't want to turn that slippery stone over unless she absolutely had to.

"I think we really need to look at where she went after the trailer park, and there's only one address listed for Belinda Rose after that," Josie said.

According to the report, the year that Josie turned fifteen, her mother had lived in an apartment in Philadelphia, two hours away from Denton. "After that, there's nothing," Josie added. "She used this identity until 2002, and then stopped."

"Maybe she died," Noah said.

"I wouldn't be that lucky," Josie mumbled.

"What's that?"

"Nothing, nothing. She must have found another identity to assume. Or went back to her real identity—whatever that is."

"Did she have any family?" Noah asked.

Josie shook her head. "No. I mean, if she did, she never told me about them. I was a kid. I never asked her." *I tried not to talk to her at all.*

"I'll send someone to all the places on this list, see if we can come up with anything," Noah said. "Even if we don't find anything that way, we'll dig into the real Belinda Rose's life. Maybe they knew one another."

CHAPTER 18

JOSIE – SIX YEARS OLD

Fingers trailed over Josie's scalp, stroking her hair gently. Nestled in her bed, her small hands clutched the fuzzy pink blanket her gram had given her for Christmas. It was her favorite thing in the world after Wolfie. Poor Wolfie, she hadn't seen him since the night at the hospital.

"JoJo," her daddy whispered.

Her eyes snapped open and she smiled, a hot spike of pain shooting from her ear all the way down to her chin, making her wince. She'd nearly forgotten. Her daddy's face floated above her bed, half-smiling, half-worried. She knew his worried look. One of his eyebrows always went up like a fuzzy caterpillar bending in the middle. Reaching up, she traced a finger over it, trying to smooth it down.

"Daddy," she said. "Is it wake-up time?"

Again, he brushed her hair away from her face, careful to avoid the dressing. "No, honey, it's still nighttime."

"Don't you have to go to work?" Josie asked.

He smiled, and his worried caterpillar brow arched more. "Not tonight, sweetie. I need to talk to you. We're going to go to Gram's, okay?"

"Will Mommy come?" she asked.

Her daddy looked away from her, at the closed door, and then back. "No. Mommy's staying here."

Josie tried to hide how happy this made her.

"JoJo," her daddy said, shifting on the edge of her bed. "I need you to be very quiet, okay? At least until we get out to my truck. Can you do that for me?"

Wide-eyed, Josie nodded.

He got up and walked over to a small duffel bag near the door, shoving things into it—her clothes and toys. She was just about to ask how long they were going to be at Gram's house, when there was a thump against her bedroom door. Both of them jumped. Her daddy turned just as another loud blow shook the door. Then her mother's voice shouted, "Goddamnit, Eli, what are you doing in there?"

Her daddy didn't answer. He just stood there in the middle of Josie's room, duffel bag in one hand.

"Unlock this door, Eli. Right now," she snarled.

"Daddy," Josie whispered. "I'm scared."

CHAPTER 19

One week later, Josie found Gretchen and Noah standing awkwardly in front of her desk. "What do you mean we have a problem?" she asked.

Noah sat in the guest chair while Gretchen began pacing, her notepad in hand. She took out a pair of reading glasses and perched them on the bridge of her nose before flipping a few pages. She read off the names of every person she had talked to at the Department of Human Services. None of them meant anything to Josie.

"Stop," Josie said. "You're telling me you talked to all of those people, and they *all* told you the same thing?"

Gretchen looked up at her. "Yes. The Belinda Rose file is not there. The Department of Human Services does not have it."

"Not there?" Noah asked. "Meaning it could be somewhere else? Do they have off-site storage?"

"No, they don't. All the county records are stored in one place—at the main office in Bellewood—and Belinda Rose's file is not among them," Gretchen said.

"So, they lost it," Josie said.

"They wouldn't go that far," Gretchen replied.

Noah laughed. "Which means they lost it. Or it was destroyed somehow, and they don't want to take the heat."

Josie ran a hand through her hair. "Okay, well, surely they had some kind of file for Maggie Smith. She ran the home Belinda lived in."

Gretchen waved her pen in the air. "Yes. That's the only lead we've got at this point. Turns out Maggie Smith got married in the late '90s, moved on from the foster home program, and became Maggie Lane. She and her husband traveled the country in an RV until he died of a heart attack."

"That was in her personnel file?" Noah asked, perplexed.

Gretchen smiled. "No, I got that from one of the DHS workers. Office gossip. She was new to the office when Maggie left to get married. Maggie had been running the group home for almost thirty years, so it was quite the hot topic of conversation at the time."

Josie asked, "How old was Maggie when she got married?"

"In her sixties. That was the other reason for all the gossip. She waited her whole life to get married, and then her husband was dead within ten years. It's terrible."

"She gave up her position at the group home in the late '90s," Josie remarked. "That was twenty years ago. Which means she would be in her mid-eighties. Is she—is she still alive?"

"Yes," Gretchen said. "She is currently a resident at Rockview Ridge, right here in Denton."

CHAPTER 20

JOSIE – SIX YEARS OLD

Josie pulled the covers over her head, curling into the tightest ball she could manage. Smaller, she needed to be smaller. The shouts from just outside her door punched through the air, penetrating the flimsy wood and slapping against her small bed. Again, Josie wished she had Wolfie.

"She is my daughter too, Belinda," her daddy said.

"So what? You're just going to take her and leave me? Leave me here alone?"

"I told you last week this wasn't working."

Her mother's voice became a screech. "Go then. Leave!"

Something thudded against Josie's door. She squeezed her body tighter, pressing her forehead to her knees.

"I'm taking my daughter," her daddy said.

"She's not yours! She's mine!"

"The hell she is."

There was a series of thuds and then a crash, and Josie heard what sounded like glass breaking. Then her mother's voice, mean this time, like the way it sounded in the hospital when she grabbed Josie's face. "I told you, you're not taking her. She stays here with me."

"You forfeited your right to be her parent when you put a blade against her face. You think I don't know you did that? Twenty-seven stitches, you sadistic bitch."

"You can't prove a goddamn thing. Now get out. You're not taking her."

"Get out of my way, Belinda."

"You think you can take the only thing I have and leave?"

"That's what I'm doing, isn't it? You've got some real serious problems, Belinda. Josie's not safe here. I'm taking her to my mother's."

"Oh sure, run to your mommy."

Josie heard a rustling, then a thump. Then her daddy said, "I don't want to hurt you, Belinda, but I will if it means protecting Josie. I'm taking her. Now get out of my way."

Her mother laughed, and Josie's body stiffened. Her heart felt like it was taking too long between beats.

More crashing. Then her daddy's voice came again, and this time he sounded different. "Belinda," he said. "Where did you get that?"

"You're not taking her, Eli."

"Let's talk about this."

More of her mother's laughter. Josie felt a strange feeling like she might pee herself. She tried to hold it in. Her mother would be *really* mad if she wet the bed.

"Oh, sure, now you want to talk," came her mother's voice from the other side of the door.

"But not here," her daddy said. "Let's take a walk, okay? Get some fresh air? We can talk this through."

"We can talk all you want, Eli, but you're not taking her."

CHAPTER 21

Sitting high on a rock-strewn hill at the edge of town, Rockview Ridge was Denton's one and only skilled nursing facility. Josie's grandmother, Lisette Matson, had been a resident there for several years now. Lisette was Josie's last living relative—besides Josie's mother—and her best friend. Josie visited her regularly and knew exactly where to find her at this time of day. She spotted Lisette's silver curls the moment she walked into Rockview's cafeteria; lunch was over, but several residents lingered, reading magazines, watching the communal television and, like Lisette, playing cards. She looked up and smiled, waving Josie over.

"You're never here this early in the day," she said as Josie leaned in for a kiss.

"I know. Work stuff." Josie took a seat across from her grandmother.

A game of solitaire was spread out before Lisette. She snapped a card down onto one of the piles and said, "I guess you don't have time to play."

"Sorry, Gram. Listen, I need to ask you some questions."

Lisette frowned. "Is everything okay? What's going on?"

Josie reached across the table and patted Lisette's hand. "Don't worry. No one is missing, or shot, or dead. Okay, well, that's not entirely true."

She told Lisette about the discovery of the real Belinda Rose's remains behind the trailer park. "We believe that my mother stole this girl's identity. I need you to tell me everything you remember about her."

Lisette's gaze slipped to the table. Slowly, she gathered her cards and began shuffling them. "Josie," she said, and her tone filled Josie with dread. It was the tone she had used when she caught Josie drinking at age sixteen, the tone she had used when she found out that Josie and Ray were having sex; it was her warning tone, the tone that said, "I can't stop you from traveling the path you're on, but I'm telling you to be careful."

Josie's heart did a quick double tap. "Gram," she said softly. "If my mother did something to this girl, I have to know."

Lisette still didn't look at her. "That woman is best left in your past, Josie. Have you forgotten how hard it was to get her out of our lives?"

"Of course I haven't. Believe me, if I had a choice, I would run screaming in the other direction. I don't even care that she's not who she said she was—but I have a murder to solve, and she has a connection to the victim."

Lisette stopped shuffling and placed her deck on the table, tapping the sides one by one until the cards were in perfect order. Josie thought she saw her eyes glisten over.

"Gram, please."

Suddenly her grandmother's fingers were digging into Josie's forearm with a strength and fierceness that belied her eighty-five years. Eyes wide, voice low, Lisette leaned in and said, "You think I don't know the things she did to you, Josie?"

Josie resisted the urge to pull away, even as pain spiked through her arm. "Don't," she choked out.

"I know, Josie. I know about what she did."

"Please, Gram. Don't."

"That's why I fought so hard for you. That's why I did the things I did. You remember that."

Josie couldn't catch her breath. Lisette's fingers dug in deeper, and Josie swore she felt her skin bruising.

"I should have killed her when I had the chance," Lisette added.

"Gram!"

Josie looked around, but none of the residents in the room were paying attention, and Gretchen, who had accompanied her to the home, was still at the front desk making inquiries about Maggie Lane.

"I would have," Lisette went on. "I wanted to, believe me. It would have been the best thing for all of us, but I was afraid I'd get caught and then you'd have no one."

Josie peeled her grandmother's fingers from her arm one by one and placed Lisette's hand on the table. "Gram, please. That's in the past. Just like you said. I'm not trying to resurrect all of that, but this case has to be solved."

"You can't be the one, Josie. You have to stay away from her. You've got officers beneath you. Let them do this."

Josie covered Lisette's hand with her own. "And they'll come in here and ask you the same questions I'm about to ask. I'm the chief of police, Gram. No, I don't have to lead the investigation, but I do have to oversee it. Just tell me what you can remember."

"You promise to stay away from her?" Lisette said.

"As much as I can," Josie answered.

Lisette pulled her hand away and stared down at her lap. "I don't know much more than you do, I'm afraid. Your father brought her over a few times in the beginning, introduced her as Belinda Rose. We had no reason to disbelieve her."

"What about her past?" Josie asked. "Did she ever talk about family or where she was from?"

Lisette was silent for a moment, and Josie could tell by the way her gaze drifted upward to the ceiling that she was searching her memory for any scraps that remained from before Josie's birth. "She didn't have any family," Lisette said. "That's what she said. Grew up in foster care. I remember that because I felt sorry for her. She was quite beautiful, your mother. When I met her, she was young, and I remember wondering why wouldn't any family adopt such a sweet, pretty girl?" She humphed. "Well, now we both know why. Unfortunately."

"I thought I heard her tell people her family was dead," Josie said.

Lisette shrugged. "She told a lot of different stories. She told your father and me that she had grown up in foster care. But after she left, I talked with the attorney who represented her in all the custody disputes. He said he didn't even know where to begin looking for her because she'd told him that her entire family perished in a house fire."

"Did she ever say where she was from?"

"Bellewood. Said she grew up around there, but that she had been moved from home to home all over the state."

"Did she have friends? A job?"

"No friends that I ever met. She used to clean houses though, I remember that."

"For a company or on her own?"

"Oh, I don't remember. I didn't ask. She stopped working after you were born anyway."

"Where did she and my father meet?"

Lisette gave a wan smile. "Where else? A bar. There used to be one down the way from the trailer park, but it was torn down ages ago."

"The trailer we lived in—whose was it?"

"Your father's. Well, he rented it from the park owner. When he died, she just kept making the payments. The owner tried to charge me for the damage to the place when she left since it was still in Eli's name."

"Do you know if she lived in the trailer park also? Before she met Dad?"

"I really don't know, love," Lisette answered. "I don't think she did. Your father said there were a lot of drugs in the park back then. He always worried about that with you. I wanted him to move back in with me after you were born, but he said your mother wouldn't allow it. Anyway, I think maybe she knew people from the bar who lived in the trailer park or went there to get high."

Josie sighed. The bar her grandmother referred to was long gone, and the drug activity that had plagued the trailer park had been eradicated during Chief Harris's tenure. Josie could have someone canvass the park, but she doubted anyone would have useful information sixteen years after the fact. Besides, by the time Josie's mother met her father, she had already been using the Belinda Rose identity for over a year, at least.

"Gram, do you have any photos of her?"

Lisette's mouth formed a straight line. A moment later, she said, "I don't think so. Your mother didn't like having her photo taken, and back then we didn't have phones with cameras, so we didn't take pictures every single day of our lives. We had actual cameras with rolls of film that had to be developed, and that cost money—"

"Gram," Josie said, trying to keep Lisette on track.

Lisette smiled. "I'll give you my photo albums before you leave, and you can go through them."

Gretchen appeared in the doorway of the cafeteria. She nodded at Lisette, and Lisette waved back at her. "You're not just here to talk to me, are you?" Lisette asked Josie.

"I'm afraid not, Gram. Do you know Maggie Lane?"

"I know who she is—she doesn't come out of her room much. Had a stroke a couple of years ago and hasn't felt like socializing since. Therapy brought her brain and her speech back, but she doesn't get around very well now. Only ever talked about her husband, and he's been gone a few years now. Don't worry, she's still lucid, but I think she's just one of those who's waiting to die. I can take you to her room if you like?"

CHAPTER 22

JOSIE – SIX YEARS OLD

Her mother shook her from sleep, pinching Josie's shoulder so hard that pain shot all the way down her arm. Josie opened her bleary eyes to see her mother's face floating above her in the lamplight. "JoJo," she whispered. "Wake up."

Josie felt her body stiffen. Slowly she sat up in the bed and looked at her mother. Strands of her mother's black hair floated around her head. Frizzies, her mother called them. They only appeared when it rained. Wet black streaks ran down each of her cheeks. She was crying.

Something was wrong. Very wrong.

"Mommy?" Josie said.

Her mother's soft, sympathetic smile punched fear into Josie's heart faster than if she'd held the shiny knife to Josie's face again. "Wh-where's Daddy?" Josie asked.

Her mother shifted on the bed and took Josie's hand. "Baby, I'm so sorry…your daddy did something very bad tonight."

Josie stared at her, confused. "What happened?"

Her hand gently stroked Josie's forearm, causing the hairs to stand to attention. Josie suddenly wished her mother wouldn't answer; each word of her reply was like a barb in Josie's skin.

"Your daddy left us tonight, JoJo. He's gone forever and ever. Do you know what it means when someone dies?"

Josie didn't answer, but she sort of knew. She knew that when people died they went to a place called heaven. That's what her daddy and her gram said. Heaven was really, really good, except that you didn't get to see your family anymore.

CHAPTER 23

Frail and thin, Maggie Lane sat hunched in a wheelchair, her long gray hair tied back in a ponytail. Although Josie knew Maggie was about the same age as her grandmother, time had been far less kind to her. Maggie's face seemed to have twice as many wrinkles as Lisette's, and her hands curled in her lap, fingers knobby and bent permanently inward toward her palms. Contractures, Josie knew they were called—when the joints or muscles shortened from lack of movement, causing permanent deformities. Josie glanced at Maggie's feet, turned inward toward one another in a pair of plain white sneakers, and suspected she probably had them in her feet as well.

Maggie raised her head up as Josie and Gretchen entered the room, and Lisette shuffled off back to the cafeteria with her walker. "Mrs. Lane," Gretchen said.

Maggie stared at them, her rheumy eyes flitting back and forth between the two unexpected visitors. Her wheelchair was sandwiched between her bed and a small dresser. Beside the dresser was a recliner, which Gretchen sat in while Josie remained standing. They introduced themselves, and Gretchen explained that they were there to talk to her about a girl who used to be in her care.

"In my care?" she said in a voice that sounded scratchy, perhaps from years of smoking cigarettes.

"A girl who lived with you in the group home on Powell Street in Bellewood," Gretchen said. "This would have been the late '70s, early '80s. Her name was Belinda Rose." Gretchen pulled out her trusty notepad and flipped through a few pages. "Birthday, October 15th."

Maggie lifted a gnarled hand and waved it. "I remember Belli. That's what I called her. Sweet thing. Till she got to be a teenager. Then she was hell on wheels."

Gretchen and Josie exchanged a look. Josie said, "How long did she live with you?"

A series of coughs erupted from her lungs, causing her whole body to shudder. Just as Josie was wondering if she should fetch one of the nurses, Maggie settled. "When I got Belli, she was about five. She was in a couple of foster homes before that, with families looking to adopt her, but it never worked out. One of them foster dads had different ideas about raising a girl, if you know what I mean."

Josie's stomach turned.

"So, you got her at five," Gretchen said. "Did they tell you anything about her real parents? Why she was in foster care to begin with?"

"Well, they don't tell you much, but if I'm remembering correctly, she was one of the girls that came from a couple of teenagers fooling around who weren't ready to be parents. Back then, having kids when you was a kid was…what do they say? Frowned upon. So we got quite a few kids come to us from teenage parents."

"What was she like?" Josie asked.

Maggie smiled, and her top dentures slipped a bit. She clamped her mouth shut, sucking them back into place. Then she said, "Sweet. She was a sweet one. Liked to help me around the home. Liked to do things for the other girls. Could always count on her for chores and such. She was affectionate too. A lot of those girls didn't have no affection growing up, and so they didn't want none or give it out. Some of them been hurt real bad—only knew a 'bad touch,' if you know what I'm sayin'."

"You said Belinda was a sweet girl until she became a teenager," Gretchen said. "What happened then?"

Maggie shrugged. Her shoulder blades rose as if she were going to have another coughing fit, but when she exhaled, all that came out was a long wheeze. She replied, "Don't know, really. Sometimes girls just go bad once they get a certain age. She started failing in school, staying out past curfew, smoking and drinking. Police caught her out in the woods drinking with some other kids a bunch of times."

In that part of Pennsylvania, it seemed every high school had an area out in the woods where teens congregated to get drunk or high, smoke cigarettes, or simply cut school. When Josie was in high school, they all went to a place known as The Stacks, a spot where multiple slabs of rock had fallen from the side of a mountain in stacks. "So, she went to school in Bellewood?" Josie asked.

"All my girls did," Maggie answered.

"Do you remember any of the kids she hung around with?" Gretchen asked.

"Had plenty of girls of my own to keep track of," Maggie said. "I couldn't be doing with their friends."

Josie said, "What about the girls in your care? Was she close to any of them?"

Maggie's lungs whistled again. She held up a hand, and they waited several seconds for her to catch her breath and speak again. "Not really. She kept to herself. She shared a room with Angie… oh dear, I don't remember her last name, although she went and got married after college, moved out by Philadelphia. Belli was closer to Angie than any of them."

If Angie had gone to college, gotten married, and moved to Philadelphia, then she wasn't Josie's mother. Still, they'd find her and see what she knew about Belinda and the people she associated with. "I'm sure we can track Angie down through the old files," Josie said. "That's very helpful."

Gretchen asked, "What did Belinda look like?"

"My Belli was short and chunky, with the curliest blond hair you ever saw. A nuisance it was."

"How long was she in your care?" Gretchen asked.

"Well, she was supposed to be with me till she was eighteen, but she ran away a couple of times."

Again, Josie's and Gretchen's eyes met. "When was that?" Josie asked Maggie.

Maggie leaned her head back and gave a tired sigh. Her face was ashen. The interview was taking a lot out of her. "Well, once for a few months when she was about fifteen or sixteen. Can't remember exactly. I was so mad at her. Someone at the high school had got her this job at the courthouse doing filing and answering phones a few hours a week. She did so well at first and was bringing in her own money. She stopped cutting school, stayed out of trouble, mostly. But she started fighting with my other girls a lot."

"About what?" Gretchen asked.

Another shrug. "Who knows? What do teenage girls fight about? There were always squabbles about their things—this one used the other one's hairbrush, that one took the other one's sweater. Then the other girls said she thought she was better than them 'cause she had a fancy job. Silly kid stuff. Then they teased her 'cause she put on some weight after she started working. She started eating everything in sight; I couldn't keep up. I never got paid that much for any of my girls. I had to stretch what little the state gave me to feed all of them. Anyway, we had a fight 'cause I said she was eating me out of house and home, and she started crying and ran off. Came back a few months later."

"Was she still overweight when she returned?" Josie asked.

"A little. But she'd calmed down a bit."

Gretchen wrote something down in her notebook, and Josie knew she was marking the timeline. Belinda Rose had suddenly gained weight and started overeating after working at the courthouse for a while. She'd left and come back thinner and with less of an appetite. Perhaps it hadn't been obvious to Maggie, but Josie knew exactly what had happened. "Mrs. Lane, did Belinda ever have any…health issues?"

Maggie turned her head in Josie's direction. "What do you mean, health problems?"

Josie shrugged. "I don't know. Anything."

Gretchen saw where Josie was trying to go and reached forward, placing a palm on Maggie's thin forearm. "Mrs. Lane, we have reason to believe that Belinda may have given birth at some point."

Maggie stared at her, uncomprehending. Then she laughed, her thin shoulders bouncing. "You're mistaken," she told Gretchen. "Belli never had no baby."

Gretchen looked to Josie, and Josie gave a swift shake of her head. Clearly, Maggie hadn't known about the pregnancy, so there was no point in pursuing that line of questioning with her. Gretchen asked, "Did you report her missing?"

"Course I did," Maggie said. "I had to. Police never found her. One day she just came back."

"Did she talk about where she had been?" Gretchen asked.

"No, and I didn't have time to pry it out of her. I had a lot of girls, and if you don't know, teenage girls aren't exactly easy."

"Mrs. Lane, can you try to remember exactly when that was? Was Belinda fifteen or sixteen?" Josie asked.

Maggie sucked on her upper dentures again. "Sixteen. She just turned sixteen."

"So, it was the fall?" Gretchen prodded.

She took a moment, then said, "It must have been. It was real cold. I remember 'cause we had all these extra heaters in the house, and I was afraid one of my girls was gonna start a fire with 'em. It was right before Christmas too. They were all just waitin' for that Christmas break to come, but holidays were hard 'cause they were all foster kids. A lot of 'em got depressed around the holidays—led to a lot more fights. I hate to say it, but when Belli ran off that first time, it was sort of a relief."

So Belinda Rose had been fairly late in her pregnancy in the fall of 1982, just after she turned sixteen, and had gone off to give birth and returned with no one the wiser.

"Can you tell me," Gretchen asked, "did she have a boyfriend? Any lads she hung around with regularly or was interested in?"

"There was one she went to high school with. Oh, what was his name? Lonnie or Lyle or something. He had two first names."

Josie suppressed a groan. "Lloyd Todd?"

Maggie raised an arthritic finger in the air. "Yes, that's it! They were together almost a year."

Josie knew that Lloyd Todd had grown up in Bellewood. He had moved to Denton when he started his business, because Denton was significantly larger than Bellewood and offered many more clients for both his contracting business and his drug venture.

Gretchen made another notation. "You said the first time— when did she go missing the second time?"

"Couple years later. She was seventeen; had about six months to go till she was eighteen. I remember 'cause we were trying hard to figure out what she was gonna do after she aged out. She wanted to stay with me, but I told her she couldn't. It was around Easter, I remember that. She went to work at the courthouse after school like she always did. She was supposed to be home around seven, but she never came back. I called the police again, made a report."

"We've checked records for the entire county," Josie said. "She's not listed as a missing person."

"Oh, 'cause she's not, dear. I got a postcard from her a few months after she left. It was after her eighteenth birthday, so she was free to do what she wanted. Never gave an address and never came to pick up any of her stuff though."

Josie felt a tingle race up her spine. "Where was the postcard from?"

"Philadelphia. Said she was sorry she left suddenly, but she met a man there and they were getting married. Thanked me for everything."

Gretchen said, "You don't still have that postcard by any chance, do you?"

Maggie laughed. "Oh honey, I didn't keep anything from my care home days once I married my husband. We took the RV on the road. Wasn't a lot of room for nostalgia. But I did give it to the police so they could mark their case closed."

CHAPTER 24

JOSIE – SEVEN YEARS OLD

Josie woke, thrashing and sweat-covered from a nightmare. Her eyes snapped open, and she had a moment of terror at the unfamiliar surroundings before the fog of sleep receded and she remembered where she was—at Gram's house, in Gram's bed. Ever since her daddy died, she had been staying here. She had her own room, but she usually preferred to curl up beside Gram. Josie sat up and blinked, her hands searching the bed covers for her grandmother's warmth, but it wasn't there.

"Gram?" she called.

There was no answer. Fear wrapped its calloused fingers around her heart, squeezing hard. She climbed down from the bed and tiptoed along the hallway toward the sliver of light coming from beneath the bathroom door. As she got closer, she heard her grandmother wailing, a high-pitched keening sound that made goosebumps break out all over her skin. She stood frozen in the hall, wondering if she should knock or call out to her. The pressure in her chest got tighter, and she ran back to Gram's bed and pulled the covers all the way over her head. She wished more than anything that her daddy would come back from heaven, but deep down she knew she would never see him again.

She was just wondering if Wolfie was in heaven with him when she heard her gram's footsteps in the hall. Josie shut her eyes and pretended to be asleep when Gram returned, not moving an inch when she climbed back into bed and wrapped her arms tightly around her.

When she woke, Gram was gone again, and sunlight streamed through the windows of the bedroom. Hearing voices downstairs, Josie hopped out of bed and went to the top of the steps to listen.

The sound of her mother's voice made Josie's whole body go cold. "She's mine. You'll never get her, Lisette."

"Please, Belinda," answered her gram. "She's happy here. I'll take care of her."

"Over my dead body," Josie's mother said. Then she shouted, "JoJo! Come down here."

Slowly, like her limbs were moving through mud, Josie made her way down the stairs. Her mother smiled at her. Not in the scary way she sometimes did just before she did something mean, but in the way she did on the rare occasion that she was nice to Josie—like when she gave her the coloring book. She knelt so that she was face to face with Josie and gently smoothed Josie's hair out of her eyes. "JoJo, you want to come home with Mommy, right?"

Josie didn't know what to say. She didn't want to leave Gram, but she liked it when her mother was nice to her. When she didn't answer, her mother said, "I've missed you, JoJo. Don't you want to come home with me? We'll color and play games and do girl stuff together; what do you say?"

Josie looked at Gram, whose face had gone all stiff.

"JoJo?" her mother said.

She wanted to do all those things with her mother. They could play hide and seek and tag, and maybe they could paint their nails together. One of Josie's friends from school had spa days with her mother where they played with makeup and did each other's hair. Josie wanted that more than anything.

Josie nodded, and before she knew it, her mother was stuffing her into the passenger's seat of her blue Chevette and slamming the door. Josie looked up to where Gram stood on the porch, tears glittering in her eyes, waving slowly. Josie's mother got into the driver's side and started the engine.

"Mommy," Josie said. "I forgot my clothes and my blanket."
"Shut up, JoJo."

CHAPTER 25

It took nearly four hours to get their hands on the Belinda Rose file. Josie considered it a miracle that the tiny Bellewood Police Department still had it. Their chief was gracious enough to let Josie, Noah, and Gretchen search their dusty back room filled with old, closed files. It didn't appear that they had ever thrown anything away.

"Gotta love small-town departments," Noah remarked as he pulled box after box off the storage shelves for Josie and Gretchen to look through.

Josie was just beginning to lose hope of ever finding it when she finally put her fingers on it. The ink on the yellowed file tab was so faded that Josie could barely make it out, but there it was: Belinda Rose.

After signing the requisite forms, the three of them left with the file in hand and headed back to their own station house, Gretchen sneezing the entire time from the hours spent kicking up dust. Josie's eyes burned like hell. They rode most of the way back to Denton with the windows of Josie's Escape all the way down, letting the cool March air blow away the past for a little while.

Once in Josie's office, they spread the contents of the file across her desk. It was thin, and the reports were faded and typewritten with an old-fashioned typewriter. There wasn't much more than what Maggie Lane had told them. Josie noted the names of the officers who had taken the two missing persons reports. A quick call to Bellewood PD revealed that both had retired long ago.

"Here," Noah said, plucking an old color photograph from the pile of pages. It was slightly bigger than an index card and showed a heavyset teenage girl standing in the small garden outside the care home. Sunlight streamed down on her, the light bouncing off her tight blond curls, and she squinted against it, smiling. A shapeless floral-print dress draped over her large middle, stopping midway down two pale, thick thighs. Josie saw the strap of a backpack on one shoulder, and in one of her hands she held a brown paper bag.

"First day of school," Gretchen said.

Josie took the photo from Noah's hand and turned it over. Someone had written *September 1982*.

"She was pregnant in this photo," Josie said. "If we've got our timeline correct."

"Is there another photo?" Gretchen asked, her fingers shuffling the contents of the file once more. "From before the second time she ran away?"

Josie found it paper-clipped to a second set of reports that had been prepared over a year after the first set. In the photo, Belinda was descending a flight of stairs in what Josie guessed was the foster home—the background was all dark wood paneling and ratty gray carpet. The photo didn't look posed for as the last one had—more like someone had caught her coming down the steps and snapped the photo. Belinda was considerably smaller and thinner than in the first photo they had found—she looked half the size she had been in September of 1982. Her hair hadn't changed; tight blond ringlets hung to her shoulders, offering a splash of life to the otherwise drab background. Without the sunlight in her face, her blue eyes shone wide and clear over a thin smile. This time she wore a tight pair of jeans and the same nylon windbreaker that Dr. Feist had unearthed along with her body. Peeking out from the collar of the jacket was a small gold locket in the shape of a heart.

"Look at that," Josie said, pointing to it. "That wasn't found in the grave."

"Maybe she wasn't wearing it when she died," Gretchen offered.

"She was a foster kid. It's quite a nice locket," Josie pointed out.

"Could be costume jewelry, Boss," Noah pointed out.

"It could also be important," Josie insisted.

She herself hadn't grown up in foster care, but her situation hadn't been much better; not until after her mother left. Josie hadn't owned jewelry even remotely as nice as that locket until she'd turned eighteen, when Ray had given her a diamond pendant he'd saved up for months to buy. She'd worn it nonstop through most of college. She still had it.

"Gretchen," Josie said, "when we're done here, take a picture of this photo with your phone and go back to Rockview and talk to Maggie Lane. She said that Belinda left her things the second time she disappeared. Ask her if this locket was among them, would you?"

"Sure thing, Boss," Gretchen said, snapping a picture of the photo with her cell phone.

"When was that picture taken?" Noah asked.

Josie took the photo back from Gretchen, turned it over, and read off the month and year. "March 1984."

"Maggie said she went missing around Easter in 1984," Gretchen said, bringing up the internet browser on her phone. Josie watched over her shoulder as she punched in her query. "Easter was April 22nd of that year," Gretchen added.

Josie picked up the report that Maggie had made. "This is dated the 26th," she said.

"So we can estimate the date of the murder then," Noah said. "Sometime on or after April 26, 1984."

"Yeah, but that doesn't tell us anything about who did it," Josie answered. "But there are names here of people who were interviewed back then. Here—" she snatched up another piece of paper. "They interviewed Lloyd Todd and his brother, Damon." She skimmed the faded typewritten words. "Lloyd said they'd been dating on and off since early 1983, broke things off around Christmas of 1983. He saw her at school that day and she seemed fine. He was at track and field practice that evening. His brother and father confirmed this as they were both at the athletic field that night too."

"It's going to be impossible to talk to Lloyd Todd," Gretchen noted. "I mean, he's in county jail right now awaiting trial. No way is he going to talk to any cops about anything without his lawyer."

Josie nodded. "He might not even agree to speak with us. Track down the brother then. If the Bellewood PD thought he was worth interviewing back then, maybe he can help us now."

Gretchen marked down the brother's name on her notepad. Then she said, "There are some names of people she worked with at the courthouse here too."

"Track them down as well," Josie said. "Someone might know who she used to hang around with. Also, see if the DHS has a list of all the girls under Maggie Lane's care for the time period that Belinda was there. I want names and photos if you can get them. Track as many of them down as you can. I want the most complete picture we can get of this girl's life in the months before she was killed."

Noah searched through the rest of the file as Josie spoke. Finally, he came up with a postcard. The Liberty Bell took up one side, the words *Greetings from Philadelphia* in red letters above it. He handed it to Josie, and she turned it over, staring at the writing on the back of it while her blood turned to ice in her veins.

Maggie: I'm sorry I left without telling you. I met the most wonderful man. We're in love! He's whisked me away to Philadelphia and we're getting married! Please don't worry about me. Thank you for everything! Belinda

It was dated the day after Belinda Rose's eighteenth birthday, postmarked out of Philadelphia, and written in Josie's mother's handwriting.

CHAPTER 26

JOSIE – SEVEN YEARS OLD

Josie's stomach clenched and burned. She didn't remember ever being so hungry. Her mother hadn't come out of her room in days. Inside the fort of sheets she had made in her bedroom, her belly groaned and felt like it was trying to fold in on itself. She squeezed her eyes shut and pressed her hands together, whispering, "Dear God in heaven, please bring my daddy back, and Wolfie too, and let me see Gram again, and also please bring more food for me and my mommy."

As she said the words, she heard voices outside her door. Her mother and a man; it must be Needle. She couldn't hear what they were saying, but she heard them walk past her door, and then heard her mother's bedroom door close.

Then she smelled it. Pizza. It was unmistakable, and her favorite. The smell of it filled her mouth with saliva. As quietly as she could, she opened her door and snuck into the hallway. Her feet were light and soundless on the worn carpet that led from the hall into the living room, ending at the kitchen tile.

The big white box sat on the kitchen table, smells of deliciousness seeping from its creases. Josie's stomach made a noise so loud, she was sure her mother and Needle heard it. But no sound came from the back of the trailer. She climbed onto a kitchen chair and opened the box. Glancing back to make sure they were still in the bedroom, she picked up a slice that seemed bigger than her head and started eating. She ate until she felt sick and woozy but fuller than she had felt in weeks.

She was on her third slice when a hand came down hard on the back of her head, knocking her from the chair she squatted on.

"Jesus, Belinda," Needle said as her mother grabbed her by the arm and dragged her out of the kitchen.

"Did I say you could eat that pizza?"

Josie said nothing. Her throat felt like it was full of concrete. Tears stung the backs of her eyes, and she concentrated as hard as she could on not letting them fall.

"Belinda," Needle said. "Come on."

"You shut up," she told him.

The closet door opened in front of Josie, coats hanging from a bar above a dusty, brown bit of carpet. It smelled like cigarette smoke and stale air. Josie screamed, "No! Mommy, no!"

Josie's mother pushed her inside. "Shut up."

The carpet was scratchy against Josie's cheek. "Mommy, you said," Josie choked out, unable to stop the tears now, "you said if I didn't tell, I wouldn't have to go in the closet. Mommy!"

Needle said, "Jesus, Belinda. She's a kid."

Her mother pointed a finger at Needle. "You stay out of it."

"Mommy, please!" Josie cried.

Then the door slammed shut, and the darkness closed in all around her.

CHAPTER 27

"Are you sure this is your mother's handwriting?" Noah asked.

Josie plopped into her chair, the first painful throbs of a headache starting behind her eyes. When Josie didn't answer him, he said, "Do you have a sample? Something that has her handwriting on it so we could compare?"

"I don't need a sample," Josie said.

From the guest chair in front of Josie's desk, Gretchen said, "Lieutenant Fraley, did you learn to forge your parents' signatures when you were a teenager?"

He looked at her. "What? No. Why would I need to forge their signatures?"

Gretchen shook her head, a look of mock sadness turning the corners of her mouth downward. "Well," she said gravely, "you must come from a long line of goody-goodies."

In spite of herself, Josie laughed long and loud, grateful to Gretchen for easing the tension in the room. Josie felt the tight muscles in her shoulder blades loosen a fraction as she laughed.

Noah raised a brow. "What?"

Josie said, "You're kidding, right? You can't forge *either* one of your parents' signatures?"

His gaze snapped from Gretchen to Josie. "No. What are you—"

Gretchen cut him off by standing and flipping her open notebook to face him. Josie stood so she could see the page too. On it, in two radically different types of handwriting, Gretchen had written: *Agnes Palmer* and *Fred Palmer*. "My grandparents' signatures," she offered. "I lived with them during high school.

How do you think I successfully cut school seventeen days of my senior year?"

Noah shook his head, but a small smile played on his lips. "So you were an overachiever then, were you?"

Gretchen slapped his shoulder with her notebook but laughed just the same.

Josie took a piece of paper out of the printer on the corner of her desk and signed her mother's name as she had known it: *Belinda Rose.*

Both Gretchen and Noah stared at it, wide-eyed. It was a near-perfect match to the handwriting on the postcard. "I started cutting school when I was twelve," Josie explained. "Also, my mom wasn't around much, and she didn't care about school or doctor's appointments or much else when it came to me, so learning to forge her signature came in pretty handy until she left. Then when I moved in with my grandmother, she caught me trying to learn her handwriting and grounded me for a week."

The levity in the room leached away as Josie placed her forged signature next to the postcard. She didn't look at her officers. The throbbing behind her eyes had become a full-on pounding, like a heartbeat. She choked out the words, "Looks like my mother just graduated from person of interest to prime suspect."

CHAPTER 28

JOSIE – EIGHT YEARS OLD

Josie pounded her fists against the closet door. "Mommy, please!" she cried. "I have to finish my homework."

There was the sound of something sliding across the living room carpet, then a bang against the closet door. Josie jumped back. The shard of light at the bottom of the door disappeared. Her breath froze in her lungs. The last few times she'd locked Josie in the closet, her mother had pushed one of the living room chairs up against the door so Josie couldn't get out.

Josie put her hand in front of her face, but she couldn't see it. Her heart pounded so hard, the sound seemed to fill up the tiny dark space. She sank to the floor, curling into a ball and trying desperately to think of things that made her feel happy, like visiting Gram and going to school. The thought of school made tears sting her eyes; her teacher was going to be disappointed in her when her homework wasn't finished. It was so unfair. She hadn't even done anything wrong. She'd come home from school and started her homework, then her mother had stormed in like a tornado, tossing Josie into the closet like an old coat.

When Josie heard the muffled voice of a man, she suddenly understood why. One of her mother's special friends was there. Josie always had to go into the closet when they came. Sweet-smelling smoke wafted under the door and made her dizzy. The man's voice was loud and angry. "I told you to have my fucking money, Belinda," he said. "Where's my money?"

It wasn't Needle. Josie had heard this man's voice before, but she had never seen his face.

Her mother said, "Relax. I told you, I'm good for it."

"No, you're not. If you were good for it, you would have it and I wouldn't have to wait. What do you think this is? I don't give shit away for free. What do you have? What can you give me right now?"

There was the sound of rustling, drawers being pulled out, things being knocked over. Then her mother said, "All I got is seven dollars."

A louder sound came; a heavy crash. Josie heard her mother cry out. When she next spoke, her voice sounded all squeezed and strange. "Come…on…let go…we'll work something out, I promise."

"Oh yeah? Like what? I want payment now, and I'm going to get it one way or another."

"You know what—I don't have money, but there are other things I can do to pay you back."

"Yeah? Like what?"

"I have a girl. You can take her in the back. Do whatever you want."

"What do you mean, a girl?"

"What do you think I mean? A kid. You can have her. I'll talk to her. She'll do whatever you want."

"How old?"

Her mother didn't answer.

"Wait a minute," the man said. "You mean that little kid? The one with dark hair just like you?"

"I only got one kid," said her mother.

There was a long, silent moment. Josie knew they were talking about her, but she didn't understand what they were saying.

When the man spoke next, his voice was filled with disgust. For a moment, he reminded Josie of the way her daddy talked to her mother near the end, before he went away to heaven. "Are you kidding me? You're kidding, right? You think I'm some kind of pervert?"

"No, no. I didn't say that."

"I don't mess with little kids. That's disgusting. You're fucked up, you know that? Give me my shit back."

Josie heard crashing sounds, grunts, gasps, and then her mother, breathless, begging, "No, please. I can pay you. Just wait." There was more rustling, the sound of a zipper being pulled down, and then the man took in a sharp breath. Josie's mother said, "I can take care of the payment myself."

CHAPTER 29

"You didn't find any pictures of your mother in your grandmother's photo albums?" Gretchen asked.

Josie stared straight ahead from her place in the passenger's seat of Gretchen's department-issue Cruze. "I found two photos of her in profile—she was with my dad—but that was it. In both, her face was turned too far away from the camera for them to be of any use to us. My grandmother never liked her and never got along with her, so I'm not surprised she didn't take that many photos of her."

"Sounds like a lot of people didn't get along with her," Gretchen noted.

Josie turned her gaze toward the window, watching the working-class neighborhoods of Denton give way to the more affluent areas. They were entering the mayor's neighborhood, where the houses stood tall and regal on acres of meticulously kept land. Apparently, Damon Todd had also moved from Bellewood to Denton after high school, and had done quite well for himself. It had only taken Gretchen a day to locate him, and when she called him, he had agreed to speak to them with the understanding that it had nothing to do with the charges pending against his brother.

When Josie didn't speak, Gretchen said, "Boss, I know you don't want to talk about her, and I don't need to know…the things she did, but I am one of the lead investigators on this case. It would help if I had a better idea of what she was like."

Josie knew Gretchen was right. In any investigation Josie ran herself, she would ask family members the same questions. You had to know who you were dealing with—what you were walking into when the day came to confront the person you were hunting.

Gretchen pulled over in front of a large white-and-brick colonial with pillars holding up a portico, bougainvillea lining the front of it. She turned the car off and shifted in her seat, pulling her polo shirt from where it was tucked into her khaki pants and lifting it up, revealing pale flesh beneath.

"What are you doing?" Josie asked.

Gretchen was in her forties and carried some excess weight around her middle. Rolls of doughy skin jostled as she lifted her shirt up to just beneath her breasts.

"Gretchen," Josie said, slightly alarmed. "I don't think—"

She stopped speaking when she saw the scars. They crisscrossed Gretchen's upper abdomen, some of them silver and thin and others purple-pink and thick like cords of rope. "Exploratory abdominal surgery," Gretchen explained. "Do you know what Munchausen by proxy is?"

Josie swallowed. "That's that syndrome where parents make their children sick for attention?"

Gretchen smiled and lowered her shirt, tucking it back into her waistband. "Yes, exactly."

"Your—your mother did that to you?" Josie asked.

Gretchen shook her head. "No, various doctors did it over many years. My mother made them think I needed it."

"I'm so sorry," Josie said, feeling stunned, as though Gretchen had just punched her. Gretchen was notoriously private. She had been with them almost a year, and no one knew anything about her. Most of the time she wore a beat-up leather jacket that, combined with her short, spiked hair, gave her the look of a biker, but as far as Josie knew, she didn't own a motorcycle. The jacket clearly had a story behind it, but no one on the police force had had the nerve to ask about it. Josie understood this need for privacy; she was the same way. Gretchen had always done her job well, and neither Josie nor anyone else on the team had felt the need to pry.

"Look," Gretchen said, "I know this stuff isn't easy to talk about. It's not easy to bare your scars, yeah?"

Josie swallowed and gave a stiff nod.

"Even when those scars are here." Gretchen tapped an index finger to her temple. "Or here," she added, tapping the same finger against her heart. "But I know a thing or two about toxic mothers."

"How did—when did your mother stop?" Josie asked.

"When she killed my sister," Gretchen said. "She's been in prison ever since. Muncy. Inmate number OY8977."

Josie said nothing.

The front door of the colonial opened, and a tall man in his late forties with wavy salt-and-pepper hair walked toward the car.

"Well," Josie said as she opened her door, "maybe my mother will join her."

Gretchen smiled as she opened her own door. They met Damon Todd halfway up his driveway and made introductions. Up close, Josie could see that he was good-looking for his age—tan and fit with an easy smile. The polar opposite of his burly, gristle-faced brother. He wore a blue polo shirt and khaki pants, as if he were about to head out golfing. He invited them inside, walking them through a large, high-ceilinged foyer with bags of sports equipment pushed up against one wall.

Damon smiled sheepishly as he motioned to it. "Sorry. I've got three teenage boys and they all play sports—and now I've got Lloyd's boys as well. The foyer is kind of the dumping ground when they come in."

To the left of the foyer was the living room. The hardwood floors were dominated by a gray microfiber U-shaped sectional that faced a large television. Josie counted three different video game systems on the entertainment center beneath the television. The sleek, dark coffee table with matching pedestal tables on either side of the room boasted faux floral arrangements. Between those and the heavy, gray, pleated drapes, it was obvious that the messy, sports-loving Todd men still had a woman in their lives. Josie knew from the research that Gretchen had done that Damon was now a physical therapist who worked closely with the student athletes on Denton University's campus.

"So," Damon said, taking a seat on one side of the sectional. "You're here to talk about Belinda Rose. I always wondered what happened to her."

"I'm sorry to tell you that she was murdered," Gretchen said, taking a seat across from him. Josie remained standing.

Beneath the tan, Damon's skin paled. "What? When…How?"

"We believe she was killed sometime on or after the night she disappeared," Josie cut in. "April 26, 1984."

His brow furrowed. "Disappeared? Word at school was she met someone, and they ran off to Philadelphia together. How do you know she was murdered?"

"We recently found her remains in the woods out behind the trailer park," Josie answered.

He hung his head. "My God. I don't know what to say." They gave him a moment. He took in a few breaths, and when he looked back up at them, he said, "What does this have to do with me?"

Gretchen said, "We're trying to get a picture of Belinda's life before she died—who she hung around with, what she was like, places she went, that sort of thing."

"Oh, well, we didn't know each other that well."

"Her foster mother said she dated your brother, Lloyd," Josie said. "Your brother gave a statement to a police officer after she disappeared stating he was her boyfriend, and you confirmed it."

"I wouldn't have said that, and neither would Lloyd. Maybe that's what the police inferred. That's what everyone inferred. I mean, people just assumed that."

Gretchen asked, "Why would people assume that Belinda and Lloyd were dating?"

"And why would Lloyd let them?" Josie added.

He clasped his large hands together and pressed them between his knees. "Well, she spent a lot of time at our house junior year."

"But she and Lloyd weren't an item?" Gretchen said.

"No, not the two of them."

"Then who? You and Belinda?"

His mouth twisted. "I guess it doesn't matter now," he mumbled, almost to himself.

"What doesn't matter, Mr. Todd?" Josie asked.

"Belinda was seeing our dad," he blurted. The effort of pushing the words out seemed to make him short of breath.

Josie and Gretchen looked at one another. Then Josie said, "Your dad?"

"He's dead now," Damon said. "Died a few years back of pancreatic cancer. He was an algebra teacher at the high school. Back then, my mom had left us right before my freshman year, so it was just the three of us—me, Lloyd, and Dad. He was tutoring Belinda after school, and things...progressed."

"That's one way of putting it," Gretchen said. Her notebook was out, and she began frantically making notes. "When did the affair start?"

"Right before the summer after sophomore year."

"1983?" Gretchen asked.

"Yeah. That's right. It was the summer before she disappeared."

"Did you or Lloyd ever talk to her or your dad about what was going on?" Josie asked.

"We tried. We were both pretty disgusted with him. I mean, we weren't ready for him to date at all, let alone carry on an affair with someone we went to school with. Lloyd was furious. I thought him and my dad were going to come to blows over it, but my dad made it clear he wasn't going to stop seeing her, and finally Lloyd just gave up. They didn't speak for a long while. I tried reasoning with Dad, but he said it was something I couldn't understand until

I was older. He said we could be mad at him all we wanted, but he only asked that we not tell anyone, because it would ruin his career and he could go to jail."

Josie and Gretchen stared at him.

He spread his hands in a plaintive gesture. "Look, I know it sounds terrible. Looking back, I realize how bad it was, but Lloyd and I were kids. All we had was my dad. If he went to prison, we'd be on our own. I think that's why Lloyd stopped fighting with him over it. He kept saying it would fizzle out eventually and that as upsetting as it was, it wasn't worth our dad going to jail, so I just kind of…fell in line."

"What about Belinda?" Gretchen asked. "Did you ever talk to her about their relationship?"

"Yeah, a couple times. She said she wouldn't stop seeing my dad and asked me not to tell anyone. She said Lloyd had already agreed to do the same. Like I said, ultimately, Lloyd didn't want our dad to go to jail. He was in the same year as Belinda, so when people assumed that she was coming over here to see him all the time, we let them think that. She told people at school she and Lloyd were a thing, and he didn't deny it. She followed him around, and even though he barely gave her the time of day, people saw them together and just assumed they were an item. You know, she had…this is going to sound strange, but she had fangs. Only on the top. They weren't even really noticeable, but by high school, almost everyone knew she had them."

"It was noted in the autopsy," Josie said. "Supernumerary teeth."

"Is that what they're called? Sorry. No disrespect intended. I only bring it up because she got made fun of a lot in school for them. She didn't have a lot of friends—none, really—and when Lloyd didn't deny that they were together and let her follow him around, all of the teasing stopped. I think sometimes she didn't want to bother with guys her own age because all they ever did was pick on her. She never said that. That's just my take on it. I mean, I told her she should be dating someone her own age, but she said—" He broke off and looked away from them.

"She said what?" Josie prompted.

"She said she liked older men—that they were nicer to her and more sophisticated and treated her better. She made it sound like she'd been with older men before."

Gretchen's pen hovered over her notepad. "Did she name anyone?"

Damon shook his head. "No. I thought she was making it up, trying to make herself seem more mature."

"Did your father ever give Belinda any gifts? Jewelry or anything like that?" Josie asked.

"No. He wouldn't have. He was pretty paranoid about being caught. People knew he was single, so if he bought jewelry, the town would have been talking. She always wore this locket 'round her neck, but it wasn't from him."

Josie narrowed her eyes. "Really? Did she ever say who gave it to her?"

"I never asked her, and she never talked about it. Lloyd didn't care enough about her to ask her. The other girls at school would bring it up sometimes, but she just said it was from someone special, and that's all she would say. I used to think maybe she bought it herself. Belinda was a nice person, but she liked attention, and the more mystery she could surround herself with, the more attention she drew."

"Mr. Todd," Josie said. "Did Belinda ever mention being pregnant or having had a baby?"

His eyes widened. "What? No. Never."

Josie knew that Belinda's affair with Damon Todd's father would have started four or five months after she'd given birth, but it was worth a try to see if perhaps she had mentioned it to Damon. Josie wondered if Belinda had hidden the pregnancy from everyone. Had she had even one friend to confide in? Would anyone out there know what had happened to the baby?

"So, what happened between Belinda and your father?" Gretchen asked, picking up the line of questioning once more.

"Oh, it didn't last. By the time the new year came around, they were finished."

"Who broke it off?" Gretchen asked.

"She did. My dad was crushed. I think he really liked her. She would have been eighteen that fall. They could have been together for real—at least that's what my dad kept saying. Took him months to stop talking about her. Then that fall there were rumors around town that she had met some guy in Philadelphia and was getting married. I never saw my dad so depressed—well, except for when my mom left."

"Where did these rumors come from?" Josie asked.

"One of the girls who'd lived at the care home with her was in her senior year, and after their foster mom got a postcard from Belinda, it was all the girls at the home could talk about. Word spread from there. Eventually my dad overheard some of the kids talking about it in class."

"Do you remember any of the names of the girls she lived with at the care home?" Josie asked.

He rattled off a few of them, mostly first names that were so common they'd be impossible to track down with any accuracy. But within a few days, they'd have the list of former care home girls from the Department of Human Services, and they'd be able to match those names with the names Damon remembered.

"I know you said she didn't have many friends, but do you remember if she had any close friends that she hung around with? Most teenage girls have at least one."

"I'm sorry, but no, I can't think of anyone. She wasn't popular, and she didn't really have friends at school—other than the girls who lived at the care home. I mean, if she had friends outside of school, I don't know. She had a job at the courthouse—she might have made friends there that I didn't know about. Like I said, she was seeing my dad. It was weird. We covered for them, but it wasn't like her and I were friends, you know? You could always check the yearbooks. All the girls from the foster home went to Bellewood High."

Josie wanted to kick herself for not thinking of it. "The yearbooks," she said. "Does the school keep copies that far back?"

"I don't know, but if you want, you can have my dad's. He kept one for every year he taught. They're in the garage with a bunch of his other stuff. I didn't know what to do with them. Seemed wrong to throw them away."

Gretchen stood up. "That would be great, Mr. Todd. We would certainly appreciate it."

"Sure. My wife will be happy to be rid of them."

CHAPTER 30

JOSIE – NINE YEARS OLD

Josie dragged a piece of blue chalk across the sidewalk outside of her grandmother's home. A series of squares stretched from one end of the pavement to the other in a pattern: two squares, then one, then two, then one, and so on. They played hopscotch at school all the time, but Josie had never drawn the boxes before. She'd squealed with delight when her grandmother presented her with a pack of colored sidewalk chalk. There were four colors: blue, pink, yellow, and green. Josie liked blue best of all, so that's what she started with. Once the boxes were all complete, she went to one end and started jumping. One foot, two feet, one foot, two feet—all the way to the end.

"Josie," her grandmother called from the front door. "Time to get ready."

Carefully, she put her chalk back inside its cardboard box and skipped up the front walk and inside.

"Wash your hands," Lisette told her.

Josie ran to the kitchen and did as she was told. "Do you think I'll fall, Gram?" she asked.

Lisette smiled as she pulled their jackets from the closet in the front hallway. "Probably. Everyone falls their first time roller skating. It's unavoidable."

Josie dried her hands on the dish towel and ran to Lisette so she could slide her jacket on. "How long does it take to get to the skating rink?"

"Oh, not long," Lisette told her, picking up her purse and keys. "Maybe ten minutes."

"Did you remember the present?" Josie asked.

Lisette picked up a brightly wrapped birthday present from the foyer table. "Of course, dear."

"I can't wait!" Josie exclaimed. "I never got invited to anyone's birthday before. Especially not at a skating rink!"

A bright smile stretched across Lisette's face. She knew Josie had been looking forward to this for two whole weeks. It was all they talked about. Lisette had even said that she might put skates on.

Her smile died the moment she opened the front door. Josie's mother stood on the stoop in a pair of torn jeans and a dirty blue T-shirt that hung off one shoulder. A cigarette smoldered in one hand. Her cheeks were sunken, and her long, black hair looked dull. She smiled a mirthless smile that sent a chill all the way down Josie's spine.

CHAPTER 31

Josie and Gretchen lugged several boxes of Bellewood High School yearbooks back to Josie's office at the station house. While Gretchen went to check on the warrants, Josie pored over the yearbooks from 1981 through 1985, looking for her mother's face among the hundreds of photos.

"There's nothing here," she said when Noah appeared.

He sat across from her. "So, she didn't go to school with Belinda Rose. We still have the care home girls, and I set up an interview tomorrow with a lady from the courthouse who worked there at the same time as Belinda."

With a sigh, Josie pushed the last yearbook away and spun her chair to look out the window behind her desk. Night had fallen, which meant it was time for her to go home, alone, to her empty house, a bottle of Wild Turkey, and the now stirred-up memories of a mother whose greatest kindness to her had been to leave.

"You okay, Boss?"

She spun back around and offered him a wan smile. "Fine," she lied. "What's up?"

"Maggie Lane says that Belinda's locket was not among the personal effects left behind at the care home. She says she doesn't know who gave it to her, but Belinda started wearing it around Christmas after the first time she ran off. I already had someone go back to the crime scene and take another look. Nothing turned up."

"Interesting," Josie said. "Maybe we'll find out more when we track down some of the girls who grew up with her."

"Hopefully." He motioned toward the dark window behind her. "It's pretty late, Boss."

"I know."

Noah was always looking out for her. She thought about asking him to go for a drink, but decided against it. Two years ago, she'd had an easy answer to this cloying sense of dread and anxiety: sex. Two years ago, she'd been in a committed relationship where sex with her fiancé was readily available, uncomplicated, and—above all—numbing. Her body yearned for the kind of physical sensation that would blot out the blackness creeping into her head. She knew Noah wouldn't say no, the same way she knew it was a bad idea. She pushed the thought away; she didn't need to make her life any more complicated. She stood and fished under the piles of yearbooks for her car keys.

"I'm going home," she said. "I'll see you tomorrow? I'd like to be there for the courthouse interview."

"You got it."

Josie left the station behind, wending her way through Denton's quiet streets, her mind on the bottle of Wild Turkey waiting on top of her fridge—the next best thing to sex—but she knew something was wrong as soon as she pulled into her driveway. The lights in her bedroom windows glowed bright and gold in the darkness.

Someone was in her house.

CHAPTER 32

JOSIE – NINE YEARS OLD

"Belinda," Lisette said, her voice sounding odd and stilted. "What are you doing here?"

"What do you think I'm doing here, Lisette? I came to get my kid."

Lisette glanced at Josie, and Josie took a step behind her grandmother. "Just like that? You left her here, Belinda, without a word. It's been months. Almost the entire school year!"

Her mother rolled her eyes. "So what? She's my kid." She extended a hand toward Josie. "Let's go, JoJo."

"Belinda, this coming and going, it's not good for Josie. She needs stability."

"Just shut up, Lisette, would you? No one asked you what you think."

Lisette's voice shook with anger. "You don't need to ask me what I think. You leave this child on my doorstep whenever you get tired of raising her. That means I'm involved. I'm her grandmother. I love her. I want her here."

"And I'm her mother. And I'll do whatever the hell I want. Now come on, JoJo. I said let's go."

Lisette didn't move. Her body blocked Josie from stepping toward her mother. "She's doing well here, Belinda. Her grades are up, she's happy. She's made friends at school. Just let her stay."

"Goddamnit, Lisette. Give me my kid."

"Just listen. Just let her finish the school year here with me."

Josie's mother put a hand on her thin hip and narrowed her eyes at Lisette. "I said no. Now I'm taking my daughter and we're going home."

"Belinda, please."

"Don't push me, bitch. I can make sure you never see her again."

It was then that Josie realized she wouldn't get to go to the skating party after all. She had been making calculations in her head as the two women went back and forth. There had been times that her mother agreed to do what her Gram asked, but those times were few and far between. Josie knew that this time, her mother would win. She could tell by the smoldering look in her dark blue eyes and the way she held her whole body stiff like a sharp edge. Josie was headed back to the old, smelly trailer and the dark, lonely closet. To hunger and the sounds of her mother's special friends moving in and out of the trailer at all hours. She had been silly to think she could do what other kids did. Silly to think she could have real friends. Now everyone in her class would be talking about the skating party but her. Well, her and that boy Ray who was always nice to her. She would be left out again, and she wouldn't even have her Gram to console her. Tears welled up in her eyes, but she held them back. Lisette put a hand on Josie's arm, but Josie knew it didn't matter.

"Okay," Lisette said. "Fine. Take her, but at least let her go to her friend's birthday party. We were on our way there now." Lisette held up the gift. "I even bought a present. It will only be a few hours. I'll take her and then drop her off to you afterward."

Her mother pushed Lisette aside and clamped a hand down on Josie's bicep, yanking her across the threshold. "I don't give a damn about some stupid kid's birthday party. Let's go, JoJo. And you, Lisette, I don't know who you think you are, trying to make decisions about my daughter's life. You'll never get her. I'll never let you have her. You just remember that."

CHAPTER 33

After calling in a robbery in progress, Josie parked across the street under a neighbor's large oak tree. She got her bulletproof vest out of the back of her Escape, strapping it on before checking her Glock. After that, she circled the house twice, her steps silent, her movements covered by darkness. She knew where her own motion sensor lights were and carefully avoided them. It only took one lap to figure out that whoever was in her house had broken in through one of her kitchen windows.

Anger boiled inside her, warring with the anxiety that raged beside it. Who was in her house? What were they doing in there? Just the thought of strangers in her private space, touching her things, felt like a violation. She had bought the house with her own money after she'd left Ray. It was huge and airy, with plenty of windows to let in the sunshine—the exact opposite of the coffinlike trailer she had grown up in. This home held only good memories for her. It was her safe place in a world that never ceased to horrify her—her sanctuary. Or it used to be, until tonight.

She was pulled from her thoughts by the arrival of two marked units, followed closely by Noah in his own vehicle. Vest already on, Noah jogged over to her, checked his weapon, and signaled for the uniformed officers to join them. They formed a small knot behind her Escape, heads bent together as Josie gave instructions. "There are two points of entry—front and back. The screen door out back is locked from the inside, so there's no getting in there from the outside—at least not quietly. They broke in through a kitchen window out back. I have no idea how many are in there, or if they're armed. I couldn't hear anything. Please exercise extreme caution." She held out a set of keys, which Noah took from her. "We'll go in the front using these. Lieutenant Fraley and me on one team, and two of you on another. You two stay out here and keep eyes on the house. Lieutenant, you have a notebook?"

Noah pulled a folded notepad from his back pocket. One of the other officers handed her a pen. She quickly scratched out a diagram of the layout of her house. "Lights are on here," she said, pointing to the square representing her bedroom. "Fraley and I go this way, you two go that way; we clear the first floor and then go to the second and proceed down this hall."

Nods all around.

Adrenaline shot through Josie's bloodstream as she and Noah crept up to the front door, followed by two of her uniforms. She'd done this dozens of times before, but never in her own home. Again, fear pushed itself to the front of her mind.

"Boss." Noah's whisper interrupted her thoughts.

She had to keep focus. This was just a regular house with potential burglars inside it. That was how she had to think of it. She clamped a hand onto Noah's shoulder, and he slid a key into her front door. The door swung open without a sound, and they padded over the threshold in a column, two teams splitting off, moving soundlessly until they met back up at the steps, giving all-clear signals. No one was on the first floor.

As they ascended the stairs, Josie heard the sound of voices—two, from what she could gather. Noah must have thought the same, lifting his hand to signal with his index and middle fingers—two perpetrators—then he pointed down the hall toward the last door, Josie's bedroom, where a sliver of light outlined the doorframe.

The voices coming from within were male. "Yo, is he coming back or what?"

"Nah, he said he got what he needed. We'll just mess this shit up real good and get going. He said this bitch ain't ever home anyway."

There were three empty rooms between them and the master bedroom—the bathroom, the guest bedroom, and a room full of surveillance equipment Josie used as a home office. Stealthily they checked each of the rooms with flashlights, but each one was dark and empty. Finally Noah stopped outside of Josie's bedroom, and the rest of them stilled behind him. Inside her chest, Josie's heart took two extra beats. Josie gave the hand signal for go, and then they were through the door with a bang, weapons panning the room, voices hollering, "Freeze! Police! Hands up! Get down on the ground!"

Two teenage boys in sweatpants and hoodies froze, dumbstruck. One of them stood on top of her bed, a can of red spray paint in one hand. On the wall above her headboard he had sprayed the letters S, L, and U. Josie guessed the last letter was probably a T. Across from him, the other boy had been yanking drawers out of her dresser and dumping the contents all over the floor. He immediately threw his hands up. The other boy dropped the can in his hand and made to jump down from the bed, only to fall face-first onto the carpet. Within seconds, the uniformed officers had both of them cuffed and ready to be transported to the station. Both teens were read their rights, then patted down, but they had none of Josie's personal property on them.

"Yo, dude," Spray Paint said as the officer pushed him into the hallway. "I hit my head. Hey, be careful all right?"

Her officer said nothing, and the sound of the other boy telling his friend to shut the hell up faded as they were both led out of the house. Josie stood, gun at her side, eyes roving every inch of the room. The word Whore had been spray-painted on one of the other walls. Most of her pillows had been slashed open, their stuffing pulled out and tossed all over the room. Clothes had been pulled from her closet and strewn everywhere. Muddy boot prints punctuated her clean carpet and her bedspread. The mirror over her dresser was shattered. Her nightstands were overturned, the lamps broken but still lit, casting strange shadows across the destruction. Her jewelry box lay in pieces on the dresser-top.

She strode over and sifted through the remains. "Oh God," she whispered.

Noah put a hand on her shoulder. "Boss," he said, "I think we should have the evidence response team come through. You heard what I heard in the hall, right? There was someone else working with them. You can come through after and figure out if anything is missing."

"My jewelry," she said. She didn't have much, but she had amassed a small collection of earrings, necklaces, and bracelets over the years. Gifts from her grandmother, Ray, and her fiancé Luke when they'd been together. Pieces she'd bought for herself for different events. Most of it she could live without, but there were three pieces of jewelry she owned that she really cared about.

"My wedding ring," she croaked. "My engagement ring from Luke and the diamond pendant Ray gave me when we graduated from high school. They're gone."

She couldn't stop staring at the dark wooden shards spread across her dresser. The jewelry box hadn't even had a lock on it. There was no need to break it, but they had anyway. Why? Why so much destruction? The rest of the house was untouched. Why had they destroyed the room in her home that she loved most? What had they done with her jewelry?

"Those little bastards," Josie blurted. Finally, she looked at Noah.

His face wore an uncomfortable expression. He wanted to comfort her, she realized, but he had a job to do, and he knew she would want him to do his job first. She holstered her weapon but remained in place, staring at Noah, focusing on his face instead of the detritus around her. Gently, he took hold of her elbow and guided her out of the room.

"We'll get to the bottom of this, Boss," he said as they moved down the stairs, his mouth so close to her ear she could feel his breath tickling her hair. "I promise."

CHAPTER 34

JOSIE – TEN YEARS OLD

Their steps echoed loudly in the halls of the county courthouse. Josie walked behind her mother, cold air flying up the stiff brown skirt her mother had made her wear. She stopped at a water fountain and gulped greedily before her mother could slap her and hiss at her to hurry up. But it didn't come. They were in public, in the courthouse where things were formal and official, and everything was cold and grown-ups stared at you like you were a bug.

"JoJo," her mother said sweetly, smiling. "Let's go, hon."

Josie knew she was the only person who could hear the edge beneath her mother's words. Hanging her head, she followed her mother to a set of large, wooden doors that opened into a huge, shelf-lined room filled with more books than Josie had ever seen. A massive desk sat in the middle of it. In front of the desk, several chairs were lined up. They were divided into sides, and Josie's gram sat in one of them, a man Josie didn't recognize beside her.

Josie followed her mother deeper into the room. Her gram reached over and squeezed Josie in a hug while Josie's mother glared. "Remember what I said," Lisette whispered into her ear before releasing her.

A tiny pinprick of fear spiked Josie's chest. How could she forget?

Her grandmother had decided months ago—after missing the skating party—that she would simply sue Josie's mother for custody. There had been endless meetings and appointments and lots of stuffy grown-ups asking Josie all kinds of questions she knew she couldn't answer honestly. She'd even had to meet with a psychologist. Of course, what none of them understood was that every time Josie was forced to talk to them, it made her mother more enraged and crueler than usual behind closed doors. She was careful not to leave any marks on Josie's body, but she didn't have to—she knew how much the closet terrified her daughter. The only reason Josie had coped with the increasingly long periods of time in the dark cell was the backpack Ray had given her to hide inside the closet. It contained a flashlight, extra batteries, a dog-eared copy of the first *Harry Potter* book, a Stretch Armstrong doll, and a couple of granola bars. As she waited out the endless nights, shivering in her nightdress from fear and cold, Josie liked to imagine that Ray was there with her.

The only good thing to come out of the custody battle was that Josie's mother was forced to let her spend short periods of time with Lisette. It was purely strategic on her mother's part. Josie had overheard her mother's lawyer say that in her petition to the court, Lisette had painted her mother as unreasonable, mean-spirited, and spiteful. He said that allowing Josie to spend time with her grandmother would go a long way toward debunking Lisette's claims. But Josie's time with Lisette was mostly spent being grilled over what her mother did to her. When Lisette realized that Josie would never confess the things that her mother did, she spent the rest of their time together trying to convince Josie that if she told the truth, she would get to live with Lisette forever.

"Josie, this is very important," she had said. "You have to tell the judge what your mother does to you. If you are very brave and tell the truth, your whole life will change. I know you're scared of her, but I'm telling you that you don't need to be. I can help you. I can protect you, but I can only do that if you tell the truth."

But Josie knew that no one could help her. Not her father from heaven, not her grandmother, not the teachers at school or the psychologist she had seen, and certainly not the judge who swept into the room and started shaking everyone's hands.

Josie sat beside her mother, her legs swinging nervously. She reached into the pocket of the cardigan she wore and felt for the Disney figurine Ray had given her. He had pressed the miniature fairy godmother from *Sleeping Beauty* into her hand the day before when they met in the woods between their houses. "Keep it," he told her. "Maybe a real fairy godmother will come and save you."

Now her fist closed around it, and she concentrated hard on the pain in her palm instead of the grown-ups all around her, talking in serious voices about her as though she wasn't there. Nobody had any power over her mother. She may only be ten, but Josie wasn't stupid.

"Miss Matson," the judge said. "Josie Matson."

Her mother leaned in and lightly touched Josie's arm, her hissed threat ringing in Josie's ears: "You be a good girl now, JoJo. Go on."

CHAPTER 35

Josie sat in the viewing room at the station house, staring at a large, closed-circuit television that showed one of the teenage boys they had arrested at her house. A mug of coffee sat untouched on the table beside her. She felt numb and exhausted. Her mind kept returning to the havoc they had wreaked on her bedroom, the window they had broken, the thought that strangers had been inside her home and violated her sanctuary. The door creaked open, and Gretchen stepped through it with a newly minted manila file in her hands.

"This one is Austin Jacks. Nineteen. Graduated from Denton East last year, hasn't been doing a hell of a lot since then. Works part-time at a fast-food place. Got picked up for possession of drug paraphernalia last year, but the charges didn't stick."

"No connection to Lloyd Todd?"

"Not that we can find."

"What about the other one?" Josie asked.

"Ian Colton. He's a minor. Sixteen. He's in holding till his parents get here. He's a junior at Denton East. No record. No arrests. He works with Jacks. That's how they know one another."

Josie doubted that they'd be able to get to Ian Colton. The moment his parents showed up, they'd likely demand a lawyer, who would agree to let Josie's team question the boy but then instruct him not to answer any questions. She saw it all the time.

"Our best bet to find out who else was involved is this kid," Josie told Gretchen, motioning to the screen. On it, Austin Jacks fidgeted in his seat. His heels bobbed up and down, drumming an uneasy beat on the floor. His teeth tugged at a hangnail on his thumb while his other hand rubbed the top of his head, brushing back and forth over blond hair that was short like peach fuzz.

"Noah's going in," Gretchen responded, pulling out a chair and sitting down beside Josie.

They watched the boy squirm, his movements growing more frenetic by the second until Noah sauntered in fifteen minutes later. He slid a crushed pack of cigarettes across the table, and Austin snatched them up. A lighter appeared in Noah's hand, and he gave the boy a light before pocketing it and leaning against the wall. Austin sucked in several hungry lungfuls of smoke, closing his eyes briefly to enjoy it. The fevered movements slowed a little, but not much.

Noah read him his rights again, and Austin acknowledged that he understood them. He didn't ask for a lawyer, so Noah plunged right in. "Do you know whose house you were arrested in earlier tonight?"

The boy shrugged. "Don't know. Some police lady. Don't care."

"Why were you there?"

He blew smoke in Noah's direction. "Why do you think? It don't take a rocket scientist to figure that out."

"You and Ian were there to rob this police lady, and yet neither one of you had any of her personal property on you when we arrested you. How do you explain that?"

His gaze flicked around the room, looking anywhere but at Noah. "You caught us before we could take anything, man."

Noah stepped toward the table. "Her jewelry is missing."

Austin's knees bounced beneath the table. "I don't know what to tell you."

"Who else was there with you?"

Another shrug. "You know who was there—you got him too."

Noah placed both palms on the table and leaned in toward the kid. "We know there was a third guy, Austin. He came and took the jewelry and left you and Ian behind to wreck the place. Who is he?"

A tenuous smile flitted across Austin's face and disappeared. He put out his cigarette in the ashtray Noah had provided and balled his hands up in his lap. "I don't know what you're talking about."

Noah sighed. "Fine. We'll get prints from the kitchen window. It won't take long to run them. Unless Ian tells us first and saves us the time. That kid is scared shitless. I'm sure him and his parents will be interested in the reduced charges the DA is offering for information on the third perp—and for throwing your sorry ass under the bus."

Without hesitation, Noah turned and left the room, leaving Austin's mouth hanging open, his skin paling beneath his acne.

Ten minutes later he stood beneath the eye of the camera, waving both arms. "Hey man, come back," he called. "I got something to say."

CHAPTER 36

JOSIE – TEN YEARS OLD

Josie stood frozen in place until finally a hand pushed her closer to the judge's desk, and her feet shuffled forward until she was nearly touching its edge.

"Young lady," he said, "I'm going to ask you some questions now, and I want you to answer them as truthfully as possible, do you understand?"

Josie nodded. She felt her mother's eyes on her like a white-hot laser beam. Her mother had been smiling for the benefit of the other grown-ups, but Josie had seen the glint in her eye; they both knew that no matter what she told the judge, Josie was going home with her mother. Josie also knew that what she said right now could either make things better for herself, or much worse.

So, she lied.

With each lie that poured from her lips, Lisette's frame crumpled a little bit more beside her. Guilt was a sour taste in the back of Josie's throat, so she looked away from her gram, instead focusing on her mother's face, which shone brighter with satisfaction with each one of Josie's denials.

As expected, the judge said Josie was to return home with her mother, but that Lisette should have visitation rights. Before they left the judge's chambers, Lisette grabbed Josie up in a bear hug, and Josie felt her gram's lips against her ear once more. "I'm not done, Josie. I'll get you away from her. I promise."

When Lisette let go, Josie smiled bravely at her, holding back the tears and digging the point of the plastic fairy godmother's hat deep into her palm. "It's okay, Gram," she told Lisette. "I'll be fine."

Another lie.

CHAPTER 37

Noah made Austin Jacks wait it out, let him sweat. Just when Josie expected him to start climbing the walls like some kind of jumping spider, the door to the room opened and Noah poked his head in. "Was that you hollering?" he asked.

Austin stood beneath the camera and pointed to it. "Yeah, it was me. You don't have someone watching me right now?"

"We're pretty busy right now, Mr. Jacks. I've got to use my people on witnesses who have something to say, like your buddy Ian. What do you need? Bathroom break?"

"You talked to Ian?"

"We're in with him now, yeah," Noah said, already retreating out of the room.

"He told you about the guy under the bridge?" Austin said.

Noah didn't miss a beat. "Yeah, but he said he didn't know the guy's name."

"'Cause we never knew his name," Austin replied. "He's just, like, the guy under the bridge."

Josie knew there were only two bridges in Denton that crossed the Susquehanna River, and only one of them offered enough space and privacy for homeless squatters and drug transactions. Noah knew this as well.

"Austin," Noah said patiently, "there's more than one guy under that bridge. You think we don't run busts down there once a week?"

The kid rubbed his scalp with both hands. "I can tell you what he looks like. You could get, like, an artist or whatever to come in, and I can tell him how to draw the guy. You know, like on TV."

Beside Josie, Gretchen laughed. Everyone thought real-life police work was like what they saw on television, but things like sketch artists cost money. A lot of money. The kind of money no police department would spend on a simple burglary—even for its chief of police.

Noah stepped inside the room, pulling the door closed behind him and motioning for Austin to sit again. This time, the whole chair rattled with his agitation. Noah said, "How about you just tell me what you know about the guy and we'll go from there."

Austin's teeth gnashed on his dirty fingernails. "You gonna help me out, or what? Like with the DA?"

"I can see about some reduced charges, sure."

Annoyance flashed in Austin's eyes. "Reduced charges? Come on, man. You could get me out of here. I didn't even do anything. I mean it wasn't even my idea."

Noah leaned back in his chair, relaxed. "Reduced charges is the best I can do, Austin. I don't make these decisions. You should know, the police lady whose house you broke into was Josie Quinn."

Austin's mouth dropped open. "The chief of police? The hot one who's always on the news?"

"Uh, yeah. We only have one chief of police."

"Shit."

"You see my dilemma? I want to help you out here, but my hands are tied. Unless of course you have some information about Lloyd Todd or any of his associates."

Austin's brow furrowed momentarily. "Who?"

"Lloyd Todd," Noah repeated slowly.

The creases in Austin's forehead deepened. "You mean that big drug dealer you guys busted last month? Todd's Home Construction?"

Noah nodded.

"I don't mess with Lloyd Todd," he said. "Never did."

Noah tapped his fingers on the table as though bored. "How about someone in Todd's crew? They've been pretty pissed since we put him away. Did someone in his organization ask you to do this job?"

Austin shook his head. "Nah, dude. I told you, I never messed with Lloyd Todd. I'm not trying to get involved in all that. I mean, like, one day I want to go to college and shit. Those guys get in deep with him. He like, controls them."

"Yeah, we know. How about your guy under the bridge? He work for Todd?"

"I don't think so. I never saw him talking to any of Todd's guys. He's on his own down there, I'm pretty sure about that."

"What else can you tell me about him?"

Austin rubbed at his cheeks until the skin pinkened. Finally, he said, "Reduced charges, right? What do you want to know?"

"Reduced charges," Noah repeated. "Tell me whatever you know about him."

"He's old, dude. Like, way old."

"Can you estimate his age?"

"I don't know, like fifties or sixties."

Next to Josie, Gretchen let out a lengthy sigh. "Nice to know that fifty is 'like, way old.'"

Josie laughed at her impression of the kid.

"He's really skinny," Austin continued. "I mean, dude's whacked out most of the time. You know Lloyd Todd don't take no whackos. You have to be on point to work for him. Anyway, I think this guy lives under the bridge, like, all the time. He's always got the same old green jacket on, even in the summer."

Noah narrowed his eyes. "I thought you didn't know much about him. Sounds like you see him a lot."

Austin slumped in his chair. "Come on, man. You trying to bust me for something else? So me and Ian go down to the river a lot, okay?"

"To buy drugs," Noah filled in.

"I'm not saying that. You asked me about the guy, I'm telling you about him."

"Okay, he's in his fifties or sixties, skinny, green jacket…"

"Stringy-ass gray hair, wears this old pair of work boots that look about twenty years old."

"You don't know his name?"

Austin shook his head. "The people you see down there—you don't ask for names, you get me?"

"Fair enough. How'd he get involved in your robbery?"

Austin put a hand to his chest, fingers splayed. "My robbery? Dude, that wasn't my robbery. I'm not trying to rob the chief of police and shit. It was his idea."

"Who?"

"The guy under the bridge. We get stuff from him sometimes, you know?"

"What kind of stuff?" Noah asked.

"Like stuff, you know? You really want to know? 'Cause if I tell you, you can't, like, bust me, right?"

Noah sighed. "I'm only interested in what you know about the robbery. I don't care what 'stuff' you were getting from this guy, okay?"

"Okay, okay. We were getting some weed and pills and shit from him—me and Ian—and we were a little behind in payment, so this guy said we could get caught up and get some more stuff if we did a job for him."

"He approached you with it?"

"Yeah, I guess. He said it would be easy. He'd go with us to the house, get us inside, and then we were supposed to take some shit and mess the place up. But there was nothing in there, you know? Nothing this guy wanted. He didn't want electronics or anything. He said to look in the bedroom for jewelry and cash, so we did."

"Who brought the spray paint?"

"He gave it to us. Said we should write something real nasty on the walls."

"So 'slut' and 'whore' were your idea?"

Austin's face flushed. "No, man, not ours. We didn't even know this bitch—I mean the chief. I said to him, 'What do you mean by nasty?' and he said to write 'slut' or 'whore' or something. He said, 'Bitches don't like to be called slut or whore.'"

Noah let out a heavy sigh. "Women don't like to be called bitches either."

Austin's head bobbed. "Hey, man, I know that."

Next to Josie, Gretchen hung her head. "Progressive," she muttered.

"Did this man tell you why he wanted you and Ian to do these things?" Noah asked the kid.

"No. We just figured he had a beef with the lady. I mean, he said it was a police lady and she lived alone, 'cause we were like, we don't want to go into no house if there's people there or a big dog and shit. He said she was always working. Anyway, he was there, and once we found the jewelry, he left. Said he'd meet up with us later when we were done. Ian said he should stay, 'cause what if we got caught, then we'd take the fall for all of it, so he said he might come back, but I knew he wouldn't."

Noah folded his arms across his chest. "Where were you supposed to meet up later?"

"Under the bridge, where else?"

Josie shook her head. "God, this kid is stupid."

"That's why the guy used him," Gretchen agreed.

"You think he's lying?" Josie asked. "About this man under the bridge?"

"Well, we know from what you heard in the house there's someone else involved. Hard to say if it's someone they're protecting, or if he's telling the truth about this drug-dealer guy. But there's one way to find out."

"He's not going to be under the bridge," Josie said.

"Probably not," Gretchen agreed. "But it's a good place to start. I'll head over there with a couple of marked units. Let you know what we find."

CHAPTER 38

JOSIE – ELEVEN YEARS OLD

Her mother's small blue Chevette sat outside the trailer looking like a discarded toy, slumped to one side, its front passenger-side tire flat. Red paint streaked the bumper where her mother had hit a shiny red Mustang when they left the liquor store. It had been two days, but Josie's neck still hurt.

Her homework was spread out on the kitchen table. Fractions. Josie hated fractions. They had started them in the fourth grade, and she still hadn't mastered them. Her mother paced from the kitchen through the living room and back, stopping at the front door on each pass to stare at the broken-down car and curse under her breath.

Josie heard the sound of a car jolting over the large pothole two trailers down before the same red Mustang pulled up beside the Chevette. From the kitchen window, Josie could see that it was waxed to perfection, except for the long thick streak where the paint had been gouged from the front of the driver's side to the back. Josie watched a man climb out of the Mustang, flicking a cigarette into the grass as he walked toward the front door of their trailer. He was tall and thin, older, but not as old as Josie's gram. Dull brown hair peeked from the back of a worn blue ball cap. The sleeves of his white T-shirt had been torn away, revealing wiry arms with faded black tattoos that Josie couldn't make out. Beneath a long, bulbous nose, a wide moustache stretched across his upper lip. Old stains dotted his faded blue jeans, and the toe of one of his boots had a hole in it.

When he banged on the door, the sound reverberated through the whole trailer. Her mother stood frozen between the kitchen and living room. She brought an index finger to her lips, signaling for Josie to be quiet. They waited without moving as the man kept knocking, harder and harder. The minutes ticked by. Then he began shouting, "I know you're in there, dammit. Just answer the door. You're not getting away with this. You hit my car and then drove off."

More knocking. More shouting. "I know who you are, Belinda Rose. The lady at the liquor store knows you. Told me all about you. Now come on out here or I'll call the police."

At this, her mother took a few tentative steps toward the door. "Shit," she muttered.

"I'm giving you ten seconds," the man hollered. "You don't come out in ten seconds, I'm leaving, and I'll be back with the police."

Josie's mother pulled the door open. "Okay, okay," she said. "Here I am."

"You gonna make me stand out here, or you gonna invite me in? Least you can do is offer me a drink after you wrecked my car."

Her mother rolled her eyes and stepped aside, letting the man inside. "I hardly wrecked your car," she remarked.

The man stood in the middle of the living room, eyes panning the trailer until they landed on Josie. He offered her a toothy smile. "Hey, sweetheart."

Josie lifted a hand in a half-hearted wave. Her mother went to the drainboard and snatched up a glass, filling the bottom of it with the vodka she'd bought at the store. She handed it to the man, and he knocked it back in one gulp, handing her the glass back. She put one hand on her hip and stared at him. "What do you want?"

Again, he smiled. "What do you think? I need a paint job and you're gonna pay for it."

"Oh yeah? How's that? I don't got no insurance."

He laughed, his eyes drifting to Josie and then back to Josie's mother. "Of course you don't."

"How much is a paint job?" her mother asked.

He looked out the front door at the Mustang. "For a beauty like that? At least five hundred."

"Five hundred dollars?" her mother exclaimed. "Are you shitting me? For some paint?"

"Honey, that's a 1965 Mustang GT. A classic car. Took me years to restore it."

Josie's mother sighed and threw her hands in the air. "I don't have no five hundred dollars. You come back in a week and maybe I'll have something for you."

The man walked over to the couch and sat down. "I don't do payment plans, and if I leave, I told you, I'm coming back with the cops."

Her mother followed him, standing between his legs, staring down at him. "Cops don't solve nothing," she told him. "Stop bringing them into this. This is between you and me."

He stretched his arms out across the back of the sofa and smiled at her like they were old friends. "Is that right?"

CHAPTER 39

As Josie predicted, the man Austin Jacks described was not under the bridge. Gretchen unearthed a handful of people who knew him, but only as Zeke. It wasn't a lot to go on. Josie didn't know anyone named Zeke, and she had no idea what the drug dealer would want with her—particularly if he wasn't associated with Lloyd Todd, as Austin had said. She left Noah at the station house to book the teenagers while she returned home to assess the damage and start cleaning up. She went in through her front door and moved through the first floor slowly, flipping on light switches as she went. The downstairs hadn't been disturbed at all. Everything was exactly as she had left it—it was impossible to tell that anyone had been there. But Josie knew. The house felt different to her now—emptier and colder somehow, like it was missing something. Something she didn't know if she could get back.

She hesitated before turning on the kitchen light, knowing the sight of the broken kitchen window was going to stir up all the feelings of unease and rage she'd been tamping down since the teenage boys had been taken out of her bedroom in cuffs. The entire ride home she'd been worrying about that point of entry—the glass broken now, her home open and vulnerable. Now anyone could slip inside unheard until she had it fixed. Then there was the cost of the window.

The kitchen lights flickered on, and Josie's breath caught in her throat. In the window, a large, thick board had been fitted into the window frame, sealing it off. It wasn't the responsibility of Denton PD to clean up crime scenes, and certainly not to board up windows, but her team had done it for her. She walked over and tested if it was secure. Tears of gratitude burned her tired eyes as she pressed against it and it didn't budge. She rushed upstairs, taking the steps two at a time. Her bedroom had been straightened, the night stands had been placed upright once more, her lamps reassembled as best as they could be. The stuffing torn from her pillows had been removed, and the torn pillowcases were neatly folded and placed at the foot of her bed. Someone had stripped the muddied sheets and folded them as well. Even the broken pieces of her jewelry box had been neatly arranged on the top of her dresser. She walked over to the dresser, where all the drawers had been put back in their places, clothes folded and placed inside each one. She studied the carpet and saw that someone had vacuumed. Many items would need to be replaced, but everything in the room was clean and orderly. Only the nasty red words shouted from the walls, marring the tidy room.

She sank onto the bed and squeezed her eyes closed against the sting of tears. In her jacket pocket, her cell phone made a pinging sound. A text message from Noah. *I'm outside*, it read. *Can I come in?*

He waited on her doorstep, a brown bag in hand that smelled deliciously like meatball subs. "You didn't eat," he said as he stepped past her. He gestured toward the bag as he made his way to the kitchen. "All I could get were sandwiches from that minimarket over near the college. We'll probably pay for this later."

Josie glanced at her microwave clock and saw it was almost three a.m. "Noah," she said softly. "You don't have to—"

"I think you should come stay with me for a day or two. Just until you get everything back in order here." He didn't look at her as he spread the contents of the bag across her kitchen table. Her stomach clenched as the smell grew stronger. He was right. She hadn't eaten. She was starving.

"That's not necessary," she told him.

Together they sat down and dug in. Under normal circum-stances, Josie knew she probably wouldn't enjoy a minimarket sandwich, but in that moment, the cheese- and sauce-covered meatballs were the best thing she'd ever tasted. Noah waited until her stomach was full before trying again.

"You can take my bed; I'll sleep on the couch."

"I'm fine," Josie insisted.

He raised a brow. "So, you're saying you'll be able to sleep here tonight?"

He had a point.

"I wanted to go with you guys tomorrow for the courthouse interview on the Belinda Rose case," she said.

"Then you should definitely get some sleep. Stay at my place—at least for tonight."

CHAPTER 40

JOSIE – ELEVEN YEARS OLD

Josie watched as her mother's body language changed. Her posture was looser, and she had that fake smile she often used on her special friends when she didn't have enough money for needles or pills. She moved closer to the man, her legs touching the inside of his. "Between you and me, I think we could work something out, don't you?"

"What do you mean?" he asked. "Like a trade?"

Josie's mother reached down and ran a hand up his thigh to his belt. "Something like that. I do something for you, and we forget all about the paint job. Call it even."

He chuckled. "Even, huh?"

She straddled him. His hands reached for her hips, but his eyes traveled over her shoulder to where Josie remained paralyzed at the kitchen table. Her mother followed his gaze, glancing at Josie. Then she turned back to him, using an index finger to bring his attention back to her. "We'll go in the back," she said.

His hands snaked down and around her mother's back, cupping her rear. He leaned into her and whispered something in her ear. At first she laughed, but then he whispered something else. There was a lengthy discussion that Josie couldn't make out. Then she heaved off his lap. She went back to the sink and rinsed a glass out, filling it with vodka. Josie waited for them to disappear into her mother's bedroom so she could concentrate on her fractions, but instead, the glass of vodka appeared in front of her. Her mother pushed it across the table until it was under Josie's nose. From the couch, the man smiled widely.

"JoJo," her mother said, "you drink this."

Josie stared at her mother. "Mom, I can't drink alcohol. I'm not supposed to."

Her mother tapped an index finger against the rim of the glass. Josie could feel the man's eyes on her. She looked at him again, but this time his smile looked different—hungry and a little bit greedy. Josie's heart skipped several beats and then raced ahead. The room seemed to close in on her.

Her mother said, "I'm your mother and what I say goes. Now you're gonna drink this down, and then you're gonna go into the back with this nice man."

"In-into the back?" Josie said, her voice cracking.

Her mother rolled her eyes. "Yes, the back. You can use my bedroom."

"Use it?"

She pushed the glass closer, and the liquid sloshed over the rim, spilling across Josie's math homework. She lowered her voice. "Don't ask questions, JoJo. You go into the back room with this gentleman and just do whatever he tells you to do, you got it?"

The vodka stung so badly, Josie gagged on it. "Jesus, JoJo," her mother complained. She went to the fridge and searched through it until she found a carton of orange juice. She poured some into the cup, diluting the vodka. Even with the juice, it smarted all the way down, burning Josie's mouth and throat and leaving a funny numb feeling on her tongue.

Josie's mother made her drink another glass after she finished the first. When she grabbed Josie's arm and pulled her up out of her seat, the room spun. Josie's feet wouldn't work. She couldn't tell if it was from the vodka or from the way the man was looking at her. Her mother's bedroom door was at once a million miles away and too close for comfort.

She didn't want to do whatever the man told her to do. She had a panicky feeling inside that he would want to do the disgusting things her mother did with men. Josie had seen them many times. Sometimes her mother was too drunk or high to remember to put Josie into the closet or to go to her own bedroom with her special friends. There had been several times that Josie was at the kitchen table when they started taking their clothes off. No one noticed her, and she was too afraid to try to run past them to her room and draw attention to herself. The things the men did to her mother looked painful and scary.

"Mommy, I don't want to," Josie choked out.

"Shut up, JoJo." Her mother pushed her down the hallway and she stumbled, reaching for the dark paneled walls to steady herself. The man followed.

Josie felt his hand in her hair, and she jumped. His laughter was hot on the back of her neck. "Relax, sweetheart. I'm going to make you feel good."

Nausea roiled in her stomach. The vodka and orange juice threatened to come back up. He was so close. Too close. The heat of his body closed in on her. Tears stung her eyes. His hand slid down from her neck, tracing her spine, moving down until one of his fingers hooked inside the waistband of her cotton shorts.

She stumbled again, and her shorts, caught on his finger, pulled down a little, exposing her. The man gave a low whistle. "This is gonna be fun," he said, making Josie's heart thud so hard in her chest, it hurt. She shut her eyes as she closed her hand around the handle of the bedroom door, and turned…

Suddenly, the trailer's front door banged open behind her and the man jumped back, snapping his hand away from her body. She turned, looking past him, to where Needle now stood just inside the trailer. Without moving, he looked from her mother to where Josie and the man were frozen in place. His dark beady eyes narrowed at the man in the hallway. "What the hell's going on here?" he asked.

All eyes turned to Josie's mother. For a fraction of a second, Josie thought she saw fear in her mother's eyes. It was quickly replaced with a flash of anger. She stepped toward Needle. "Nothing that concerns you," she told him.

But Needle remained rooted to the spot. He gestured toward the man. "Who the hell's that?"

Her mother rolled her eyes. "None of your goddamn business. Did you bring anything?"

Needle ignored her. "JoJo," he called.

Josie said nothing. Her fear, mixed with the effects of the vodka, robbed her of speech. Her eyes pleaded with him.

"Hey," her mother said irritably. "I told you to stay—"

"Shut up," Needle said. He held out a hand in Josie's direction. "JoJo, come on now. Come over here."

Somehow, Josie's feet scuttled toward him. His hand touched the top of her head, and he nodded toward the front door. "Go on outside and play now."

"You son of a bitch," her mother growled, but Needle ignored her, pushing Josie toward the door.

She didn't have to be told twice. She practically tumbled out into the cool air, running into the woods as quickly as her feet would carry her.

CHAPTER 41

Josie surfaced from a deep sleep, her bleary eyes taking in unfamiliar surroundings. Light-blue walls, a four-drawer dresser scuffed from top to bottom, masculine items scattered across its surface—an electric razor, cologne, a black wallet. Then there was the smell. Not unpleasant. Just different. It was Noah's smell, she realized. As the fog of sleep cleared, she sat up in his bed, listening. She thought she heard noises from downstairs. She had slept peacefully, considering she was in a strange bed and was still reeling from the intrusion of her home. She looked around the room once more, noting how little light it got compared to her own bedroom. The furnishings were utilitarian, although in the six months since she had last been to his house, Noah had outfitted the downstairs with new, modern furniture and appliances. It still had the half-finished look of a bachelor pad, but it was far more welcoming and comfortable.

A knock sounded on the door. Before Josie could answer, Noah walked in, a steaming mug of coffee in his hands. He froze when he saw her. "Oh, I'm sorry. I guess I should have waited for you to say 'Come in.'"

"It's okay," Josie said.

"You might have been changing," he pointed out. "I—uh—I'm really sorry."

He started to retreat, but Josie stood and reached for the coffee. "It's fine," she said. "Really. Thank you."

She sipped the coffee standing there, suddenly aware of how she must look wearing Ray's faded old Denton PD T-shirt and a pair of threadbare sweatpants. She put the mug on his nightstand and patted her hair down. Beneath her fingers, she felt a thick lump of knotted hair in the back of her head.

"Guess I should, uh, use your bathroom," Josie said.

She went to move past him as he tried to get out of the doorway, but they both moved in the same direction. The awkward dance continued as they tried to get out of each other's way, only succeeding in bumping chests. The heady scent of Noah's aftershave invaded her nostrils. She wished she'd had time to brush her teeth before their first conversation of the day.

"I'm sorry," Noah said, finally backing out of the room. He pointed to his left. "Bathroom's that way."

Josie smiled tightly. "Got it. Thanks."

She showered, brushed her teeth, and dressed quickly. In the kitchen, Noah whipped up a breakfast of bacon and eggs, which they ate in silence. Only once they left to meet Gretchen for the interview of the former courthouse employee did the awkwardness between them dissipate. As they drove to the Bellewood home of Alona Ortiz, the retired district court clerk who had once worked with Belinda Rose, Josie tried hard not to dwell on what had happened in her home the night before.

Ortiz lived in a two-story brick home near the courthouse in the center of Bellewood. Her front porch was cluttered with potted plants and children's toys. When Ortiz emerged, a knit shawl wrapped around her hunched shoulders, she smiled and waved at the mess. "Grandkids," she explained. "They're like little tornadoes. Come in, come in. Sit."

Her living room was equally full of plants and toddler toys— brightly colored blocks, worn stuffed animals, a plastic tool set, and a dress-up trunk filled with glittery pink and purple dresses and several sparkly tiaras. Gretchen made small talk with her while Josie and Noah found their places on her threadbare burgundy sofa. Ortiz sat in a recliner across from them, tucking strands of her shoulder-length silver hair behind her ears. Josie knew she was in her sixties, but she had a youthful look about her, her olive skin still relatively smooth except for the deep laugh lines bracketing her mouth.

"Three of you," she observed. "This must be important. What did young Belinda get up to? Is she in trouble?"

Gretchen perched on the arm of the sofa. "I'm sorry to tell you, Mrs. Ortiz, but we believe Belinda was killed in 1984, possibly the same day she went missing. We found her remains in Denton last week."

Mrs. Ortiz's mouth turned downward. Her brown eyes found the floor. "I'm sorry to hear that," she said gravely.

"We were wondering what you could tell us about Belinda and her job at the courthouse," Josie said.

Mrs. Ortiz leaned back in her chair and folded her hands over her stomach. "That was some time ago, but I wouldn't have told you to come over if I didn't remember her. Hard to forget those blond curls, but mostly I remember her because she was quite a flirt. Caused a little bit of conflict around the office while she was there."

"What did she do at the courthouse?" Noah asked.

"Oh, you know, mostly filing, getting the mail ready, making sure the coffee pot was full. It was a part-time job. Myself and one other woman worked there as clerks. We had gone to the high school to see if we could get one or two students to come in and help out. There were a handful of candidates, but Belinda got the job. She was very sunny. Never had any problems with her work. I mean, she was a bit unreliable. I didn't think we should let her come back after the few months she missed, but we needed help and she did her job well. Like I said, I never had a problem with her work."

Josie leaned forward, her elbows on her knees. "But you had other problems with her?"

Mrs. Ortiz gave a tight smile. "Well, not just me. We had several judges, some assistant district attorneys, and some public defenders who worked out of the courthouse. They had their own staff who didn't appreciate the way Belinda flirted with their bosses."

Noah asked, "Was the staff primarily female?"

Mrs. Ortiz smiled at him knowingly. "We're talking the early eighties, son. The judges and lawyers were male, and the staff was female. So yes, all female. I think many of them were just jealous. She was a very vivacious young woman, and she did turn the heads of a lot of men."

Josie said, "Did Belinda have relationships with any of the men?"

Mrs. Ortiz frowned. "She was a teenager," she said, as if that precluded the possibility of an affair.

"Well, was there anyone she flirted with more than the others?" Gretchen asked.

"I suppose she had quite an interest in Judge Bowen."

The name was vaguely familiar to Josie, but she couldn't place it.

Gretchen scribbled something on her notepad. "How did Judge Bowen react to her interest?"

Mrs. Ortiz waved her hand. "Oh, he loved it. Of course, he had to be careful because he had a young wife, and she worked there too, as a secretary. The flirting caused some arguments between them at first, but then Mrs. Bowen became friendly with Belinda. They were close in age."

"How close?" Josie asked.

"Oh, well, Mrs. Bowen was only twenty. It was quite the scandal when she and the judge got married because he was fifteen years older than her, but she was of age and they seemed in love."

"How old was Mrs. Bowen when they got married?" Noah asked.

"Eighteen," Mrs. Ortiz answered.

Noah looked at Josie with a raised brow. She knew what he was thinking. If the girl was eighteen when the judge married her, they had likely been seeing one another before she became of age. Which meant he may have had a predilection for young girls. Belinda had gotten pregnant shortly after starting her job at the courthouse. It was too big a coincidence to ignore.

"What was Mrs. Bowen's first name?" Gretchen asked.

"Sophia."

"Did the Bowens stay married?" Noah asked.

Mrs. Ortiz nodded. "Oh yes. They were married right up until Judge Bowen passed. Cancer. That was about ten years ago. Their children were already grown, thank goodness. They had two boys."

"Do you remember Belinda being pregnant?" Gretchen asked, steering the conversation back to their reason for being there.

Three horizontal lines appeared on Mrs. Ortiz's forehead. "Pregnant? Belinda was never pregnant. She was just a child."

Josie wondered if Belinda had really been that skilled at hiding the pregnancy, or if all the adults in her life had simply been that oblivious. Mrs. Ortiz seemed a bit naïve in Josie's estimation, although what Josie saw in her job day in and day out had made her jaded. Josie said, "You said that Belinda was friends with Sophia Bowen. Was there anyone else she was close to? Someone she may have confided in?"

Two of Mrs. Ortiz's fingers tapped her chin as she thought about it. "There was that one young lady from the cleaning service. Oh, what was her name?" She pursed her lips. Several seconds slipped past. She sighed. "I can't remember her name. She worked for the housekeeping company that came in in the afternoons and evenings to clean. Actually, the three of them were thick as thieves now that I think about it. I used to catch them out back smoking cigarettes and giggling about this or that. No one would have noticed if it was just Belinda and the cleaning girl, but Sophia—well, people expected a judge's wife to act a certain way. I talked with her a few times about not acting like a teenager cutting school."

"Do you remember the name of the cleaning service?" Josie asked.

"No, no I don't."

"What about the girl from the service that Belinda and Sophia used to hang out with?" Noah asked. "What did she look like?"

"Oh, she was very pretty," said Mrs. Ortiz. "She had long, black hair. Almost down to her rear end. Blue eyes. She was very thin—not like Belinda or Sophia. No, the cleaning girl was thin as a rail."

"How old was she?"

"I'm not sure, dear, but she was young. Maybe in her twenties."

Josie felt Noah's eyes on her but didn't look at him. Her mother had to have been young enough to pass for eighteen when she stole Belinda's identity. She had blue eyes and had always worn her black hair down to her backside. By fourteen, Josie had outweighed her mother. It was the drugs, Josie knew now. Her mother had survived almost entirely on drugs, and not much else. Food had never been a priority in their trailer. Josie shot Noah a quick glance, communicating with her eyes. It could be her. He nodded almost imperceptibly.

"Do you remember who owned the cleaning service?" Noah asked. "Or the names of anyone else who worked there?"

Mrs. Ortiz shook her head. "I'm sorry, I don't. They went out of business decades ago. Maybe someone on your staff would remember? They had municipal contracts with all the police departments in the county as well. They had different cleaning crews that went to different buildings, but if you're just looking for the name of the company, any one of the police departments would have had a contract with them in the early '80s."

CHAPTER 42

Sergeant Dan Lamay ran a hand over his thinning gray hair and shook his head slowly. "A cleaning service?" he said. "In the '80s?" He took another moment to think about it while Josie, Gretchen, and Noah stared at him. Lamay was the oldest officer on the force, and the only one who had been around in the 1980s. His career had survived the ushering in and out of four different chiefs of police, as well as one mighty scandal. He was nearing retirement age, with a bad knee and a paunch that stretched his uniform shirt more each day. But Josie knew that with his wife battling cancer, and a daughter in college, he needed both his income and health benefits, so she kept him on and assigned him to the lobby desk.

"Anything you can remember would be helpful," Josie prodded.

He scratched over his left ear. "I'm sorry, Boss," he said. "I don't remember. I don't even remember there being a cleaning service back then. I was on patrol, you know? Brand new from the academy. Didn't spend much time in the station house."

Josie sighed and waved toward her office door. "Thanks anyway, Sergeant."

Lamay lumbered toward the door but stopped before crossing the threshold. "Boss," he said, "I bet there are records of it upstairs. I had to go up there last year to get an old case file. There were records going back to the '70s—not just closed cases, but receipts and stuff too."

Excitement propelled Josie out of her chair. "Let's take a look," she said.

*

They hardly ever used the third floor of the Denton Police Department. The old, historic building didn't have elevators, and no one particularly wanted to climb another set of steps, so it was used primarily for storage. Josie had only been up there a few times, mostly to help the women from the historical society lug holiday decorations back and forth from one of the storage closets. She had never noticed all the document boxes stacked in the hallways—or rather, she had never noticed just how many of them spilled out of the various rooms and into the hallway.

She, Noah, and Gretchen stood at the mouth of one of the hallways, staring at the stacks of boxes. Beside her, Gretchen said, "This is worse than the Bellewood PD storage room."

Noah said, "This looks like a fire hazard."

"Do we really have that many closed files and old records?" Josie asked.

They moved down the hallway, and Josie swung the door to the first room open. Inside were shelves along each wall, all of them packed with more boxes covered in dust nearly a quarter-inch thick.

Noah said, "Chief Harris kept everything."

"So did everyone who came before him, by the looks of it," Josie said.

Gretchen sneezed.

"I think none of them had the time to organize any of it and shred the old stuff," Noah explained.

Josie sighed. "Well, I'm not authorizing overtime to clean up this mess, that's for sure, but have a couple of people start doing it bit by bit on the slow days, would you?"

"Sure thing," Noah said.

"All right, let's see what we can find."

They split up, each one taking a different room, quickly searching the boxes for old receipts and contracts from the mid

'80s. An hour later, Josie's back ached from leaning over the boxes and riffling through their contents, when she heard Gretchen call from the hallway, "I got it!"

Josie and Noah met her in the hallway, where she dragged an old white document box along the floor. "Here," Gretchen said, wiping sweat from her forehead with the back of one hand. "Handy Helpers Cleaning Service. They had contracts to clean the building after hours in 1981, 1982, and looks like 1983. No personnel records, only the contract between the service and the police department. I don't see anything after 1983. It must be in a different box."

Josie said, "That's okay. Pull what you've got. What we really need is the name of the owner. I doubt they'd keep personnel records over thirty years old, but the owner might remember my mother, or know someone who would."

CHAPTER 43

"You've got to be kidding me," Josie said, looking from Gretchen to Noah, who stood in front of her desk like a couple of school children being reprimanded by the principal.

Noah shook his head, a mournful look in his eye. "I'm sorry, Boss. Handy Helpers Cleaning Service went out of business in 1984, when the owner died. Car accident. Not long after Belinda disappeared."

"I talked to a couple of his relatives—a niece and nephew. No one kept any of the records from the business," Gretchen said.

"So there wouldn't be any personnel records," Josie said.

"Sorry, Boss," Noah offered.

Gretchen said, "There is still Sophia Bowen, the judge's wife. If she used to hang around with Belinda and the girl from the cleaning service, maybe she can offer us a lead. She said she can meet with us later today, and she lives in Denton now."

Josie considered this. Interviewing Sophia Bowen had been a priority to begin with, but she had really hoped that the cleaning service personnel records would give them something more solid than someone's memories. A first and last name. A date of birth. A social security number. Anything that might tell them the identity of Josie's mother before she stole Belinda Rose's life.

"I'll go with you," Josie said. "Where are you with the list of girls who lived in Maggie Lane's care home during the time Belinda was there?"

"Well, that's the good news," Gretchen said, pulling a sheaf of papers from her back pocket and handing them to Josie. "I have a complete list, and Angie is on her way to the station to talk to us."

The disappointment Josie felt just moments earlier gave way to hope. "That's great."

Gretchen helped Josie spread the pages across her desk. "There are fourteen girls in all who lived at Maggie Lane's care home while Belinda was there. Two of them we can eliminate because they were adopted out before Belinda turned ten. Three of them are dead. One is in prison. Two were moved to different foster homes before Belinda reached high-school age. That leaves six of them, including Angie Dobson—that's her married name—who is on her way here."

Gretchen pointed to a photo of a woman in her early fifties with long brown hair just starting to show strands of gray. The photo looked as though it had been pulled from a social media account. In it, Dobson stood on a beach at sunset, smiling with sunburned cheeks, a Hawaiian-print sleeveless sundress wrapped around her thick frame. The straps of her bathing suit peeked from beneath the dress, cutting into her tan shoulders. "She lives outside of Philadelphia, but her daughter goes to college here, and she's in town to visit. She graduated the same year that Belinda would have graduated."

"What about the others?" Josie asked, studying each of the photos, most of which had been pulled from social media. There was one mug shot and the photos of the three women who had already passed on, accompanied their obituaries. All looked to be in their forties or fifties. None resembled Josie's mother.

"I've spoken to them all," Gretchen said. "They didn't have much to offer. Belinda did her own thing. Most of them didn't like her because Mrs. Lane seemed to favor her. Then she got the job at the courthouse and was hardly ever home. They confirmed her gaining weight shortly after she started at the courthouse, running away for three months, and then when she came back, always being over at Lloyd Todd's place. A couple of them said they suspected that she was pregnant, but they couldn't say for sure. None of them recall her talking about where she went when she ran away. Two of them said they thought she had a few friends at the courthouse, but they don't remember any names. None of them remembered the names of any of her friends other than Lloyd and Damon Todd."

"So, this Angie is our last hope as far as the care home girls go," Josie said.

Gretchen nodded. "Yeah, hopefully she knows something the others didn't."

"Well if Belinda didn't confide in anyone at the care home," Noah piped up, "there's still Judge Bowen's wife."

CHAPTER 44

Angela Dobson made herself comfortable at the head of the conference room table while Gretchen flipped to a new page in her trusty notebook and Noah got them all coffee. Her shoulder-length hair showed even more gray than in the Facebook photo that Gretchen had found. When she smiled, clusters of crow's feet appeared at the corners of her brown eyes. A variety of colorful butterflies dotted the sweater she wore over a pair of pressed jeans. "I always wondered what happened to Belinda," she told Josie and Gretchen. Her hair swished as she shook her head. "So sad. I didn't believe she had met prince charming and gotten married, but I never thought she was dead. Murdered too. How sad. How did it…how did it happen?"

Gretchen and Josie exchanged a look. Josie said, "I'm sorry, Mrs. Dobson, we're not at liberty to divulge those details yet."

Angie nodded sagely. "I understand. I guess it will all come out eventually anyway."

Noah appeared with three coffee-filled paper cups squished together between his palms. He doled them out and then produced packets of sugar, creamers, and plastic stirrers from his pockets. Angie smiled at him. "My kind of guy," she remarked.

Leaving her coffee untouched, Gretchen began, "How well did you know Belinda?"

Angie dumped three sugars into her coffee and stirred. "Pretty well, I guess. We were the same age, you know. Our birthdays were only a month apart. I came to the care home two years after Belli though. That's what Maggie called her. Did she tell you that?"

"Yes, she did," Josie answered.

Angie rolled her eyes. "None of the rest of us had nicknames, but Belinda did. Maggie would never say it, but we all thought Belinda was her favorite. She was a nice lady, Maggie was, but she didn't hide her preference for her precious Belli."

"Maggie said that Belli became quite the troublemaker in her teens, though," Noah remarked.

Angie waved a dismissive hand. "Oh sure, we all were. Belinda just got caught more often."

"Did you and Belinda spend a lot of time together?" Gretchen asked.

"At Maggie's we did, but that was about it. Especially once she got the job at the courthouse. She was never home."

Josie said, "Did Belinda ever talk to you about her pregnancy?"

She expected shock and surprise, but Angie simply laughed and said, "She didn't talk to anyone about that pregnancy."

"You knew about the pregnancy?" Noah asked.

"Well, I suspected. She never came out and admitted it, but she didn't deny it either. One time I caught her raiding the fridge in the middle of the night, and she asked me not to tell Maggie. I said, 'I won't tell her you were sneaking food, but that's the least of your worries 'cause she is gonna flip when she finds out you're pregnant,' and she didn't say anything. Didn't even blink. She just waddled off to bed. That's when I knew I was right."

"Did you ever ask her about who the father was or what she intended to do about the baby?" Gretchen asked.

Angie shook her head. "No, not like that, anyway. I got her in private a few times and told her if she wanted to talk about it, she could tell me anything and I wouldn't tell Maggie, but she always walked away from me."

"You noticed she was pregnant," Josie said. "How come no one else did?"

Angie shrugged and sipped her coffee. "Belinda was one of those girls who gained weight all over when she was pregnant. She didn't really have a belly, she just got wider everywhere, so it looked like she was just putting on weight. I only knew because we shared a room, and she was always throwing up in our trash can. Plus, the foster mother I was with before Maggie got pregnant right before I was transferred, so I knew what to look for. Actually, that's why I ended up at the care home, because once she had her own baby, she was finished with us foster kids. I guess I just knew the signs—the morning sickness, the big appetite, the weight gain—and like I said, if we didn't share a bedroom, I might not have even known. We hardly saw her at the care home. She worked all the time back then. She'd leave for school with the rest of us in the morning and not come home till half the girls were already in bed. Maggie was so overwhelmed, she didn't have time for noticing things."

This last statement was without malice. Even when Angie complained of Maggie playing favorites, her tone betrayed quite an affection for the foster mom.

"Did you say anything to anyone when she ran away in the winter of 1982?" Gretchen asked.

"No," Angie said. "It wasn't my place."

"You were a couple of fifteen-year-olds," Noah said. "Your foster sister was hiding a pregnancy. You didn't mention it to Maggie when Belinda disappeared? Weren't you worried about her?"

"Look," Angie replied, "Belinda was pretty independent, you know? Yeah, she hid the pregnancy, but she didn't seem like she was in trouble. She wasn't the kind of girl you worried about. She always got by. Sure, Maggie was worried about her, but Maggie also had the rest of us to care for, and before Belinda left, the fights those two used to have were off the charts. I hate to say this, but it was kind of a relief when Belinda took off. I knew she was getting close to delivering, and I figured she had made arrangements. Plus, it wasn't my secret to tell, you know? Then she was back a few months later like nothing ever happened."

"Did you ask her what happened to her baby?" Josie asked.

"Of course I did. She would only say that everything worked out. She was really cryptic about the whole thing."

"She didn't tell you what she did with the baby?" Gretchen asked.

"No, not a word."

"She never gave you any indication as to where she was during those three months?" Josie asked.

"None. She just said that she was fine and that everything had worked out."

"Assuming she carried to term and the baby was born healthy, she couldn't have gone through any official channels," Noah remarked. "No way she gave birth at a hospital. If a minor showed up at a hospital—particularly one who's already in the foster-care system—to give birth, there's no way that would have gone unnoticed or unreported. And an adoption—the courts would have had to be involved."

Angie finished off her coffee and set her cup on the table. "That is true."

"What do you think happened to the baby?" Gretchen asked.

Angie thought for a moment. "I honestly don't know. But someone must have helped her. I mean, she had to stay somewhere those last few months, right? Maybe someone took the baby from her. Did you know that if you have a home birth, you can fill out the birth certificate whenever and mail it in to the state?"

Josie frowned. "Don't you need a midwife to file that paperwork?"

"No, you can have an unassisted birth in Pennsylvania. I had my first daughter at home in the bathtub. Same thing. I mean, I went to a real doctor throughout my pregnancy, but my husband helped me deliver. We were lucky there were no complications. But all I had to do was fill out the paperwork to file for a birth certificate. I don't know what the laws are now, but back then, you just needed two witnesses to sign a form saying you were pregnant. Not impossible to come up with."

"You think that's what happened to Belinda's baby?" Noah asked. "That she found someone to take it?"

Angie stared at the table, her face looking drawn. "It's better than the alternative, isn't it?"

"Which is what?" Noah asked.

Josie knew what Angie was going to say before she said it. "That the baby died, and Belinda buried it somewhere."

"Do you think she was capable of dealing with something like that?" Josie asked.

Angie held her gaze, dark eyes penetrating, sending a chill from Josie's scalp to her toes. "When you're a fifteen-year-old foster kid with no resources and no good choices, you're capable of dealing with just about anything."

"Did she ever talk about who the father was?" Gretchen asked.

"No. She wouldn't talk about him."

"Was she seeing anyone before she got pregnant?"

Again, Angie shook her head. "No, not that I know of. Maggie would have killed her anyway. We weren't allowed to date until we were seventeen. Most of us did anyway, starting at thirteen or fourteen, but we kept it a secret. Obviously, Belinda was seeing someone, or she couldn't have gotten pregnant, but I don't know who it could have been."

Gretchen said, "Or she could have been sexually assaulted."

Angie considered this. "I guess that's true, but I think she was seeing someone. I mean, she wasn't torn up or anything. Although by that age, most of us had been assaulted or molested at one point or another."

Angie said this in such a matter-of-fact way, Josie didn't know whether to be saddened or in awe of her strength and candor. "Come to think of it," Angie went on, "she did come home after the pregnancy with this pretty little locket. She never took it off and would never tell anyone who gave it to her. So, wherever she was and whoever helped her—I don't think it was against her will."

Josie said, "What about friends? Do you remember who she hung out with?"

Angie's lips twisted as she thought for a long minute. Then she said, "No one at school, that's for sure. People teased her mercilessly, especially about her teeth. You know about those, right?"

"We're aware," Noah said.

"In her junior year she started seeing that Todd kid—I think he's the same one who just got arrested. That's something isn't it?"

Steering her back to the topic of Belinda, Gretchen said, "How about people she worked with?"

"Oh yeah, there were a couple of girls she was friendly with at the courthouse. One was a judge's wife, if I'm not mistaken. The other one worked there too."

"Do you remember their names?" Josie asked.

"I'm sorry, I don't."

"We have the name of the judge's wife," Gretchen told her. "Sophia Bowen. We don't know the name of the other woman she hung out with."

Angie said, "I know it began with an L, but that's all. Linda? Lilly? Laura? Something like that. She was a few years older than Belinda. I remember that because Belinda kept talking about how cool she was that she had her own apartment."

"Did she say where that apartment was?" Josie asked.

"No. I just assumed it was in Bellewood."

Gretchen made a note on her pad. "Do you remember anything else that Belinda said about her?"

"I'm really sorry, but I don't."

CHAPTER 45

Noah drove them to Sophia Bowen's home, recapping what they knew as they moved through the streets of Denton. "Belinda starts working part-time after school at the courthouse sometime in early 1982. By the fall, she is pregnant, but the only person who notices is her roommate. She disappears for three months and returns no longer pregnant, but with a nice locket for her trouble. We have no idea where she went, who she stayed with, or what happened to her baby. As far as we know from the people we've talked to, she never told anyone what happened. She came home and resumed her normal life. A few months after that, she starts having an affair with a teacher, whose sons help to cover it up. Eventually she dumps the teacher, and three or four months after that, someone smashes her head in with a tire iron, or something similar, and buries her in the woods. Six months later, the boss's mother starts using her identity here in Denton."

"Belinda kept a lot of secrets," Gretchen said. "Any one of them could have gotten her killed."

"Or none of them," Josie muttered.

She felt Noah's eyes on her. "What do you mean?"

"I mean my mother could be impulsive, crazy even. It's possible that none of the things we've learned about the real Belinda Rose did anything to set her off. Maybe she just looked at my mother the wrong way that particular day, and she decided to smash her head in."

As the campus of Denton University passed by outside her window, Josie became aware of the heavy, awkward silence in the car. She turned to see Noah glancing at her out of the corner of his eye and then craned her neck toward the backseat where Gretchen was studying her. With a sigh, she said, "You guys said you needed to know more about her."

"According to Angie and Mrs. Ortiz, they were friends," Noah said.

Josie laughed drily. "My mother didn't have friends. She was only interested in what people could do for her."

"Well, obviously she had a relationship with Belinda long before she stole her identity," Gretchen said. "So, what would Belinda have been able to do for her?"

Josie didn't have time to answer as Noah pulled up in front of a large gable-style house with a faux-stone patterned exterior, complete with curved windows bracketed by board and batten shutters and hemmed in by wrought-iron window boxes. They were empty, but Josie could imagine them filled with colorful flowers come springtime. The front door opened before they were even out of their car, and a woman stepped out onto the stone steps. She was short and rotund, dressed tastefully in a long red skirt and white blouse with a red scarf draped around her neck. Thin blond hair swept away from her face, pinned in a bun at the back of her head.

"Mrs. Bowen?" Noah said, extending a hand for her to shake as they climbed the steps.

Introductions were made, and Mrs. Bowen ushered them inside her home. It was large and tastefully decorated in muted pastel colors. Potted plants dominated the foyer and the large sitting room, which was bright and airy. Two light-gray, button-tufted Chesterfield sofas sandwiched a circular, glass-topped coffee table with a large vase at its center, fresh flowers reaching out from it.

The three officers sat on one sofa, and Mrs. Bowen sat across from them, perched on the edge of the opposite sofa, her ankles crossed primly, hands clasped in her lap. "Can I offer you some coffee or tea?" she asked.

"Thank you, but we're fine," Gretchen said, notebook and pen ready in her hands.

Sophia's gaze dropped to her lap momentarily. "I'm so sorry to hear what happened to Belinda. I would never have suspected. Everyone thought she ran off with a man."

"Where did you hear that from?" Josie asked.

Sophia shrugged. "Oh, I'm not sure now. I think Mrs. Lane came around and told someone at the courthouse. We were all concerned. She stopped coming to work. Malcolm and I had brought home our first son by then, so I had stopped working, but I heard all the office news when Malcolm came home each night. So, what can I help you with all these years later?"

Gretchen said, "We're just trying to get a sense of what Belinda's life was like in the weeks leading up to her death. The people she spent the most time with, that sort of thing. Alona Ortiz mentioned that you and Belinda were good friends."

"Oh yes. We were quite close. We used to take smoking breaks together and talk about what had happened on *Dynasty*."

"Mrs. Ortiz mentioned that Belinda was very flirtatious with your husband," Noah said. "Was that a problem between you two?"

Sophia laughed, the sound like wind chimes tinkling, and waved a hand in the air. "Oh that. Yes, well, Belinda flirted with everyone. That's just how she was. She liked attention, just like all of us young girls did. It is true that at first, I was concerned with how much attention Malcolm paid to her. I was a young bride and quite insecure. What I didn't understand at the time was how difficult things were for girls like Belinda."

"Girls like Belinda?" Josie echoed.

Sophia smiled. "Foster children. No family or support system. She had a foster mother of course, but no father figure in her life at all. My Malcolm was just trying to provide guidance to her, give a strong male figure to look up to. He used to say it was the Christian thing to do."

Josie wondered what else Malcolm had tried to provide for Belinda Rose, but she kept silent. Gretchen said, "So you became friends with Belinda."

Sophia nodded.

"Did she confide in you?" Gretchen continued.

"Well, sure."

Josie asked, "Did she talk to you about her baby?"

Sophia's measured smile froze on her face. "Her what?"

"Her baby," Noah said.

Sophia's eyelids fluttered as she struggled to keep a polite smile on her face. "Belinda didn't have a baby."

Josie said, "Her autopsy showed she gave birth before she died."

"No," Sophia said. "That can't be. Belinda was never pregnant."

"It would have been in 1982," Josie told her. "She would have given birth sometime in late 1982."

Sophia placed a manicured hand on her chest. "My God. I didn't know. I knew she went missing that winter. She had been fighting a lot with her foster mom, I remember that much. But I certainly don't remember her being pregnant."

"She came back to work at the courthouse afterward. Did you ever ask her where she had been?"

"Yes, of course I did. We all did. She didn't want to talk about it. I didn't push. You know, she probably just stayed with a friend, but Belinda loved to generate drama."

"Yes," Josie said. "We've heard that."

"Speaking of friends," Gretchen said. "Who else did Belinda hang around with?"

"Oh, I don't know who her friends were; well, besides the girl she roomed with at the care home. I'm sure she had friends at school, but I only ever saw her at the courthouse, so I really couldn't say."

Josie said, "We understand she hung around with one of the girls from the cleaning service, as did you."

Sophia did her wind-chime laugh again. "Oh, Handsy's helpers?"

Noah said, "You mean Handy Helpers."

"No, we called them Handsy's helpers because the owner was a little…um…handsy, if you know what I mean."

"You mean he sexually harassed his workers?" Gretchen asked pointedly.

Her smile still in place, Sophia humphed. "I suppose that's what it would be called today. He had a lot of young girls working for him, and word was that he couldn't keep his hands to himself. That's why the turnover was so big. For such little pay, who would want to deal with their boss groping them all the time?"

Josie swallowed the biting replies that came to mind, as well as the lecture about why your pay shouldn't matter—a woman should never be groped or harassed, in her workplace or anywhere else. It seemed completely lost on Sophia that she had been a teenage secretary to the judge before they were married. Instead of pointing this out, Josie asked, "Were you friendly with any of the young women from the cleaning service?"

"Oh, well, not really. Like I said, there was a big turnover so none of them were around for very long. Plus they really only came right toward the end of the day when the rest of us were getting ready to leave."

"Mrs. Ortiz said you and Belinda were quite close with one of the young ladies," Noah said. "Thin, with long, dark hair and blue eyes. Does that ring a bell?"

Josie added, "Her name perhaps began with an L? Linda, Lilly? Something like that? Laura, perhaps?"

Sophia's brow furrowed. Her gaze flitted up to the ceiling. "Hmmm," she said. "That does sound familiar. I mean, I wouldn't say I was 'quite close' with any of them, but there were probably one or two who were there longer than the rest that I talked with. I'm ashamed to say that I used to smoke, and those cleaning girls would sometimes join Belinda and me outside for a cigarette."

Gretchen asked, "Do you remember a specific woman whose name began with an L?"

"I don't doubt that there was a young woman, a Linda or a Lilly—that sounds a bit familiar—but I don't specifically remember one. I'm so sorry."

Another dead end. How was it possible that Josie's mother had been so forgettable to so many people that none of them even remembered her name? Had it been by design? Or was someone lying? Were multiple people lying? If so, why? Josie couldn't see any reason for Mrs. Ortiz to lie. Damon Todd also had no reason to lie, especially after divulging his father's scandalous secret. He, his brother, and their father all had alibis for the night that Belinda disappeared. Angie Dobson had been more forthcoming than anyone they'd talked with. She had given them their first real clue as to Josie's mother's real identity—or at least the identity she'd been using before she stole Belinda's. Josie couldn't think of any reason for Sophia Bowen to lie, but she was certain she wasn't being entirely truthful.

"When did you stop working at the courthouse?" Josie asked her.

"Oh, it would have been the summer of 1983 when we brought our eldest son home. Then a couple of years later, our other son was born, and I never looked back. They're grown now, of course. Andrew is a lawyer, you know, right here in Denton."

It was then that Josie realized why the name Bowen was so familiar to her. Andrew Bowen had been to the police station many times to defend his clients. Josie had never spoken directly with him, but she had passed by him many times over the years. "Does your son practice criminal law?" Josie asked.

Sophia's smile widened. "Yes, that's right. He does a little family law and other civil matters, but his primary area of practice is criminal defense. My other son is a doctor. He lives in San Francisco."

There were a few more minutes of conversation between Sophia and Gretchen that Josie didn't bother to pay attention to. She was on her feet, wandering around the room, aware that Sophia's eyes kept darting toward her, although she couldn't imagine why she was making Sophia nervous. They thanked her for her time, asked her to call them if she remembered anything else, and started toward the front door.

It was then that Josie noticed the framed photographs hanging on the wall toward the back of the foyer. There were several of two handsome young men, probably only a few years older than Josie, one brown-haired and the other blond—high school graduations, college graduations, candid shots of them playing various sports, and even a photo of one of them on top of a mountain peak. Josie recognized Andrew Bowen. It was an impressive display of the accomplishments of Sophia Bowen's seemingly perfect offspring, but that wasn't what made Josie's throat seize up. Her finger pointed to the large portrait that presided over all the other photos—Sophia Bowen as a much younger woman seated in a rigid pose next to her husband, Judge Malcolm Bowen.

Noah stepped up beside her. "What is it, Boss?"

Josie's mouth opened, but no words would come.

"Boss?" Noah repeated.

She squeezed out, "Him."

Sophia walked over to them. "That was my Malcolm," she said lovingly. "Of course, that was taken ages ago."

Gretchen sidled up to Josie on her other side, looking from Josie to the portrait and back. "You knew Judge Bowen?" she asked.

"What's that?" Sophia asked, an edge of uncertainty creeping into her tone.

Finally, Josie's voice came to her. "I didn't know him, but he knew my mother."

"Oh, did he? Who was your mother?" Sophia asked.

"Boss," Noah said, a note of concern in his voice.

Josie ignored Sophia and turned to Noah. "There was a custody hearing. No, not a hearing, a private mediation. Just me, my mother, my grandmother, their attorneys, and Judge Bowen. I was nine or ten. My grandmother wanted custody. She lost. Mostly because I lied about all the things my mother did to me. I was too afraid to tell the truth."

Now Josie wondered if telling the truth would have made a difference. Her grandmother had sued her mother under the name Belinda Rose, and Judge Bowen had known the real Belinda Rose who had worked at the courthouse in 1982. Josie was now willing to bet that he was the father of Belinda's baby. He would have known in 1997 when Josie's mother appeared before him that she wasn't Belinda Rose. He might have even remembered her from her days on the Handy Helpers' staff. Or had he simply believed there was more than one woman by that name in the county?

Josie tried hard to think back to that day, examining her memories for any small clue that the judge and her mother had been in league together. If Josie was right, and it was Judge Bowen who had impregnated Belinda Rose, it was possible that her mother had known about the affair and used it to blackmail the judge. There were a number of judges in the county. Why had her case fallen on his docket, and for a private mediation rather than a hearing?

Again Sophia asked, "Who was your mother?"

But now the judge was dead. His records and the docket would only reflect that a woman named Belinda Rose was awarded custody of her own daughter. Josie wondered if he had been the judge to sign off on the custody order when her mother finally left once and for all. The only person who knew that her mother wasn't who she said she was had passed away, leaving Josie with nothing but a ghost and more questions than answers.

"I don't know," Josie answered. "I have no idea who she was."

CHAPTER 46

"She's lying," Josie said.

Back at the station house, she, Noah, and Gretchen had gotten takeout and planted themselves in the conference room, their notes and materials from the Belinda Rose case spread out over the table.

"Boss," Noah said, "she stopped working at the courthouse long before your grandmother tried to get custody of you. I doubt she even knew about any of it."

"Unless Malcolm came home and told her," Gretchen said. "It seems like he liked to come home and share the office gossip with her. You don't think it would have occurred to him to come home and say, 'Hey, remember that girl who used to work at the courthouse who disappeared? Well, she showed up today at the courthouse only she wasn't the same girl.'"

"Or," Noah said, "there's more than one Belinda Rose in the state. We don't even know that Malcolm Bowen knew Josie's mother from when she worked for the cleaning service. Do men like that really notice the help?"

"He noticed Belinda Rose," Josie pointed out. "My money's on him as the baby's father."

Gretchen nodded her agreement. "I was thinking that too."

Noah made a noise of frustration. "That still doesn't mean he knew your mother in the early 1980s, or remembered her."

"My mother had something on him," Josie said with certainty. "I know she did. How ballsy was it to go to the courthouse you used to clean using the identity of a girl you used to work with there?"

"We're talking fifteen years later, Boss," Noah said.

Josie was going to argue her point, but her cell phone vibrated, dancing noisily across the glass-topped table. Seeing Misty's name flash across the screen, Josie snatched it up and answered, listened for a moment, then said, "I'll do it. Give me a half hour, okay?"

She hung up and, as she stood, she noticed Noah and Gretchen staring at her. "Misty needs me," she explained. "Both her and the baby are sick. Mrs. Quinn took them to the doctor, but she has to work. Misty needs me to pick up a prescription for the baby."

They continued to stare, and Josie realized that it was out of character for her to walk away from work in the middle of an active case, even though as chief, she didn't need to be there. She was supposed to be getting better at delegating. "I'll be back in an hour," she said. "In the meantime, draw up some warrants. I want a search for any female foster children in the care of the state between 1962 and 1982 whose first name is Linda, Lilly, or Laura."

Noah groaned. "Boss, with all due respect, that's like looking for a needle in a haystack."

Gretchen was already taking notes. Josie raised a brow at Noah. "Do you have any better ideas?"

"Is there anyone else your mother knew who might be able to shed some light on who she was or what happened to her?" Noah asked.

"No," Josie said. "Everyone who knew her would have known her as Belinda Rose. That doesn't help me. Most of the people she knew were heavily involved in drugs in one way or another. I don't know their names. I only know them by the nicknames I gave them when I was a child. Most of them are probably dead now."

Gretchen asked, "Did she have any boyfriends? After your father passed?"

Again, Dexter McMann rose up in her mind. "There was a man," she admitted. "A boyfriend. But I don't think he will give us much to work with. He would only have known her as Belinda Rose, same as me. I don't know what happened to him."

"Do you have his name?" Gretchen asked.

"I don't—I don't remember," Josie lied.

Gretchen gave her a penetrating look. Then she said, "Try to remember. People you date usually keep photos. Could be worth paying him a visit. In the meantime, we'll get to work tracking down the Lindas, Lillys, and Lauras of the foster care system."

CHAPTER 47

JOSIE – THIRTEEN YEARS OLD

There was a man in her mother's bed. This wasn't at all unusual, except that it was the same man who had been in her mother's bed every morning for the last two weeks. The noise of their vigorous nighttime activities was hard to sleep through in the tiny trailer, but she made sure to be up, showered, dressed, and out the door every morning before either of them got up, taking the shortcut through the woods to wait for Ray on his back porch. Josie's mother and the new guy weren't around in the afternoons, usually returning to the trailer after dinner, by which time Josie was firmly barricaded in her room. Josie didn't like it when men stayed over, but she loved it when her mother had a reason to ignore her.

When she finally met him, it was by accident. A stomach virus had kept her up most of the night, and as she was stumbling from the bathroom to the kitchen to get a glass of water, she stumbled smack into his bare chest. The impact sent Josie flying backward, her ass hitting hard against the kitchen tiles. The lights switched on, and Josie threw up a forearm to avoid the sudden glare. Standing over her, looking impossibly tall, was a guy who had to be closer to Josie's age than her mother's. Shaggy brown hair fell across his face. He wore only boxer shorts, and the muscles of his long torso rippled when he reached down to help her up.

"Hey," he said. "You okay?"

She nodded, suddenly very aware that she must smell like vomit.

"You don't look so good," he told her. "I'm Dex, by the way. Your mom said she'd introduce me, but you're never here."

Oh, I'm here, Josie thought. All her mother had to do was knock on her bedroom door, but now Josie saw why her mother wouldn't want them to meet. She couldn't take her eyes off his flat stomach and the trail of hair that dipped into the front of his boxers. She'd seen Ray shirtless a dozen times, but Ray didn't look like this. "How—how old are you?" Josie asked.

Dex laughed. "I'm twenty. I know, I know, there's a bit of an age difference, but your mom, you know, she's really cool."

Josie didn't bother responding to that. Dex didn't seem like he was there as the result of a drug-and-alcohol-fueled bender like most of them. He actually wanted to be there, which made him either really stupid or every bit as cold-hearted as Josie's mother. Josie's money was on stupid; she'd seen her mother manipulate men before. She pushed past him and got a glass from the overhead cabinet, filling it with water and gulping it down. Immediately she regretted it as nausea roiled in her stomach.

"You sick?" Dex asked.

Yeah, he definitely wasn't the brightest.

Ignoring him, Josie tried to push past him, but before she could get through the living room, the nausea overcame her and vomit exploded across the carpet in front of her. Holding her stomach, she swayed on her feet. It was only the water she'd just had, but the smell was rank. Her mother was really going to make her pay for this.

Then Dex was at her feet, blotting the carpet with paper towels. He left and came back with cleaner he'd found under the kitchen sink. "You should go lie down," he said. "I got this."

Josie knew she should thank him, but she was afraid if she didn't get into her bed that instant, she might not make it. She ran to her room and clambered into her bed, pulling the covers up to her neck, letting the illness pull her under its choppy waves.

She didn't even remember falling asleep, but when she woke up, on her nightstand were four cans of ginger ale and two sleeves of saltine crackers. She sat up, confused and sure she must be dreaming. Reaching over to examine one of the cans, her feet bumped into something hard and plastic beside her bed. A bucket. For her to throw up in. For a moment, Josie wondered if her grandmother had been there in the night, but she knew better. Her mother never allowed Lisette inside the trailer. There was no chance it was her mother, so it had to be…Dex?

It was two weeks before their paths crossed again, and when they did, she only managed a mumbled "Thanks." It made her nervous when men were nice to her. It always came at such a heavy price—her mother's rage, a bargaining chip, or something worse. Occasionally Dex would invite her to join him and her mother while they ate or watched television, but she always declined. He invited her to go to the movies with them or out to eat, but again she refused. He always looked a little disappointed, but he had no idea of the way things worked in her mother's world.

Then he started approaching her when her mother wasn't home. He had practically moved in by this point, and while her mother was off doing whatever she did to earn money to keep the trailer roof over their heads, Dex tried to draw Josie out, offering her rides to and from school, wanting to take her for ice cream, asking if she needed help with her homework, trying to get her to watch TV with him. One day he brought home a dozen donuts and offered her some, pointing out that he had gotten six of her favorite kind: French crullers. How he even knew that was beyond her. Had she told him?

As if sensing her question, he said, "The last two times your mom got donuts, the French crullers mysteriously disappeared. I took a wild guess."

Josie stood in the middle of the tiny trailer kitchen, her stomach growling at the sight of the donuts, and put a hand on her hip.

"Look," she told him, "I've already got a boyfriend, I don't need anyone's help, and I sure as hell don't need another one of my mom's pervy boyfriends trying to be 'nice' to me. I wouldn't touch you for a million donuts, so just cut it out. Okay?"

For a moment, he stared at her wide-eyed, shock slackening his jaw. Then, slowly, a smile spread across his face and he began to laugh. He bent at the waist, holding his belly, just laughing his ass off. Josie shot him the dirtiest look she could muster.

Finally, he said, "You're pretty sassy, you know that? How many 'pervy boyfriends' did your mom have before I moved in?"

Josie walked away from him, taking up position on the living-room couch where her homework was spread out. "Enough," she said.

"I'm not being nice to you because I want something from you, and I'm certainly not a pervert."

"That's what they all say," she muttered as she picked up her pencil and tried to focus on her homework.

A French cruller on a folded paper towel appeared next to the worksheet in front of her. "We're living together," he said. "I'm dating your mom. I don't want anything from you. I'm just trying to talk to you, to maybe make you look less miserable once in a while."

"Well, don't try being my dad either," Josie snapped.

"I'm not trying to be anyone's dad," Dex replied. "Your mom and I, we're just having fun."

"I know," Josie said. "I hear you every night."

Again, he laughed. "You're a whip," he said. "Anyway, have some donuts, don't have some donuts. I'm going out. If you want a ride to school tomorrow, I can take you."

He flashed a smile at her, his green eyes vibrant beneath a shock of dark hair, and left the trailer. Josie listened to the sound of his car pulling away and wondered how long he would be in their lives.

CHAPTER 48

Josie emerged from the pharmacy with Harris's antibiotics in one hand and her cell phone in the other. Misty rattled on while Harris screamed in the background, the sound making Josie want to race to him and scoop him into her arms. But when he was sick, she knew all he wanted was his mother. Fetching the medication was the best way she could help. "I got some more infant Tylenol too," Josie said. "I'm only a few minutes away."

"Oh great," Misty said. "You're a lifesaver."

A man stood leaning against the driver's-side door of Josie's Escape as she found her vehicle in the parking lot. She hung up with Misty and stopped dead in front of him. It was dark, and the parking lot was deserted except for them and a couple of other vehicles, but Josie could see dark eyes glinting from beneath his baseball cap. He wore faded blue jeans and a blue down vest over a flannel shirt. She estimated him to be in his forties. His hands were hooked in the belt loops of his jeans, one of his feet flat against the door of her car. A smile snaked across his face as she looked him up and down.

"Can I help you?" Josie asked.

He kept smiling at her in a way that made the hairs on the back of her neck stand up. One of her hands slipped inside her jacket and rested on the handle of her service weapon.

"Now that's not very nice, is it, Chief?" he said.

"Do I know you?" Josie asked.

"No," he said, "but you want to."

"Yeah, I don't think so," Josie said. "Out of my way. There's someplace I need to be."

He stepped aside slightly and put a hand on the door handle, as if to open it, but Josie hadn't disengaged the locks yet. She didn't want to get any closer to him, much less cross his path to get into her vehicle. "Allow me," he said with fake politeness.

"I can take it from here," Josie told him.

The hand on her gun was reassuring, but she knew she had to be careful—the mayor would have her ass if the chief of police was caught pulling a gun on a guy who was simply trying to open her door for her.

The man didn't move, so Josie said, "What do you want?"

"Just trying to have a conversation with you, sweet thing."

Josie kept her voice clear and firm. "My name's not sweet thing, and I really don't have time for this. I told you, there's somewhere I need to go. Someone is waiting for me."

"You know, you could be nicer to a gentleman just trying to be polite," he told her, his sickening smile holding firm.

She'd had enough already. "Get out of my way," Josie told him.

The punch came fast and hard, whizzing past the left side of her head as she ducked under it just in time, barreling into him with the full weight of her body and slamming him against her Escape. Josie heard him gasp the word, "Bitch." Then everything else happened at once—she took a step back, her hand emerging from her jacket with the Glock, but before she could take a shooter's stance, his fist swung out wildly, catching her on the side of her face. She felt the skin of her cheek swell. Stumbling to the side, she tried to keep her balance, lifting the Glock toward him once more. Lightning-fast, his other arm lashed out at her wrist. The Glock clattered to the ground and the man's hands closed around Josie's throat. He swung her around, and her body crashed into the side of the vehicle. Pain shot across the back of her skull.

The man held her there, squeezing her throat until her vision started to gray as she clawed at his fingers. "You said you wanted it," he breathed into her face. "I'm gonna give it to you, Chief."

Josie's heart froze in her chest and then kicked into overdrive, jackhammering against her sternum. One of his hands left her throat and reached between her legs, tearing at her jeans, pulling them downward. It was all the opening Josie needed. She brought one elbow up and sliced downward onto the man's forearm, breaking his hold. Her other elbow came up fast, smashing into his nose. He staggered backward, muttering the word "bitch" once more and holding his hands to his face. They came away bloody. He stared at them and then looked back at her. "Oh, so you really want this to be real, then. Well, now I'm taking what I came for."

He lunged toward her, and she stepped out of the way, snagging one of his wrists and twisting his arm high behind his back. She kicked between his feet, spreading his legs and putting him off balance. Her forearm knocked his face into the window of the Escape once, and then again for good measure. Josie didn't have cuffs, but she took his other wrist and twisted that behind his back as well. "Get on your knees," she commanded.

She felt him struggle against her hold, and she twisted his wrists until he cried out in pain and his knees buckled. Pushing him onto the ground, she readjusted her grip on his wrists, both now bent at unnatural angles. Josie knew the pain was the only thing keeping him from coming after her again. Once his face was against the asphalt, she put one knee on his back and one on his neck. "You're under arrest," she said, and read him his rights.

"What the fuck is this?" he cried.

Josie took one hand away long enough to fish her phone out of her pocket and dial 911, dropping the phone onto the pavement so she could keep him pinned as she shouted into it. She rattled off the address. "Officer needs immediate assistance. Send nearest units. Contact Lieutenant Fraley."

The man squirmed beneath her. "Are you fucking kidding me?" he spat. "This was not what we agreed on. This wasn't part of the deal."

Josie leaned closer to his face. "What?"

"You promised not to arrest me," he cried.

"Promised not to arrest you? I don't even know you."

"It's me," he said. "Keith. I answered your ad."

Josie felt her stomach sink. "My ad? What ad?"

He continued to struggle, bucking against her, grunting. "Your ad on craigslist, you crazy bitch."

CHAPTER 49

Noah arrived just behind two marked units, jumping out of his car and racing toward her before the patrol officers were even out of their seatbelts. Blue and red lights pulsed in the darkness. Dropping to his knees, Noah grabbed the man's wrists, securing them with two plastic zip ties he pulled from his pocket.

"I've already read him his rights," Josie told Noah as they lifted Keith from the ground and handed him over to the patrol officers to put in the back of a cruiser. Josie stalked around the perimeter of the Escape, locating her gun and holstering it before going in search of the pharmacy bag she'd discarded during the attack. Luckily it hadn't been crushed. She held it up as Noah approached. "I need to get this to Misty," she said.

Noah studied her, and she saw the change in his face—the hardened professionalism giving way to shock. Even under the whirring red and blue lights, she could see his pallor. Looking down, she saw that the zipper on her jeans was torn open to reveal the waistband of her black panties beneath.

"Josie," Noah said.

She held out her free hand. "Give me your jacket, Fraley."

Slowly he took it off and handed it to her. Trading him the pharmacy bag for his jacket, she tied the jacket around her waist, knotting the sleeves at the small of her back. "Misty needs that, do you understand?"

He stepped closer to her. The patrol officers waited several feet away, standing by their cruiser. "I don't care about Misty right now," Noah said.

Josie looked away from him. "Well, you should. If you want to help me right now, you can get that to her and meet me at the station." She signaled for one of the officers, and he jogged over. "The store probably has footage of what just happened. Go in and see if they've got cameras out here in the parking lot. I want whatever they have."

"You got it, Boss," he said, and headed off to the store.

Noah's face was set with frustration. Josie raised a brow at him. "Do we have a problem, Fraley?"

He shook his head, but a muscle ticked in his jaw.

"Good," Josie said. She panned the ground again. "I need you to get to work. That guy was answering an ad, and I'm pretty sure this time it was for much more than 'kinky fun.'"

Noah swallowed. "What are you saying?"

"I think the ad that was posted was for a rape fantasy."

CHAPTER 50

"His name is Keith Gibbs," Noah said. "He's forty-four, a resident of Denton. Single, no kids. Works at the potato-chip factory. He says he found your ad a few days ago, that the two of you exchanged emails and set up the scenario. That was all I could get out of him before he asked for an attorney."

Josie followed Noah into the closed-circuit viewing room, smoothing down the T-shirt and jeans she had changed into in her office. Unfortunately, these extra clothes had been stuffed inside one of her desk drawers for so long, they were plagued with wrinkles. But they would have to do. "Did you get the emails?" Josie asked.

"He sent them to Gretchen from his phone. She's printing them now."

They watched the large television screen that provided them with a view into their interrogation room, where Keith Gibbs paced.

"Did you find the ad?" Josie asked.

She glanced at him just long enough to notice the flush creeping from his throat to the roots of his hair. He handed her a sheet of paper. On it, the subject line of the ad read: *Fulfill My Fantasy… Looking for a Forced Connection.* Beneath that, the text went on, *Thirty-something hot female cop looking for a big, strong stud to fulfill rape fantasy. Don't reply unless you're willing to come at me hard and you like a good fight. If you want something fun and taboo, hit me up.*

Nausea stirred the dinner Josie had eaten an hour earlier in the conference room. "My God," she said.

Noah took the page from her hand and placed it facedown on the table. "I read the emails. There are only four of them. Basically, whoever is posing as you gives your name and address, says you're the chief of police. Lays out this scenario where he follows you for a day or two and approaches you in a public place and rapes you. You will fight back, but he is not to stop, and you promise not to arrest him."

"The email address?" Josie asked.

"It's a free email address anyone can open with a dummy name. It's registered in your name, obviously. I drew up a warrant—for the email provider and craigslist—but I doubt we'll turn up much. Whoever is doing this is tech-savvy enough to remain anonymous. I mean, maybe if we were a bigger department or the FBI, but we don't have a lot of resources for this kind of thing. I can pass this along to the state police or ask someone at the college to consult, if you want."

Josie shook her head. She had someone else in mind. "I'll handle it. Just get me what you can, okay?"

"You know someone?"

"I know someone who knows people," she answered. She took out her phone and fired off a text to Trinity Payne. *Hey, are you still coming to town? Still interested in that Lloyd Todd story? I'll give you an exclusive, but I need your help with something. ASAP.*

To Noah, she said, "I want to talk to Lloyd Todd."

"Boss."

"I don't care what you have to do, get me a meeting with him. I'll drive over to the county jail and talk to him. He can have seven lawyers if he wants. This ends now."

Her cell phone rang. It was Trinity. "I'm coming into town this evening," she said when Josie answered. "I'll be staying at the Eudora, and yes, I'm still interested in the Lloyd Todd story. I'm more interested in doing a story on you."

"Don't hold your breath," Josie said.

Trinity laughed. "Never say never, my dear. I know you well enough by now to know that you don't call me unless you need something. What am I trading for the Todd story?"

"I need your help with some…computer crimes. You have connections, right?"

"Oh, honey, I know some of the best hackers you'll never meet. But I'm not sure the Todd story is big enough to warrant me calling in those favors."

Josie groaned. "You can't be serious."

"You've been involved in some of the most intriguing cases in the entire country just in the last two years. The network thinks a story on you would bring in huge ratings."

"I really don't have time for this, Trinity. Not to mention that I have absolutely zero interest in having my face splashed all over the national news again."

"I knew you would say that. Just hear me out. We'll talk about it in person. Alone. No producers, no cameramen. Just me. Just come over tomorrow, okay? I'll help you with your computer crimes case."

Josie felt Noah's eyes on her. She really didn't have the time or inclination to hear Trinity out about this particular matter. She hated doing press, and the last thing she needed was to be under a microscope on national television. But she knew that Trinity's contacts would locate whoever was placing the craigslist ads in a matter of hours, where it could take weeks through official channels. After the last few days, she was desperate for this assault on her life to stop, even if that meant humoring Trinity's pitch for a few hours.

With a heavy sigh, Josie said, "Fine. Text me your room number when you get here."

The squeal of delight Trinity gave could be heard all the way across the room where Noah stood. It startled him.

She knew it was futile, but Josie pushed the phone closer to her mouth to remind Trinity, "I didn't say I'd do it. I only said I would hear you out." But Josie could picture Trinity's predatory grin. She always got what she wanted.

"Whatever," she told Josie, hanging up just as Gretchen came in with a sheaf of papers in her hand. Josie took the pages from her but didn't read them.

Gretchen said, "Your would-be rapist, Keith Gibbs, has no known association with Lloyd Todd. He was just a twisted guy answering an ad."

"I figured that," Josie said. "We'll find out who's behind the ads and go after them."

Gretchen looked at the CCTV screen, where Gibbs had finally taken a seat, then back to Josie. "Boss," she said, "we can't hold him."

Josie stepped toward Gretchen. "What?"

"You know this," Noah said. "He thought he was answering an ad for a consensual sexual encounter. Technically, he did nothing wrong. At least, that's what his attorney will argue."

"I don't give a shit about his attorney," Josie snapped. "He assaulted me. He stuck his grimy hands on me. He did not take no for an answer."

"Because he thought that was the arrangement," Gretchen said. "Look, I agree, the guy's a shithead, and he assaulted you, yes, but he thought this was an arrangement the two of you had agreed on. He had no reason to believe that you were not the person behind the ad or emails. He's got no priors. Not even traffic tickets. Clean as a whistle."

"I want to press charges," Josie said.

"The DA will toss them out," Noah told her. "I know you know this, Boss."

Anger flared in Josie's chest, burning up her skin. "I don't give a shit. I'll talk to the DA myself if I have to. He is not leaving here tonight. Charge him."

Gretchen and Noah looked at one another and seemed to come to some kind of agreement. "Okay," Gretchen said. "I'll do the paperwork."

CHAPTER 51

The glowing numbers on Noah's cable box showed it was nearly one a.m. Curled beneath a blanket on his couch, Josie shook herself awake long enough to register the old 1990s sitcom playing on the television. She tried to focus on it, but every cell in her body felt heavy with longing to go back to sleep. Her ears tuned to the sounds coming from the kitchen—dishes clinking, the microwave whirring, and another sound that Josie couldn't identify. A warm sense of calm pulled her back toward sleep again. She was safe here. She could relax—just for a little while. She picked up the remote and turned the volume up a little, filling the room with canned laughter and letting her eyelids flutter closed once more. She was almost there, almost all the way under, when she felt Keith Gibbs's hands press down on her, smelled his moist breath. Her insides curdled, and she thrashed against him.

"Boss!" Noah's voice startled her awake. He stood over her looking worried, two large coffee mugs in his hands.

Josie shifted to sit up and wiped sweat from her brow. "Sorry," she said. "I-I, uh, fell asleep."

"You were dreaming," Noah said.

Not dreaming, she thought. *Remembering.* Her mind was trying to process those terrifying, chaotic moments now that it wasn't focused on work.

"You okay, Boss?" Noah asked.

Ignoring his question, she said, "You know, you can call me Josie—I mean, at least when we're here together."

She patted the space next to her, and Noah sat down, handing her a cup. White foam with what looked like ground cinnamon steamed from inside. It smelled sweet and spicy, with a faint scent of whiskey. "What is this?"

Noah smiled and lifted his cup. "A dirty chai latte—coffee, spices, and single malt. I thought you might like it. I can make you something to eat too, if you want."

Josie smiled and sipped the drink, slowly savoring it. "Not necessary," she said. "This is perfect, thank you."

They drank in silence, lost in the images playing on television for several moments. Then Noah said, "Are we going to talk about tonight?"

"No," Josie replied.

"Bos—Josie, you know you can talk to me."

"And you know that I'm not a talker."

He laughed. "True. All right, how about that detail we talked about? One unit on you all the time until we get this sorted out?"

She was grateful to him for not pushing. The only way she had survived what she had was by blocking out the terrible things that had happened and all the dark feelings that went with them. The only option she had ever had was to keep moving forward. She knew this wasn't healthy—a therapist she'd been forced to see in college had told her that one day it would all catch up with her, but so far she had been able to stay just ahead of her demons. She planned on keeping it that way.

The latte made her feel warm and drowsy. She put her coffee mug onto the table and stood, offering him a small smile. "Can we not talk about that right now? I think the best thing for me right now is just to go to bed."

Looking surprised, Noah set his own cup on the table. "Oh, sure, okay. I mean, unless you want to hang out. We don't have to talk about work."

"Thank you, but I really just need some sleep."

She felt his eyes on her back as she left the room. Upstairs, she collapsed into his bed and straight into a deep, dreamless sleep.

*

A few hours later, she woke; her back and neck felt stiff from the assault, but the memory of Keith Gibbs attacking her was a little duller in her mind than it was before. Soon the memory would be small enough to lock away in her mental vault with all the other horrors she'd endured.

Heading downstairs, Josie tiptoed past Noah, who lay sprawled on the couch snoring, and found her phone charging in the kitchen. It was almost the time she would normally get ready for work. There was a text message from Gretchen from twenty minutes earlier.

Todd has agreed to meet with you. Ten a.m. county prison.

There was also a text from Trinity. *Room 227. I'll see you later today, right?* Josie didn't answer it.

She went back into the living room and gently shook Noah awake. "Fraley," she said. "Wake up. You're my detail today."

CHAPTER 52

The Alcott County Jail was located in Bellewood and managed by the sheriff's office. The jail acted as a hub for all the police departments in the county, processing their prisoners and holding them over for trial. Although Denton police had a holding area in their station house, it was mostly for drunk college students and other people guilty of minor offenses. Once it came time for someone to be arraigned and booked, the sheriff transported them from Denton and processed them through the county facility.

Because Lloyd Todd's lawyer insisted on being present for their meeting, the deputies had placed them in a private meeting room. Lloyd sat hunched over the table, his hands cuffed and threaded through an iron loop fixed to the tabletop. The orange jumpsuit he wore stretched tight across his broad shoulders. Dark eyes glared from beneath a pair of bushy eyebrows, and gray shot through his short, spiked brown hair and the patchy beard that stubbled his cheeks. He looked much older than his brother, although Josie knew they were only two years apart. Noah waited outside.

"This is highly irregular," Lloyd's attorney said from where he stood behind his client, looking sharp and imposing with his slicked-back black hair and a charcoal suit that probably cost more than Josie's car.

"Your client agreed to it," she said.

The attorney bristled. "I advised him against it."

No one was more surprised than Josie that Lloyd had agreed to meet with her, but as Trinity Payne often said: *People always want something, you just have to figure out what it is.* It wasn't normally

Josie's style to bargain with people, but she had two major issues she needed to address with Todd, and whenever possible, she preferred to go directly to the source.

Lloyd, however, gave nothing away.

Josie started close to home. "I met with your brother the other day."

Nothing.

"Your boys are doing well there."

A flicker in his eyes, barely perceptible. He folded his hands together, chains clinking. Josie forged ahead. "I was there to talk to him about Belinda Rose. Do you remember her?"

"We went to high school together," Lloyd said.

"That's right," Josie said. She recapped everything Damon had told them, and Lloyd agreed that all of it was accurate.

"You wouldn't be coming around asking about her unless something bad happened to her," Lloyd said.

"She's dead," Josie told him. "Someone caved her head in thirty-three years ago and buried her in the woods in Denton."

Lloyd's expression didn't change, but he offered, "Sorry to hear that."

"Mr. Todd," Josie said, "do you remember anyone that Belinda hung out with? Any of her friends? Perhaps from the courthouse?"

"Why are you asking me?"

"Damon said you and Belinda spent a lot of time together," Josie said.

"Damon also told you she was seeing our father, so you know that me spending time with her—it was all fake."

Josie raised a brow. "But you did spend time with her. Surely the two of you talked now and then."

Lloyd chuckled. "Belinda talked a lot, Chief. I don't remember everything she said."

"I'm not asking you to remember everything she said," Josie told him. "I'm asking one question. Surely you remember Belinda talking about her friends."

Lloyd sighed. "She was friends with a chick named Angie from the foster home," he said.

"Anyone else?" Josie prodded.

"That's more than one question."

"It's the same question. I want to know who Belinda's friends were."

"There were a couple of girls from the courthouse."

"Names?" Josie asked.

"Come on, Chief—" he began.

"You remembered the name of her friend from the care home; what were the names of her friends from the courthouse?"

He sighed, shaking his head as though what she was asking was ridiculous, but seemed to give it some thought. Lines creased his forehead until, finally, he said, "Sophia. Sophia and Lila. That was the other one, Lila."

Josie hoped her excitement didn't show on her face. Her spine straightened, and she leaned forward slightly. She hadn't expected him to remember. Not Linda or Lilly or Laura.

Lila.

It was like unlocking a secret code. She felt slightly breathless. "Do you remember Lila's last name?"

He shook his head. "Nah, sorry. I never met her or the other one. Just heard Belinda talk about them all the time. She talked a lot, and like Damon told you, I let her follow me around at school sometimes so no one would get the wrong idea about her and my dad."

Josie was sure that Noah was already on his phone, asking Gretchen to get into the county foster-care records, but she glanced meaningfully at the camera over the door anyway. "There's one more thing," she told him.

"I think that's quite enough," the attorney interjected. "My client has been more than helpful on this matter. He didn't have to meet with you today."

Lloyd glanced over his shoulder and silenced the man with a look. He turned back to Josie and opened his palms, inviting her to go on.

"I want you to get word to your people to stop harassing me. You crossed a line last night."

"Chief Quinn," the attorney said, approaching the table.

Once again, Lloyd silenced him. "I'm afraid I don't know what you're talking about," he said.

"Okay, fair enough," Josie said. "Maybe your minions don't keep you abreast of all their activities in here, but since your arrest, the department's vehicles have been vandalized, the station house has been egged, someone put shit under the handles of my car doors, robbed my house and destroyed my personal property, and worst of all, someone placed sick personal ads on craigslist under my name. Last night, a man tried to assault me in the parking lot of a pharmacy because he was responding to an ad someone placed in my name for a rape fantasy."

The attorney said, "These are very serious allegations."

Josie kept her eyes fixed on Lloyd, whose expression had not changed. "I'm not accusing him of anything," she said. "I'm accusing people he associates with. I believe if he had a conversation with these people and encouraged them to stop these behaviors, it would greatly help his situation."

The attorney opened his mouth to speak, but Lloyd said, "My situation?"

Josie leaned forward again, both elbows on the table. "I'm not stupid, Mr. Todd. I know you didn't have to meet with me. You didn't have to talk to me about Belinda Rose. You did something for me. Now, what can I do for you? What can I do for you that might make you more amenable to talking to these associates?"

"I don't have associates," he responded. "But if I did, they wouldn't be doing shit like robbing your house or putting ads online."

"What are you saying?"

"I'm saying, anyone I associated with might pull off some harmless pranks."

"Slashed tires and shattered windshields of the department's entire fleet is hardly minor," Josie pointed out.

Lloyd shrugged. "I told you, I don't have associates. I'm speaking hypothetically."

Josie resisted the urge to roll her eyes. "Okay, hypothetically, what are you telling me?"

"That the other stuff you're talking about—robbery and personal ads—my hypothetical associates had nothing to do with that."

"The man who robbed my house is in his fifties or sixties, thin, with gray hair, always wears a green jacket, can be found under the bridge, and goes by Zeke. Hypothetically, he wouldn't be someone you associate with?"

Lloyd laughed, his shoulders shaking. "You're talking about Larry Ezekiel Fox. He's an old burnout. No one associates with him. He's a pirate with absolutely no loyalty. He's been using since you and I were in diapers. Used to go by Larry. Started using his middle name a few years back. Now everyone calls him Zeke."

"So, hypothetically, he wouldn't have robbed my house in retribution for my department arresting you?"

The attorney's face flamed red. "Really, Chief, this is highly irregular. I must—"

This time Josie put a hand up to silence him.

Lloyd answered, "Hypothetically, no. If Zeke wanted to rob your house, he had his own reasons."

"Where can I find him?" Josie asked.

"Can't help you there."

"But you can help me with my hypothetical problem with the vandalism and 'minor' property damage?"

A smile slid across his face. "If you can help me with my son. My oldest. You see, he got caught up in this mess—me being falsely accused and all that. He's been charged with some things he didn't do."

"I'm sure he has a good lawyer," Josie said pointedly.

"Oh, he does. But it never hurts to have the chief of police have a conversation with the district attorney."

Normally, Josie would have taken great pleasure in telling a man like Lloyd Todd to go fuck himself. Somehow she doubted his oldest son was as innocent as Todd portrayed him, but she understood a parent's need to protect his child. She also knew that Todd wouldn't offer everything he knew and then ask for a favor after the fact. He was holding on to something, and the only way to get it was to make a show of good faith.

"Let me make some phone calls," she said.

*

Two hours later, she was back in the conference room across from Lloyd, handing his attorney the paperwork concerning Lloyd Todd Jr. "I couldn't get the charges dropped," she told him. "But I did get them reduced. Plus, he can enter an accelerated rehabilitation program. He goes to therapy, drug and alcohol counseling, job training. He does community service and pays some fines, and if he completes all the requirements, his record is expunged of these charges. That's the best I can do. He'll still get a clean slate. This time."

Lloyd bristled at the barb, but looked over the paperwork his attorney pushed in front of him, nodding as Josie spoke. He didn't hurry. After a solid five minutes, he looked up at her and said, "There's a strip mall on Sixth Street. That laundromat that's been there for decades."

"I know the one," Josie said.

"Zeke hangs out there when he's not under the bridge. So I've heard. Hypothetically."

Josie stood. She couldn't believe the words were coming out of her mouth, but they did: "Thank you, Mr. Todd."

Her hand was on the doorknob when Lloyd called out to her one last time. "Bowen and Jensen," he said.

Josie turned her head. "What?"

"Belinda's friends. Their last names. Bowen and Jensen. I remember because together they made the initials B.J. You know, like blow job?"

CHAPTER 53

"Lila Jensen."

Noah drove as Josie sat in the passenger seat, staring straight ahead but seeing nothing. She kept saying the name. Trying it out. It wasn't what she'd expected. Then again, Josie wasn't sure what she had expected. Lila Jensen sounded so normal, pretty even. Not at all like the devil she knew her mother to be.

"Lila Jensen," she said again.

"Gretchen's already on the phone with DHS trying to expedite a search of their records. She's also checking the databases to see how many Lila Jensens there are, or were, in the state, looking for any born between 1958 and 1964—assuming she was between eighteen and twenty-four when Belinda first met her at the courthouse. We know she was older than Belinda, but not by much."

Josie blinked, the flashing mountain scenery coming back into focus. "That won't help you find her."

"What?"

"So we know who she was before she stole Belinda's identity. She shed her own identity for a reason. She wouldn't go back to it. She doesn't want to be found."

The strange exhilaration of discovering one of her mother's secrets was now replaced with a sense of disappointment. Maybe they would find out some things about Josie's mother before she had become Josie's mother, but she knew in her gut it would not lead them to her. They still had no way to track her. No photos, even.

"Dex," she whispered.

Noah looked over at her for a second. "What's that?"

Josie cleared her throat and spoke more loudly. "Dexter McMann. The boyfriend I mentioned to you. I remembered his name. I need you to find a current address for him. He would be thirty-seven now."

"You think he would have photos?"

"I doubt it," Josie said. "It's probably a dead end, but Gretchen is right, I have to at least try talking to him. But first, I want to find Larry Ezekiel Fox and have a little chat with him."

CHAPTER 54

JOSIE – FOURTEEN YEARS OLD

Her biggest mistake was letting herself enjoy life with Dex around. He'd been living with them for almost a year, and he was right: he wasn't a pervert, and he didn't want to be her father. They'd developed a strange kind of friendship restricted to the hours that Josie's mother was out of the trailer. She watched *ER* with him, and he watched *Ally McBeal* with her. Lisette would have said Josie was too young to watch television shows with such adult themes, but Dex didn't seem to think it was an issue. He drove her to school each day, picking up Ray along the way, and sometimes even picking them up at the end of the day as well. He took her for ice cream sundaes, swimming in the river during the summer, and sledding in the winter. Once during a snowstorm he'd driven into an empty parking lot and done donuts in the icy slush, provoking screams and giggles from Josie and somehow not crashing the car into any of the light poles.

If her mother noticed their rapport, she didn't comment on it. As usual, Josie stayed out of her way, and Dex focused all of his attention on her when she was there. For a time, Josie thought they could go on forever that way. But it couldn't last forever. That was the silly dream of a naïve fourteen-year-old.

The first signal came the day Josie sliced her hand open working on a science project. She had chosen to take and compare fingerprints and, after taking her own and Dex's prints, had broken a glass while reaching for some paper towels.

A wedge of glass protruded from the meat of her palm. There was a lot of blood, but she didn't even feel the pain until she heard Dex say, "Holy shit!" He sprang into action, wrapping her hand up in a dish towel and rushing her to the hospital. At the ER, they removed the glass, stitched her up, and sent her home, where her mother was waiting for them.

Josie could smell the booze on her before they were even through the door. She stood next to the bloody glass debris they had abandoned in the kitchen, hands on her hips, glaring at the two of them. Josie knew from the way her eyes narrowed that she was in deep shit now. But when her mother spoke, she was looking at Dex. "Just what the hell do you think you're doing?"

From the corner of her eye, Josie glanced at him, seeing the confusion on his face. He smiled as though he wasn't sure if this was some kind of joke. "I'm sorry," he said. "What did you say?"

"Where were you?"

"I took JoJo to the hospital. She cut her hand pretty bad. She had to get stitches. I—"

"Did I give you permission to take my fourteen-year-old daughter to the hospital?" Her mother's voice was hard and cold, sending a shudder up Josie's spine.

Dex looked mystified. "Didn't you hear what I said? She needed stitches. She was bleeding all over the place."

"I didn't hire you to be a babysitter, Dex," her mother said. "You're mine."

He placed a hand on his chest. "I'm sorry, what?"

"JoJo takes care of herself. She doesn't need your help with anything. You're here for me."

"She's a kid," Dex argued.

"Yes, she's my kid. Not yours. You stay away from her and stay out of our business, you got that? I don't care if her goddamn hand is hanging off. And what the hell is all this?" she waved toward the makeshift fingerprint kit that Josie had left on the coffee table.

"I was helping her with a science project," Dex said. "But let me guess, you don't want me doing that either?"

A smile curved her mother's lips. "Now you're catching on."

Dex took a step toward her. "Let me ask you, Belinda, when's the last time you helped your kid with her science project? Or helped her with her homework, or—"

"Dex," Josie said, "don't."

The smile dropped from her mother's face, replaced by a look of pure rage. She looked from Josie to Dex and back again. Then, in a mocking tone, she mimicked Josie: "Dex, don't."

"Belinda," Dex said.

"I see what's going on here. You thought that JoJo was part of the deal. And you"—she turned her wrath toward Josie—"you're just a little whore after all, aren't you?"

"Hey!" Dex shouted. He moved in front of Josie and pointed a finger at her mother's chest. "Watch it."

Her mother looked him up and down as though he was beneath her. "Oh? What if I don't?"

He sniffed the air, moving his face closer to hers. "You're drunk," he said.

"So? That doesn't make what you're doing right."

"I'm not doing anything, and neither is JoJo. She's a kid, Belinda."

"And so are you. Get the *hell* out of my house."

With that, she sauntered off to her bedroom at the back of the trailer. Josie let out the breath she'd been holding. The center of her palm was on fire. Dex stared at her for a long moment. "You okay?" he asked.

Josie nodded.

She assumed he would leave. They always did. But she was wrong. Instead, he followed her mother down the hallway, kicking open her door with a loud bang and slamming it closed behind him. Josie stood rooted to the spot, listening as the shouting turned to gasping, and the familiar sound of her mother's bed springs creaking filled the small trailer—faster, louder, and longer than Josie had ever heard before. She fled to Ray's house, staying until well after midnight, but when she came home, she could still hear them.

CHAPTER 55

As much as Josie wanted to arrest Zeke herself, if she intended to press charges against him for the robbery of her house, she knew it would make things much easier on the district attorney if she had one of her patrol officers pick him up. Just as Lloyd Todd had promised, they found Zeke sleeping across two plastic chairs in the back corner of the laundromat.

Once he was brought in, Noah had him put into the interrogation room. He didn't ask for an attorney. As his teenage accomplice had told them, he wore a drab green jacket, frayed at the edges and missing all of its buttons. His face was creased with lines from age and hard living, and his long gray beard was yellow at the end. Across his forehead he wore a bandana that had lost all of its color and was now a dingy gray with a faded pattern on it, scraggly white hair snaking out from beneath it. Josie watched him on the closed-circuit television as he chain-smoked the cigarettes Noah had left with him, lighting one from the end of the last.

"A thousand cigarettes will not cover up his stink," Noah remarked as he walked in, handing her a file. "This guy needed a bath ten years ago. Homeless most of the last decade. Did a handful of stints for drug possession, manufacture, intent to sell—that sort of thing. No known associations with Lloyd Todd, just like Todd said."

Josie flipped through the pages of the file, which contained arrest reports, docket entries from his various convictions, and a few old mugshots. There was one photo from seven years earlier that caught Josie's eye, and something niggled at the back of her mind.

She riffled through more pages until she found another one from thirteen years ago. With fewer lines on his face, his features were a little clearer. They were familiar, she realized. But why?

"Do you think Todd was telling the truth about the robbery and the ads?" Noah asked.

Josie didn't take her eyes off the file in her hands as she looked for more photos. "You know I don't make a habit of trusting lowlifes like Todd, but I don't see why he would give me so much information but lie about something like that. He hypothetically admitted to the most costly of the incidents. Why hold out on the other stuff? There's no benefit."

"I guess. But that begs the question: Who is behind the robbery and the craigslist ads?"

Josie motioned to the television. "Maybe Zeke can tell us."

She suddenly found what she was looking for: a third mug shot, this one taken twenty years earlier when Josie was ten. A gasp escaped her throat as the rest of the contents of the file fluttered to the floor.

"Boss?" Noah said. "What is it?"

Josie could hardly get the word out: "Needle."

"What's that?"

She looked up at the television screen. "I have to talk to him."

Noah was hot on her heels as she dashed out of the viewing room and down the hall to the interrogation room. "Boss," he called out, but he wasn't fast enough.

The door banged open and Needle stared up at her. She walked slowly to the table as Noah slipped in behind her and closed the door. She could sense that he wanted to say something, to stop her, but he kept silent. Josie placed a palm flat on the table and leaned toward him, the smell of smoke and stale body odor nearly overpowering her. "Do you remember me?"

He stared at her, a toothless smile splitting his face.

"Do you?" Josie demanded.

"Little JoJo."

Behind her, Josie sensed Noah startle. No one ever called her anything but Josie or Boss. Only Ray had had the privilege of shortening her name to Jo. Hearing her childhood nickname after so many years gave her a jolt as well, but she did her best to hide it.

"You knew my mother," Josie said. "What was her name?"

Needle laughed. "You know your mother's name."

"I want to hear it from you."

"Belinda," he said easily. "Belinda Rose."

"Her real name," Josie demanded.

A look of genuine confusion crossed his face. "Be-linda Rose," he repeated.

So her mother hadn't confided in this man. Josie changed tactics. "Why did you rob my house?"

"I didn't rob no one's house."

Josie rolled her eyes. She slapped her palm against the surface of the table to keep his attention focused on her. "Cut the shit, Zeke," she said. "I have two witnesses who not only put you there, but will testify that you put them up to it. Why? Why me? Why now?"

His fingers fumbled to get a cigarette out of the crushed pack in front of him and light it off his last. "You were a cute kid, you know that, JoJo?"

Josie said nothing.

"Made your mom a little crazy, I think. Having such a pretty thing around. Everyone always paying so much attention to you. Your dad—he didn't care a lick for your mom once you came along. That never sat well with her, you know."

Without conscious thought, Josie's hand reached up and traced the scar that went down her jawline. Needle motioned to her face. "That was the worst I ever seen her," he said. "Well, up until that night."

"You stopped her," Josie said.

He nodded. "She scared me that night. I seen her do a lot of things, but that was something different."

"Did you take me to the hospital?"

"Yes."

Josie's throat felt like it was in danger of closing up altogether. When she asked her next question, it came out nearly a whisper. "Why didn't you go inside and tell them what she did?"

He shrugged. "Wasn't my place. Besides, you don't cross a woman like that." He took a long drag from his cigarette, the ash glowing bright orange. "You oughta know that better than most."

She said nothing. Smoke hung in the air, unmoving. Quietly, Noah took a step closer to the table, watching the two of them. Finally, he shifted his gaze to Needle and said, "Zeke, we've got you on the robbery. Just tell us what you did with the jewelry. Did you sell it?"

Needle shook his head.

Noah said, "You didn't sell it?"

"I don't know what happened to it."

"It just disappeared from your hands, did it?" Noah asked.

"Did you know it was my house?" Josie interjected.

Needle met her eyes, and she was taken back to her childhood, hiding behind the couch or under the kitchen table, Needle catching her eyes, smiling at her, offering her a piece of his sandwich or a sip of his soda. She was always hungry. Then there was the day he had walked in on her mother trying to sell her for a paint job and told her to go outside and play. Josie never knew what had transpired after she ran off, but when she'd returned home, the man was gone. The paint job was never spoken of again. Needle had been in the right place at the right time. He had been kind to her. As kind as someone like him could be.

He smiled a sad smile. "I'm sorry, little JoJo."

"Why were you nice to me when I was a kid?" she asked.

He shrugged. "No reason not to be. Seemed like you were in a pretty bad situation there, especially after your dad passed."

Again, she was struck by the fact that his kindness and sympathy had only gone so far. Yes, he had been nice to her, had recognized what could only be called abuse, but he hadn't gone so far as to help her out of the situation. The world was full of people like Needle. People who noticed when others were in trouble, but whose sense of self-preservation ultimately outweighed their sense of justice.

"Why?" Josie tried again. "Why did you rob my house?"

Needle shook the pack of cigarettes, but there were no more left. He stubbed out the last butt in the ashtray Noah had provided and let out a lengthy sigh. "You're smart, JoJo. You can't figure it out? You haven't figured it out yet?"

Josie felt the cold fingers of fear scuttle up her spine. "Figured what out?"

Needle leaned back in his chair and folded his nicotine-stained hands over his stomach. "I'm about done here. If you're gonna charge me, charge me, and I'll take that lawyer you said would be appointed for me if I can't afford one. I got nothing else to say."

Noah and Josie stared at him for a long moment, waiting to see if he would change his mind or ask for something, but he was relaxed in his seat, whistling an unrecognizable tune to himself. Finally, Noah walked to the door and Josie followed. He held the door open for her, and she was about to step through it when Needle spoke again.

"Don't know what you ever did to her, little JoJo."

Her heart seized in her chest. She turned back to him. "What did you say?"

"She said you'd find me. I said no you wouldn't, you'd never know I was involved. But she was right. You got me. You even recognized me."

"Who said I'd find you?" Josie asked, frozen in the doorway. "What are you talking about?"

He met her eyes. "She wanted me to give you a message. She said she'll destroy everything you love."

CHAPTER 56

"Boss," Noah said as she fled past him down the hallway. The distance from the interrogation room to her office seemed endless, like she was in one of those nightmares where no matter how fast you ran, you never moved, and the end was always just out of reach. Breath came in short gasps, her palm clammy as it closed around the door handle at last.

Noah was only a few feet behind; she heard the sound of his feet slowing on the tiles behind her. "Boss," he called again. "What the hell was that about?"

She slammed the door in his face, locked it, slumped against it, and slid down to the floor. Her heartbeat thundered in her chest. Too fast—it was going too fast. Dizziness assailed her. Noah called to her from the other side of the door, but she couldn't answer. She looked around her office, but all she saw were flashes from her childhood—her mother stalking the darkness of the trailer, waiting for Josie's dad to return, muttering words Josie would never forget:

I'll destroy everything you love.

It was her all along. How long had she been back? What had brought her back after all these years? Where was she? The memories of the things Belinda—no, Lila—had done to her awoke and screamed into Josie's mind, black and cloying. She squeezed her eyes shut, but that only made it worse. Clambering to her feet, she moved behind her desk, hands searching for the framed photo of her and Ray as nine-year-olds. She focused on his face, remembering all the ways he had helped her face the monsters in her head. She was suddenly glad Ray was dead—it meant her mother couldn't hurt him.

She looked up to the corkboard above her desk where she had pinned several photos—Josie and her predecessor, Chief Harris, at one of her promotion ceremonies years earlier. Photos of people she'd never met—victims whose grateful families had written her letters after she'd solved their cases. A photo of Josie and Lisette from Lisette's last birthday. The most recent photo was a candid shot of little Harris Quinn, giggling with smashed baby peas all over his face.

"Oh Jesus," Josie mumbled to herself.

She sprang up and opened the door to her office to find Noah still there, his arms folded across his chest, his eyes piercing.

"I need a detail on Misty Derossi and my grandmother," she said.

"What was that guy talking about, Boss?" Noah asked.

"He's talking about my mother. She's back. She's here, or somewhere nearby. She's behind all of this—the ads, the robbery. She's coming after me and the people I love; no one is safe. You need to get someone over to Rockview. I'd bring Gram home with me, but it's not safe. And Misty and Harris—she'll find out about them. I can't let anything happen to them. Not because of me."

Noah's arms dropped to his sides as she spoke. "Let me go at this guy. He must know where she is. We'll get to her first."

"No," Josie said. "He doesn't know where she is. Not that he would tell you anyway. She's smarter than that. She would have come to him. If she knew that I was going to find him, she wouldn't make it that easy."

Behind Noah, Gretchen approached, a piece of paper in her hand. She reached past Noah and handed it to Josie. "Found that boyfriend. Fraley told me his name. Dexter McMann lives in Fairfield now."

It was a little over an hour away. Josie could get there in half that time.

"There's a phone number there," Gretchen said.

"I don't need it," Josie told her. She went to her desk and found her car keys. "I'll be back in a few hours."

"I'm going with you," Noah said.

"No, you're not. I need you to stay here, make sure Zeke gets properly booked, get someone out to Misty's place and Rockview."

Her phone buzzed in her pocket. She pulled it out and saw another text from Trinity reminding her she had agreed to meet that day. *Something came up at work*, Josie shot back. *I'll try to stop by tonight, but it will probably have to wait till tomorrow.* In reply, Trinity sent her a pouty-face emoji. Josie rolled her eyes, pocketed her phone, and left the building.

CHAPTER 57

JOSIE – FOURTEEN YEARS OLD

There were other instances that caused cracks in the tenuous peace inside the trailer since Dex had moved in. One evening her mother had come home early from work and found them sitting side by side on the couch, laughing at a movie on television. She had flown at Josie, raining down open-hand slaps onto her head until Dex pulled her away. Josie had fled to her room and stayed there until the arguing died down. That night Dex did leave, and he didn't come back for a week.

There was the time it was raining—pouring in sheets—and Dex left her mother at the trailer to pick Josie up from school so she wouldn't have to walk home through it. At first, her mother hadn't made much of it, but when Dex was asleep she had burst into Josie's bedroom, pouring a bucket of cold water over her as she slept. Startled awake, Josie found herself on the wrong end of an expletive-laced tirade. If Dex had noticed how tired Josie was the next few days while her mattress dried out and she slept on the floor, he didn't comment.

The forensic science books that Dex had found at a thrift shop for Josie were burned in the metal barrel outside of the trailer while he was at work. When he asked if she was enjoying them, she didn't have the heart to tell him what her mother had done. Maybe she should have. Maybe he would have left. Or maybe he would have simply followed her mother into her room and banged her some more. Josie never understood their strange relationship. She never understood anyone's relationship with her mother. Except Lisette's—her gram hated her mother fiercely.

The death knell of that mostly bright year was all Josie's fault. Perhaps having someone there to talk to her, to care about her, to show interest in her, had made her bolder. Or perhaps it had simply made her just as stupid as Dex. There was a freshman dance coming up—a formal dance—and Ray had asked her to go with him. His father had been gone for a year, and he was finally feeling his freedom—he wanted them to be normal and go to a dance like boyfriend and girl-friend. Josie figured she could do her own hair and makeup, like she'd seen a few of the other girls at school doing theirs in the bathroom. But she knew she needed a dress, and she didn't have much money.

She had asked Dex if he would drive her to the thrift store and then, later that evening, drive her and Ray to the dance. But Dex, being Dex, had gone above and beyond, dropping her outside a dress shop and telling her there was a deposit behind the counter for whatever dress she wanted. Her heart sang as she chose a slinky but fairly modest blue dress that the saleswoman said brought out her eyes. Dex also had a cousin who owned a salon, and he'd arranged an appointment for her there once she was done.

Josie barely recognized herself in the mirror as Dex picked her up to take her back home so she could change before the dance. "Ray won't know what hit him," he told her, smiling.

Josie couldn't wait to see Ray's face when they picked him up. In her bedroom, she put on her dress and twirled in front of her mirror, feeling pretty for the first time in her life. Her bedside clock showed that she only had a few minutes before Dex would take her to get Ray. Her mother would be at work all night, and Josie hoped she would never find out about the dance, or the dress, or the makeup, or the way Ray had made her feel when he asked her to be his date.

Dex's eyes lit up when he saw her. "Wow," he said. "You look amazing."

"Thanks," Josie replied.

They were standing by the front door, ready to leave, when Dex stopped her. "Wait," he said. He took her shoulders and peered into her face. For a moment, a bolt of fear shot through her, and she flinched as he lifted a hand, licked the pad of his thumb, and rubbed at a spot just below her left eye. "Mascara," he said.

Josie laughed nervously. The palm that remained on her one shoulder was warm. She hadn't ever been this close to Dex. The proximity—mixed with her anticipation of going to the dance— was dizzying. He grinned at her. "JoJo," he said softly. "You make sure you have a good time tonight, okay?"

She nodded.

"Ray's a lucky guy, kiddo."

A sudden impulse made Josie rock up onto her toes and plant a kiss on Dex's cheek. Surprise lit his face, and they stood frozen in time for a moment—Josie's lipstick on his cheek, his hand on her shoulder—smiling stupidly at one another. And that's when the door opened; her mother stood there, a six-pack of beer in her arms. She stared at them for a long time, taking everything in: Josie's dress, makeup, and hair, the way they stood close to one another, Dex's car keys now dangling from his free hand.

Josie's heart stopped, and she counted two long seconds before it thundered back to life like an angry beast trying to claw its way out of her chest. She waited for her mother's fury, for her to throw the beer cans at Josie's head, or to fly at her, tearing at her dress and hair until Josie was too unkempt to be seen in public.

But her mother did nothing. She simply stood there. Then she asked, "What's going on here?"

Dex said, "JoJo has a school dance. She's going with Ray. I told them I'd drop them off."

Her mother turned her gaze to Josie. "Your grandmother sneak you that stuff? That interfering bitch."

Josie would have let it go. That would have been best. But Dex jumped in before she had a chance to formulate her response. "No,

I did, and I didn't sneak it. JoJo needed a dress for the dance, and my cousin does hair and makeup, so I asked her to help out."

Her mother narrowed her eyes at him. "*You* did this?"

"Come on, Belinda. You never went to a school dance? Give the kid a break. You won't let her see her grandmother. Her dad's dead. The only person she ever sees is that scrawny little Ray. So she wants to go to a dance; let her have some fun."

Josie braced herself for the attack she knew was inevitable. She closed her eyes and took a deep breath, waiting for the blows, the tearing of her beautiful dress, the bruises on her face that would render her makeup useless.

But it didn't come. She felt something brush by her, and when she opened her eyes, her mother was seated on the couch, popping a can of beer. Both Josie and Dex stared at her in shock, but she simply sipped her beer, picked up the remote control, and turned on the television. When she realized they were both still looking at her, she said, "Well, you better get going then."

They walked outside, letting the trailer door flap closed behind them, a fizz in the air like they had narrowly escaped something huge. They didn't speak or look at one another the entire route to Ray's house.

Ray seemed oblivious, possibly mistaking her nervous energy for jitters about the dance. She tried to have a good time, to focus on Ray and the way he kept looking at her like buried treasure, but her mind kept returning to the terrifying calm of her mother, sitting placidly on the sofa, drinking beer.

When Dex brought Josie home from the dance later that night, her mother looked as though she hadn't moved an inch, except for the bottle of vodka in front of her. Dex said, "I'm going to bed. You coming?"

"No," she said. "I think I'll stay up awhile. Might sleep out here by the TV."

CHAPTER 58

Anxiety gnawed at Josie's insides as she drove alone to the address Gretchen had given her for Dexter McMann. Before she had made it to her car, Noah had redoubled his efforts to come along, but ultimately he did as he was told, staying behind and sending patrol cars to monitor Rockview Ridge and Misty Derossi's house. From the car, Josie called Misty and awkwardly explained that some people had been harassing her lately because of her job, and that she wanted to make sure that harassment didn't extend to those around her. Luckily for Josie, Misty was too ill and too exhausted from dealing with a sick baby to ask many questions. Josie had a similar conversation with the administrator of Rockview, who promised to tighten up their security measures. Gretchen was busy finishing up the paperwork on Needle's arrest. They would have their hands full until Josie returned.

Fairfield was a tiny town in Lenore County, which was south of Alcott County. Most of Lenore County was made up of farms and state gameland. The Escape hugged the curves of the winding mountain roads until they gave way to rolling one-lane roads snaking across miles of farmland. If the thought of seeing Dex again wasn't making her sick to her stomach, Josie would have enjoyed the idyllic scenery.

The address Gretchen gave her brought her to a one-story house with dingy white siding and several poorly constructed additions built onto the side. It sat two acres back from the road at the end of a gravel driveway. An old red pickup truck sat outside the front porch. Josie saw several cut tree trunks standing like sentries in the grass in front of the house. As she got closer, she saw that several of them had been carved into the shapes of animals—a bear, an eagle, and a large owl. One trunk had a man's face carved into it, with a long flowing beard that reached the ground. They were stunning. She parked her Escape and walked over to where they stood. There were several smaller ones in the long grass at her feet—a duck and a sleeping coyote.

A man's voice called out, "They start at three hundred. The eagle is already sold, I'm afraid. I've got more in the back. Just finished my first mermaid."

She heard his steps moving toward her. She didn't want to turn, to face him, but she was here, and there was no running away.

"I, uh, also have a couple of dragons if you're into that sort of thing. Lots of people looking for those these days. There's a big demand for mythical creatures all of a sudden. I was thinking I might try a unicorn, but I don't—" His words died on his lips as Josie turned to look at him.

Frozen in place, he stared at her. He'd always been tall, and in the years since she'd last seen him, he'd put on some weight. He looked sturdier now, strong and burly in a pair of stained, torn jeans and a black T-shirt that clung to his chest. He had always been handsome. Until the fire.

She had hoped that maybe the scars would get better over time, or that he'd find a plastic surgeon who could restore what had been lost, but looking at him now, his face still bore the heavy, indelible marks of her mother's wrath.

"Haven't seen you in almost twenty years, JoJo," he said, his voice husky.

"Josie," she said. "My name is Josie."

He smiled, and the side of his face that hadn't melted lifted. "I know," he said. "Josie Quinn. Married Ray after all. I was sorry to hear about his death. You were two peas in a pod."

"We turned out to be very different people," Josie said.

He nodded. "Yeah, well, I guess that's true, isn't it? I see you on the news all the time since you solved that case of all those missing girls and became chief. You've done well for yourself."

Josie took a step closer to him. She ran a finger along the side of the enormous bear sculpture. "Looks like you have too."

He shrugged. "I do okay. Beats going to a job every day and dealing with the public." He motioned to the side of his head. The burns had taken a portion of his hair behind his left temple. "It gets old answering the questions, you know?"

She didn't know, but she nodded anyway. "They gave you a glass eye," she said. "It looks good."

His fingers touched just beneath his left eye socket. "Yeah, makes me look more human, I think."

An awkward silence unfurled between them. Josie turned and looked back at the sculptures. "These are amazing, Dex. I had no idea you knew how to do this."

"What are you doing here, JoJ—Josie?"

Josie pointed to his front porch. There were no chairs, but there were a couple of steps they could perch on. "Can we sit?"

He ushered her over, and they sat side by side on the stoop. For a couple of minutes, they stared at his open front yard, watching the breeze ruffle the tops of the trees lining the road. Then Dex said, "I never told you this—never had the chance to—but it wasn't your fault."

Josie swallowed over the instant lump in her throat. "Bullshit. It was entirely my fault. I'm so, so sorry, Dex."

He knocked his thigh against hers. "Stop. We don't even know that she did it. It was just odd timing."

"Someone sets fire to your hair while you're sleeping? On a night when she just happened to fall asleep on the couch, out of harm's way? You know as well as I do that she did this to you. And she did it because of me."

"You were a kid. Belinda was crazy."

"Lila," Josie said. "Her real name was Lila Jensen."

"What? What do you mean by that?"

She told him everything, and he didn't speak for a long time after she had finished. Then he said, "Makes you wonder what else she's gotten away with, doesn't it?"

Josie nodded.

"What do you need from me?"

"A photograph," Josie answered. "If you had any—or kept any. I know it's a long shot. I probably wouldn't have kept a picture of the woman who disfigured me."

He stared out at the road. "I didn't."

Disappointment sat heavy on Josie's shoulders. Before it could settle into full-blown despair, Dex said, "But I kept a picture of you. And your mother happens to be in it as well. All this time, I thought that was unfortunate."

CHAPTER 59

JOSIE – FOURTEEN YEARS OLD

Josie woke to the sound of Dex screaming like a wild animal caught in a trap—a sound that would haunt her dreams for years to come. She sprang out of bed and ran into the hallway to find smoke billowing from her mother's room. Inside, Dex's head was a ball of flame, and he was running around throwing himself against the walls like he was stuck in a pinball machine. On the bed, one of the pillows was alight, and fire was spreading quickly across the bedspread. A gust of air from the open window billowed the curtain into the flames and set them alight too. Dex slapped his hands furiously against his skull, but the flames were taking over faster than he could snuff them.

Josie ran back to her room and snatched her comforter from her bed. Back in the main bedroom, she screamed Dex's name to get his attention, but he seemed not to hear her. Finally, she climbed onto the bed, trying to stay on the side that wasn't burning, and as he passed by her, she threw the comforter over him. Her hands found the round hardness of his skull, and she pounded it with both palms. He kept screaming. She had to get him out of the room. Jumping down off the bed, she guided him toward the door. He stumbled and fell into the hallway. Josie pulled the door closed behind her, trying to contain the fire, and tried to find his arms beneath the comforter. Her hand closed around one of his. "Dex," she said. "Come on. We have to go."

He teetered but came to his feet. The comforter was still over his head, tendrils of smoke floating from beneath it. The smell of burnt flesh singed Josie's nostrils as she guided him out into the living room, toward the front door. Her mother watched them from the couch, unmoving, a glass of vodka in one hand and a satisfied smile on her lips.

CHAPTER 60

Josie paused before getting in the car to snap a picture of Lila's face with her phone. She sent it to Noah and Gretchen so they could get it out to the news outlets as quickly as possible. As she drove, the photo sat on the passenger's seat of her Escape, drawing her gaze toward it again and again. Her mother standing outside of their trailer, slender but shapely in a pair of jeans and a lavender V-neck T-shirt. Long, shiny black hair cascaded down over her shoulders. Her thin face, high cheekbones, square chin, and blue eyes set on the slightest angle gave her a slightly exotic look. Josie remembered well the steady flow of male attention that Lila Jensen attracted—when she wanted to.

Josie's thirteen-year-old self stood beside her mother in a sleeveless sundress that was two sizes too large for her, her blue eyes vacant. I'm here but I'm not really here, said the look on her face and her stiff posture, her body leaning away from her mother even though they stood shoulder to shoulder.

Josie didn't remember the photo being taken. Few people they knew had cameras, and Lila hadn't generally allowed them when they did—now Josie understood why. Josie was grateful that Dex had kept this one photo. It was the most tangible lead yet.

Back at the station house, Gretchen reported that there were four Lila Jensens in Pennsylvania, and only one of them was within the age range that Josie's mother would be—and she'd had one apartment in Bellewood in 1983 before disappearing off the grid forever. It was a dead end. All they knew for sure was her true birth date. Not in October, but July. Josie faced a mound of paperwork on her desk from administrative duties she'd been putting off all week. Jitters ran through her body, making her fingers tap her pen in a drumbeat on her desk as she sat in her chair, trying to focus. She called and checked on Misty and Harris. Then she called Rockview again. No reports of anything out of the ordinary.

Gretchen had tracked down Lila Jensen in the foster-care system, but in a county many hours away whose DHS office was having difficulty locating such an old file. Josie had a sinking feeling that the Lila Jensen file had gone wherever the Belinda Rose file had gone. She wondered if Judge Malcolm Bowen had had anything to do with it before he died. He was the only person who would have had enough influence to make two foster care files disappear. Again, the thought that Sophia Bowen hadn't been truthful when they interviewed her niggled at Josie's mind. Now that they had a photo, perhaps they could bring her in, question her formally, and see if they could get something more from her. She called Bowen's home but got the voicemail. She left a message asking if Sophia could come to the station for formal questioning and gave her office and cell phone number. It was Sophia's move.

Giving up on the idea of getting any paperwork done, Josie decided to drive over to the Eudora and face Trinity. But there was no answer when Josie knocked on the door to her room. She waited in the hall for fifteen minutes, texting Trinity that she was there, but got no response.

Night fell around her as she drove away from the hotel and aimlessly around the city until fatigue burned her eyes. She wanted to keep moving, keep doing anything that would keep the memories at bay. But the clock on her dashboard said midnight, and Noah had texted her twice already to remind her that she needed rest; he suggested she stay with him again for her own safety.

Noah.

The lights of his little house glowed brightly as she pulled up in front of it. Wordlessly, he let her inside. His thick brown hair was still wet from a shower, and he wore shorts and a Denton PD T-shirt.

Josie went upstairs and changed into a pair of sweatpants and a T-shirt. She took up position on Noah's couch again, staring at her reflection in the blackness of the television screen: drawn face, haunted eyes.

Noah joined her on the couch. There were no dirty chai lattes. No meatball subs. He didn't even ask if she had eaten. She knew he was truly angry with her this time; she hadn't been forthcoming with him about Needle, and then she had run off to talk to Dex alone. "I'm sorry," she said.

"I'll respect your boundaries," Noah said. "You don't need to shut me out."

"I'm not—I didn't, I—"

He waved a hand. "It's okay. Just let us protect you. You've got a whole department at your disposal. If anyone on your staff had been robbed and attacked in the same week, you'd want someone on them—you know you would."

This was true. It was also true that she didn't like admitting weakness or vulnerability, and she certainly didn't want her staff to view her that way. "I'll try," she said.

"Lila Jensen's photo ran on the eleven o'clock news," Noah said. "It's already up online on all the local news sites. You'll be notified immediately if any good tips come in."

"Thank you," Josie said.

"Gretchen tried to get something out of Zeke, but he wouldn't talk."

Josie kept her eyes on her reflection in the television. "I told you he wouldn't. He's got nothing to lose. He meant what he said—he wouldn't cross my mother even if he knew where she was."

"Josie, do you really think she's that dangerous? That she would go after your grandmother or Misty and the baby?"

She shook her head. "Maybe not directly. You've seen—she had someone else rob my house. I doubt she is very computer-savvy.

She probably had someone else place the craigslist ads. One of those teenage idiots working at the Spur Mobile store has probably been giving her my number—hell, that same teenager is probably the one placing the ads. She uses people; there were always people willing to do things for her for drugs or favors or because she had something on them. She's been working at this for over a month now. She won't stop until everything I love is gone."

Noah let a moment pass. She sensed him trying to figure out a tactful way to ask the question. "Why…why does she—"

Josie met his eyes. "Why does she hate me so much?"

He looked away.

"It's okay. Look." She pulled her hair away from her face, turning so that he could see the long, silvered scar running down the side of her face. "She did this to me when I was six. The man you brought in tonight? Zeke? He stopped her. I used to call him Needle because I didn't know his name, and that's what he always brought with him."

"I'm sorry," Noah said.

"That was probably the least horrible thing she did to me. The man I visited today was her boyfriend. She was angry with him because of something I did, so she set fire to his hair when he was sleeping. Or at least, I suspect she did. There was never any proof. They both smoked, and it was assumed he must have fallen asleep with a lit cigarette in his mouth. But I just know she did it."

"Jesus."

"In my sophomore year of college, I had some…struggles. I was depressed. Drank too much. I had to see a therapist. I didn't go for long, but what I got out of that experience was the realization that my mother hates everyone—not just me." She laughed, a mirthless sound. "In other words, it's nothing personal. She only cares about herself, which means she cares about other people only if they have something she wants or needs. Once they've served their purpose, she takes pleasure in making them suffer. She is spiteful, jealous, and vengeful, and most of all, she's unpredictable. And very, very dangerous."

"I had no idea," Noah said.

"Of course you didn't. No one knows. It's not something I talk about. Ever. Only Ray knew what she was really like, and even he didn't know everything. For a long time, I was the only thing keeping my dad around. Once he was gone, she kept me from my grandmother just to be cruel. So, the answer to your question—she hates me because that's just who she is. What I don't know is why she's come back. Why now?"

A feeling of bone-deep fatigue spread through her as she spoke. She closed her eyes, and a moment later she felt Noah's hand slide into hers, squeezing gently. There was nothing he could have said to comfort her, and she appreciated the steady silence he let her have. She squeezed back.

When she opened her eyes again, she caught him staring at her intently. As tired as she was, the electricity between their clasped hands gave her a jolt. With his other hand, Noah reached over and pressed a palm to her cheek. It was warm, and Josie let her head sink into it. Tears sprang to her eyes, and she blinked them back. She wasn't sure if she could take this kind of tenderness. He searched her face and leaned in slightly, his lips inches from hers, testing the air between them. She lifted her lips to his, and he kissed her, long and slow and deep until her legs felt weak and her whole body tingled. Kissing him was strange and nothing like she had expected; it was better than anything she'd ever expected, and that terrified her.

He broke the kiss but held onto her, pressing his forehead to hers, the two of them breathing into one another for a moment.

"Noah," she said. "You don't—you shouldn't—"

"What?"

"You don't want me. You're so good and I'm too—damaged."

He moved his head back just enough so that she could see his smile. He cupped both her cheeks. "No," he said with absolute conviction. "You're not damaged. You're extraordinary."

It was like their bodies had caught fire as her mouth crashed down onto his, and then both of them were reaching, pulling at one another's clothes. With Noah's frenzied hands and mouth on her body, the trauma of the last several days fell away. There was only him and the sensations he provoked in her body. It was like trying to stop a forest fire with a watering can, but somewhere deep inside, the more reasoned part of her made her pull back. She didn't want to be this person anymore—a woman who used the heat and ecstasy of sex to hold back her demons whenever she thought they might overwhelm her.

"Stop," Josie said. "We have to stop."

Her last two relationships had been colossal failures. Maybe not entirely because of the sex and whiskey she used to escape her feelings, but they'd failed nonetheless.

Noah's mouth was hot against her throat. She pushed him away gently, disentangling herself and standing up. She needed some distance between them, even as every cell in her body yearned to be close to him again.

His chest heaved. "What is it?" he gasped, staring up at her. She'd managed to get his shirt off. The scar near his right shoulder from where she'd shot him during the missing girls case drew her gaze. He had forgiven her easily, but her guilt lived on.

"You deserve better than this," she said.

A crease appeared over the bridge of his nose. "What?"

"I'm not—I'm not good enough for you."

He jumped up. He was down to his boxer shorts, and she could see that he was ready for her. "I think that's a judgment I need to make, not you," he said.

She was suddenly aware of the air on her skin. She looked around but didn't see her T-shirt anywhere. She folded her arms over her bra and met his eyes. Emotions of every kind roiled within her. She tried to find some kind of focus. "Noah," she said, "this just isn't a good idea."

He lifted a hand to touch her, but she moved back, out of his reach. The edge of the coffee table cut into the backs of her calves. The confusion in Noah's eyes was replaced with hurt. The sight felt like a knife in her chest.

"I'm sorry," she managed. "I just don't think we should—"

The sound of their cell phones ringing simultaneously cut her off. Noah tore his eyes from her, looking around blindly for his phone.

"On the table," Josie said as she looked around for her own. She found it between the cushions of the couch. It had stopped ringing, but the missed call was from the police station. Noah was already talking to someone. "Yeah, I got it," he said. "I'm on my way."

"What is it?" Josie asked.

He sighed and pushed a hand through his hair. He wouldn't look at her. "Big college party at one of the off-campus houses. You know those big ones up on Turner Hill?"

"The ones with the big drop-off behind them?"

"Yeah, the creek runs behind them. One of the neighbors called police because of the noise. Patrol showed up, a bunch of kids ran out the back, and one of them fell from the drop-off trying to get away. He's alive but had to be life-flighted to Geisinger."

"My God."

Noah found his T-shirt on the floor next to the couch and pulled it on. "They've got a bunch of underage drinking arrests. I'm going to head over and help out."

He disappeared up the steps. Overhead, Josie could hear him opening and closing drawers in his bedroom. When he came back down, he was wearing jeans and his shoulder holster.

Arms still folded over her semi-naked torso, Josie stepped toward him. "I'll go with you."

He shook his head, snatching his keys from the coffee table. "I can handle a college party. Go upstairs. Go to sleep."

Josie watched his back as he walked away from her toward the foyer, and felt a panic start deep in her chest. "You have to be careful," she blurted, running after him. "My mother—she'll try coming after you too. She'll know—"

Noah's hand was on the doorknob, but he still wouldn't look at her. "Know what?"

She reached for his back, her fingers brushing his shirt. A hot flush crept up her cheeks. "That I..." She broke off. Beneath his shirt, she saw the muscles of his shoulders tense. She tried again. "That I care about you."

He pulled the door open. Over his shoulder he said, "Somehow, I don't think that's true." Then he was gone.

CHAPTER 61

The glowing green numbers of Noah's digital clock announced that it was after ten a.m. Josie sat up with a start, throwing the covers off her. Sunlight peeked around the edges of his bedroom shades. Why the hell hadn't he woken her up? Was he really that angry with her? Had he come home at all? Snatching her cell phone off the nightstand, she saw she had no messages. Something wasn't right. She threw on some clothes and went downstairs. Everything was exactly as she had left it when she'd trudged up to Noah's bedroom the night before. The coffee pot was empty, a sure sign he hadn't come home.

A small kernel of unease settled in the pit of her stomach. Since she had been chief, there hadn't been a single day that she hadn't gotten at least three phone calls before ten a.m. Even on her days off. She raced upstairs to grab her things before dashing to her car. Hopping into it, her right foot searched for the gas pedal but didn't find it. It was then that she noticed how far back her seat was from the steering wheel.

"What the hell?"

A slow panic tingled through her. She slid her seat back up and broke three traffic laws getting to the station house. Sergeant Lamay sat at the lobby desk. Josie could tell by his wide eyes that something wasn't right. She passed through the door that separated the public from the rest of the building and advanced on Lamay. "What the hell is going on?"

Lamay spoke in a whisper. "There's been an incident. Well, a murder. Bad one. Boss...I know it wasn't you. We all do. But the fire marshal called the mayor 'cause he didn't trust Fraley or Palmer to handle it. Least, that's what he said when he showed up here with her a few hours ago."

Josie's heart began to race, the tingle in her body now a hard vibration. "A few hours ago?" she hissed.

Lamay looked behind her to make sure they were still alone. "They were going to pick you up."

"Pick me up? You mean arrest me?"

Lamay nodded. He leaned toward her, and the chair creaked beneath his rotund frame. "You can still go, Boss," he told her. "I'll take care of the cameras."

Josie put a hand on his shoulder. "Thank you, but that's not necessary."

"Boss, it's bad."

"I'm not going anywhere. I am the chief of police in this town, and this is my department, my station house. Where are they?"

Lamay's shoulders rounded. He fidgeted with one of the buttons on his uniform shirt. "Conference room."

Josie turned to go but stopped before she reached the hall that would lead her deeper into the building and closer to her doom. She thought of her grandmother, then Misty and baby Harris. A sick feeling invaded her stomach. "Lamay," she said. "The victim. Was it a woman? Or a child?"

"No," he said. "It was the owner of that body shop over on Sixth and Seller. Not too far from where Zeke was picked up the other night."

The color drained from her face.

"You okay, Boss?" Lamay asked.

No. She was not okay. Words failed her. She steadied herself with a hand against the wall.

"Did you know him?" Lamay inquired.

Bile rose in the back of her throat. "Sort of."

CHAPTER 62

Mayor Tara Charleston presided over the conference room table with a cold stare that made Josie's skin crawl. The two had never gotten along, and Josie knew that Mayor Charleston was just waiting for any opportunity to remove her from her post as chief. Or "interim chief" as Tara liked to call her. Josie didn't know what the hell was going on, but whatever it was, there was a good chance it could end her career.

"Chief Quinn," she said when Josie walked through the door. "We were going to send someone to find you."

"I bet you were," Josie said.

Gretchen and Noah sat next to one another on one side of the table. Both looked haggard and distressed. Dark stubble covered Noah's face. When he met Josie's eyes, the look of pain and confusion was like a physical slap. She wished things hadn't ended so awkwardly between them the night before. Gone was Gretchen's easy smile. Every line etched into her face by her forty-four years was evident. Both of them looked as though they were being held against their will. Perhaps they were; she couldn't imagine either one of them not trying to warn her. Unless Noah was really that hurt. Then she saw their phones sitting side by side near Tara's right hand.

"What's going on?" Josie asked, pulling herself up straight and tall.

"Boss," Gretchen said.

"Detective," Tara cautioned.

Naked anger flared on Gretchen's face as she looked at Tara. Noah nudged her with an elbow, a silent request for her to keep her cool. She kept quiet but shook her head, a vein in her forehead throbbing. Josie couldn't remember ever seeing her so angry.

"Sit," Tara said.

Josie folded her arms across her chest. "I think I'll stand."

"Suit yourself." Tara swiveled slightly in her chair and punched a button on a department laptop, bringing the screen to life. "During the night last night, at approximately three a.m., you, or a woman looking remarkably like you, drove your Escape—or a vehicle identical to yours with your same license plate number—to Ted's Auto Body, where the owner, Ted Heinrich, was tied to a chair, beaten, and set on fire. He did not survive."

Josie swallowed but said nothing.

Tara turned the laptop toward Josie so that she could see the screen. She pressed another button and a video began to play. At the top left-hand side of the media software, Josie could make out the words ROWLAND INDUSTRIES. Ted Heinrich had obviously sprung for some high-definition video surveillance equipment. Top of the line. Her gaze returned to the bird's-eye view of the front of his body shop. A concrete driveway with a giant grease stain led to two large garage doors, their windows painted white. To the right of the garage doors was a regular door with a sign above it: OFFICE. Creeping into the corner of the frame, Josie could see part of Heinrich's red 1965 GTO Mustang. The sight of it made her feel sick.

A few seconds later, an Escape pulled up and covered the grease stain completely. When Josie saw her own license plate staring back at her, she wished she had agreed to sit down. The brake lights died, and the driver's-side door opened.

And then, Josie stepped out of the car wearing a yellow T-shirt, jeans, and a pair of white sneakers. They looked new. Josie felt three pairs of eyes drilling into her, but she maintained composure while her brain worked at warp speed to make sense of what she was seeing. For a split second, she actually questioned herself. Had she been drugged? Sleepwalking? Had she driven to Ted Heinrich's business during the night and killed him? She'd certainly fantasized about it over the years. But no, she realized, remembering that her driver's seat had been out of position when she got into her car that morning. This was something else.

On screen, the woman closed her door, took two steps away from the Escape, and looked around. Her eyes searched upward, panning until she found the camera. She looked into it, and Josie's own face stared back at her. In the conference room, Josie counted off the seconds. One, two, three, four. Then the woman reached up and gathered her long, black hair into both hands as if she were pulling it into a ponytail, dragging it to the side so that all her hair rested over her left collarbone. Her head tilted to the left a bit, almost as if she were listening to something. But she wasn't listening to anything. She was exposing her profile. The right side of her face was soft, smooth, and unblemished in the moonlight.

"Trinity," Josie murmured.

Trinity went into the office door, and Tara reached over and fast-forwarded the video, stopping it when Trinity came back out, her clothes mussed and covered in something dark—oil or blood, or both, Josie guessed. This time, in her rush to get to the Escape, she didn't bother looking at the camera. Within seconds, both Trinity and the Escape were gone. Tara closed the laptop.

Gretchen said, "The mayor ordered patrols to go to your house and collect you and your vehicle—for evidence processing—but you weren't there."

Noah had known where she was, but he hadn't told. Because he was protecting her or because he knew that if the mayor found out she'd been sleeping at his house, he'd be in the hot seat as well?

"Chief Quinn," Tara said, "the only reason you are not being booked into county jail right now is because Lieutenant Fraley tells us that that cannot possibly be you in that video. Primarily because, unlike the woman in this footage, you have a scar running down the right side of your face."

Josie lifted her hair and turned her face so that Tara could get a good look at the mark her mother had left on her at the tender age of six.

"Well," Tara said. "It seems you have a doppelganger."

"There's more," Gretchen said. "Tell her."

Tara looked reluctant but added, "We found what we believe is your old wedding ring at the scene, but Detective Palmer tells me that all of your jewelry was stolen from your home only a few days ago, so there is no way you could have left it at the scene."

"This is obviously a setup," Gretchen said.

Josie said, "You should talk to Trinity Payne, the reporter. She's staying at the Eudora Hotel. Room 227."

"Why would Trinity Payne kill a man and try to frame you for it?" Tara asked.

Why would Trinity kill a man at all? Josie wondered. What nagged at Josie even more was why Heinrich, and why now? What connection did Trinity have to the man?

The story.

Josie almost blurted the words out loud, stopping herself at the last minute. Trinity would do anything for a story, and she had wanted to do a story on Josie. But then Josie had blown her off repeatedly. Had she gone off on her own and started digging into Josie's past? Even if she had, how had she turned up the connection to Heinrich? No one knew about him. Not even Ray had known. There were only four people who knew what nearly happened between him and Josie all those years ago—Heinrich, Josie, Needle, and Lila.

Fucking Lila.

"Trinity had to be under duress," Gretchen said. "Whatever happened inside that body shop—Trinity's hand was forced. She's the face of a national network. Why would she do something like this if she wasn't under duress?"

"She didn't appear to be under duress," Tara pointed out. "And she was alone. She drove up, went inside, spent almost an hour there, and came back out alone. How could she be under duress when she went there willingly?"

Trinity would have gone willingly if it meant getting a story. Lila must have fed her something. But how? Had Trinity somehow tracked down Lila? No, the entire Denton PD hadn't been able to track the woman down. Trinity had some of the best resources for finding both people and information, but surely she hadn't been able to find Josie's mother when the rest of them had been smacking into wall after wall.

Which meant that Lila had somehow contacted Trinity. Trinity would have agreed to meet Lila. She would have been interested in Lila's take on Josie's childhood. All the juicy secrets—the juiciest of all being what Heinrich had almost done to Josie at eleven years old. Lila would lie and spin it, of course. When she told Trinity the story, she would fail to mention that she had sold Josie for a paint job. No, she would make Josie out to be some tween seductress, and she would leave out the part where Needle showed up and stopped the whole thing. But if Trinity had gone to Heinrich's for a story, why go in the middle of the night, and what had happened to result in his murder?

"Someone threatened her," Gretchen said.

"So, you're saying someone made her steal the chief's car and drive to Heinrich's to murder him. Then why would she make a point to show the camera that she doesn't have the chief's scar?" Tara argued.

"Because she knew the police would pull the video, and she wants us to know she's being coerced," Gretchen shot back.

Josie's thoughts spun on. It was one thing for Lila to lure Trinity to Heinrich's shop with the promise of a big story, but quite another for Trinity to kill him. Had she actually murdered the man? Josie tried to imagine Trinity killing him. It wasn't hard.

Josie had imagined killing the man for decades. She had also seen how ruthless Trinity could be, but did that cutthroat behavior in her work necessarily translate into being able to murder someone? Was Trinity capable of beating a man and setting him on fire while he was tied to a chair? Josie thought she knew the answer, but maybe she was wrong.

Tara shook her head. "We don't even know for sure that's Trinity. Makeup can cover up a scar."

"It's her," Gretchen insisted.

"Maybe it is," Tara said. "Or maybe it's not. Chief Quinn, do you have an alibi for last night?"

"Of course I—" Josie broke off. She didn't have an alibi. She had been at Noah's alone, and he had been here at the station house. Even if he wanted to, he couldn't lie for her, not that she would ever expect him to do that.

Tara smiled coldly. "Well, the DNA will tell. Given the unique circumstances, I've spoken with one of my high-level contacts at the state police, and he has agreed to expedite testing. We should have it back within forty-eight hours. In the meantime, I've instructed your staff to carry on with their day-to-day operations. Lieutenant Fraley and Detective Palmer will spearhead the investigation. They'll speak with Ms. Payne so that she can shed some light on this unfortunate situation."

"You've instructed my staff?" Josie said.

"In light of the fact that you are now a suspect—"

"Person of interest," Gretchen interjected, drawing a nasty glare from Tara, which she shot right back.

"Person of interest," Tara echoed. "I don't think it's appropriate for you to continue on as chief. I'm therefore suspending you pending the outcome of this investigation. You are not to leave this town, do you understand?"

Josie heard her mother's words once more. *I'll destroy everything you love.*

She had underestimated her mother, read the situation all wrong. Josie loved nothing in the entire world more than her job. It had been quite a challenge when she took over as Chief, and she often found it stressful, but if she was forced to choose between being chief and no longer being a police officer, she would choose chief every time. Lila Jensen had truly gutted her—worse than the knife slice, worse even than being sold.

Josie had sacrificed everything to become a police officer, rising through the ranks of the Denton Police Department rapidly, becoming the first female lieutenant, then the first female detective, and finally the first female chief of police in Denton history. She had fought and forfeited to bring justice, peace, and protection to the citizens she served. This was her life's work, and while she'd slept, her mother—using Trinity Payne—had taken it away from her.

"I'll need your credentials and your gun," Tara said. "And we'll need you to turn over your car so that it can be processed for evidence."

God only knew what Lila had told Trinity, but Josie was sure that Trinity would never throw away her own career to kill a pedophile. Exposing her unblemished face to the camera was a clear message to Josie. The question was: What message was Trinity trying to send?

"And you're not to set foot in this building again until I authorize it," Tara went on.

In the last two years, Trinity had tried many times to get Josie to confess the origin of her scar. She had never remarked on the resemblance between them, but if Josie noticed it every time they were together, she was certain Trinity had as well. Trinity knew that she would be mistaken for Josie. Was Trinity in league with Lila, or was she Lila's unwilling pawn? Did Lila have something on her? Was Trinity just twisting the knife in Josie's back, or was she trying to tell Josie that she hadn't gone there willingly?

"Ms. Quinn, do you understand me?"

Tara's words seemed to come from far away, and the room had gone out of focus. Josie blinked, and Tara's piercing, gleeful stare sharpened again. Josie took her badge and police ID from her pocket and tossed it onto the table. The Glock slid out of her holster. She ejected the magazine and handed it to Gretchen together with the pistol. Then she took her car key from her keychain and handed that over as well.

"I'll get this back to you," Gretchen said, ignoring the scathing look Tara sent her way.

Josie nodded. She looked at Noah, but he wouldn't meet her eyes. That hurt almost as much as giving up her gun and badge. There was nothing left for her to do but leave, so she thrust her chin forward and gave Tara one last challenging look before turning and walking out of the room, and her station house.

CHAPTER 63

With no car and no job, Josie sat on a bench across the street from the station house, staring at what just hours ago had been her domain. Her mind raced as her body went numb. Heinrich was dead. Her childhood bogeyman was gone. Finally. How many times had she wished for him to be punished for what he'd intended to do to her? Even though Needle had saved her from going into that bedroom, she still had nightmares about what might have been. She had to admit to feeling a small sense of peace now that this monster had been vanquished. But mostly she felt empty. Heinrich's death changed nothing. Her soul remained scarred. He wasn't, after all, the one who had made the deal. Lila had.

She tried to shift her focus away from the conflicting feelings raging inside. Lila was still out there, working to destroy Josie's life; and then there was Trinity. There were at least a half-dozen things she needed to do immediately, but she had no transportation. It would take a couple of days for her vehicle to be returned to her, and she had a feeling that Tara would do all she could to stretch that timeframe even longer. She didn't even have a way to get home, or to Noah's to pick up the things she had left there. Her texts to Trinity went unanswered, and when she called Trinity's cell phone, it went straight to voicemail. Josie didn't leave a message.

"Boss?"

She looked up to see Sergeant Lamay standing beside the bench. She hadn't even noticed him leaving the station house or crossing the street.

"I'm not your boss anymore, Lamay," she said.

"Would you say we're friends then?"

"Well, I wouldn't go——" She stopped, blinking to bring him into focus, concentrating on his eyes, which glinted with mischief. "I mean, of course we're friends, Dan."

He held out a set of keys to her. "Then the mayor wouldn't have an issue with me lending my friend my car. Right, Josie?"

Josie couldn't help the grin that spread across her face. As her hands closed around the keys, tears of gratitude stung the backs of her eyes. Her arm froze in midair, keys jangling. "Wait," she said. "I can't borrow your car. You need it. Your wife has chemo——"

"My daughter is away at college," Lamay interrupted. "She left her car at our house. We'll just use that until you get yours back. My wife and I pay the insurance on it anyway."

Before she could think about it, she leapt to her feet and squeezed Lamay in a quick hug. "Thank you, Dan," she said. "I won't forget this."

She drove to the Eudora, sneaking past a long line of people waiting to check in at the front desk, and made her way up to Room 227. She banged on the door several times, but there was no answer, and Josie could hear no movement behind the door. Back in the lobby, Josie waited behind the last guest in line. Once the concierge had checked the man in, Josie stepped up. The young blond man with the permanent toothy smile recognized her at once, the genial look in his eyes instantly replaced with contempt. She had stood in this very spot six months ago while working a case involving a casino mogul who had rented out the hotel's penthouse.

"Chief Quinn," the man sneered, his painted-on customer service smile still in place. "Is there something I can help you with?"

Her suspension hadn't been made public, and the concierge hadn't asked for her credentials. "I'm here for a welfare check on one of your guests—Trinity Payne in Room 227. I tried knocking on her door. There's no answer. No one has heard from her in twenty-four hours, and we have reason to believe she might be in trouble."

He eyed her skeptically. "Well, if you've knocked on her door, and she didn't answer, there's not much more I can do to help you, I'm afraid."

"You can have someone on your staff check the room," Josie said.

"We don't like to violate the privacy of our guests."

"I'm not asking you to violate the privacy of one of your guests, I'm asking you to check and make sure she's not dead or injured inside that room. What is hotel policy, by the way, if you believe one of your guests may be in imminent danger? How many hours are you required to wait before you check inside the room?"

His fake smile never faltered and yet, somehow, he managed to glare at her. "Is it the Denton Police Department policy to send the chief of police to do welfare checks?" he asked.

Josie leaned her elbows onto the counter, moving closer to him. "Trinity Payne is a close personal friend of mine. She's also a bit of a celebrity, as I'm sure you know. If she is, in fact, injured or dead inside her room, do you really want to bear the scrutiny of nationwide press because you refused to allow the police to do a proper welfare check when they made it clear to you that Ms. Payne may be in danger?" Josie read off an invisible headline above his head. "Concierge refuses welfare check. National news reporter, Trinity Payne, dies. I can see that going viral."

With a sigh, he tapped the keyboard of the computer. Then a keycard appeared in his hand. "Let me have my associate take you to her room." He made a phone call, and five minutes later a different man led Josie back to room 227.

Wordlessly, he let her into the room and stood by the door with his hands clasped at his waist while he watched Josie nose around. The bathroom and closet were clear. Trinity wasn't there. Josie felt both reassured and anxious. She hadn't really expected to find Trinity's dead body in the hotel room, but she was relieved all the same. But if Trinity wasn't in her hotel room, then where the hell was she? Where had she gone after killing Heinrich?

"Are you finished?" the man asked.

"Just a second," Josie said. Trinity's open suitcase lay across the bed. On the small circular table in the corner of the room was a closed laptop, a Gucci purse, a set of car keys, and Trinity's phone. The sight of her phone sent a prickle up Josie's spine. Trinity never went anywhere without her phone. Josie pulled a pair of latex gloves from her jacket pocket—even as chief, the habit had never died—snapped them on, and picked up Trinity's phone, pressing its power button to bring up the lock screen. It asked for a password.

Josie had no idea what Trinity might use as her password, and she couldn't spend much time trying to think of it. Tara was clearly focused on Josie for Heinrich's murder, but Josie knew that once she let Gretchen and Noah out of her sight, their first line of inquiry would be Trinity Payne. They'd be on her heels any moment. Gretchen would know how to get the phone unlocked, Josie was certain.

Josie turned to the man. "I'm going to need to see your CCTV of this hallway, the entrance, and possibly the parking lot."

The man looked bored. "Let's go back to the lobby," he told her. "I'll call the manager."

The manager, a balding blond man in his forties, was both more personable and more helpful than both the concierge and the man who had let Josie into Trinity's room. He didn't ask for her credentials either, and within moments of meeting him, Josie understood why. "I saw you on TV after the Lloyd Todd arrest," he said. "You're much more attractive in person—and I don't mean that in an inappropriate way."

Josie smiled uncomfortably as they stood behind one of his staff members in the CCTV room behind the lobby, waiting for the young woman to pull up any footage of Trinity she could find. The manager prattled on, "Anyway, I just wanted to personally thank you. My son has been hooked on drugs for years now. We haven't been able to help him. Turns out his dealer was one of Todd's guys. Soon as those guys were arrested, my son went into rehab."

"I'm glad to hear that," Josie said.

"Who knows if he'll stick with it, but we're very hopeful. You know, since the day he was born, he was always giving us trouble."

Before the manager could launch into the story, the employee seated in front of the screens said, "Here you go—she left her room yesterday afternoon around two p.m."

On screen, they watched Trinity emerge from her hotel room wearing the same clothes she had on in the Heinrich surveillance. She held nothing in her hands as she rushed down the hallway. At the elevators, she pressed the down button frantically and was through the doors before they were even fully open.

"Here she is in the lobby," the woman said, pointing to a different screen. Both Josie and the hotel manager watched as Trinity exited the elevator in the lobby. She made a beeline for the door, walking so fast she was nearly jogging.

"And here she is in the parking lot," the employee added. She indicated three of the other screens, and they watched Trinity make her way through the parking lot to the outermost edge of the camera's view, where she walked rapidly off-screen. "I'm afraid that's it," the woman said. "That's as far as these cameras go."

Where had Trinity been rushing off to without her phone or car keys or even a purse?

"What about the rest of the day and night? Can you see if she ever came back to her room?" Josie asked.

The employee turned her attention to the screen showing the hallway outside of Trinity's room, fast-forwarding the footage until it caught up to present time. Trinity never returned.

Josie turned to the hotel manager. "Thank you for your help," she said. "My colleagues will be back to collect some evidence. If you hear from Ms. Payne, please call the police department immediately."

"Of course," he said.

As Josie drove out of the parking lot in Sergeant Lamay's ten-year-old Camry, she passed Gretchen with a patrol car trailing behind her. Neither Gretchen nor the patrol officer even glanced her way.

CHAPTER 64

From the Eudora, Josie drove to Heinrich's auto body shop, but the entire building was cordoned off with police caution tape, and a patrol car sat outside. Of course. Tara knew Josie's first instinct would be to go to the scene herself and investigate. She pulled away and drove through town, pushing back the strange mixture of relief and emptiness that had come over her since she'd heard about Heinrich's death. She tried to figure out her next move. She kept coming back to Trinity. The reporter had left her hotel room willingly. There was no one with her, no gun to her head. She must have gone to meet with Lila, and from there, stolen Josie's car, driven to Heinrich's, murdered him, and then left—alone—to return Josie's Escape to the street outside Noah's house.

But if Trinity had driven the Escape back to Noah's house, why was the seat pushed all the way back? Trinity was the same size as Josie. She would have no reason to adjust the seat. Which meant that somewhere between the body shop and Noah's house, Trinity had met up with someone and turned Josie's car over to them. Someone taller than both Trinity and Lila. Lila was even shorter than Josie, so she wouldn't have pushed the seat back.

So, who had been in her car?

Josie pulled over and took her phone out. She started to text Gretchen about the car but then realized that her Evidence Response Team would print the car anyway. If the person who had driven it had left prints, they would be found. Josie put her phone away and pulled back into traffic, the need to keep moving consuming her.

Where was Trinity now? she wondered. Was she hiding because she had killed a man, or was Lila holding her somewhere? Josie had no doubt that Lila was behind Heinrich's murder somehow, and that Trinity had gone to meet Lila because Lila had promised her a story. But what would make Trinity kill a man so willingly? Josie thought about what it would take for her to throw away her life and career and commit a murder. What would make her desperate enough to do that? Not a threat against her own life. She'd rather die than go down and lose everything. But would she trade her career and her morality to save someone she loved? It was then that Josie realized she didn't know Trinity at all. She knew nothing personal about the reporter, her life, her family, her loved ones.

Josie turned the vehicle around and headed back to her home. She hadn't been inside for days, and the rooms had an empty, sterile feeling to them—as if they weren't really hers anymore. She hoped that one day it would feel like a safe place again. But until then, she would startle at every little noise, like she did when she was in the spare room booting up her laptop and her neighbor's garage door screeched open. Bringing her laptop down to the kitchen, she made herself a pot of coffee, still unable to shake the feeling that she was in someone else's space now.

As the coffee brewed, Josie pulled up her internet browser and typed in Trinity Payne's name. The search returned more results than Josie could possibly sift through in a few hours, or even a week, so she typed in *Trinity Payne biography*, and that narrowed it down somewhat. She clicked through several sites, turning up the same information again and again. She had gone to NYU, where she'd graduated summa cum laude with a degree in journalism. She started out as a roving reporter for WYEP in the Denton area, then she moved quickly to the network's morning magazine show in New York City, working as a national correspondent until a source gave her a bad story. Her fall from grace had landed her back at WYEP, until she had helped Josie crack the missing girls case two years earlier, and the network wanted her back on the national stage.

Josie knew all this. She clicked through the sites faster, skimming over repeat information, looking for something more. Finally, on an NYU alumni website, she found a more detailed article about Trinity, written three months earlier—*NYU Journalism Alum Rises from Tragedy to Network Royalty.*

The first paragraph read: *Network darling Trinity Payne is no stranger to controversy. Her travails with bad sources as well as her recent rise to fame helping to crack some of the biggest criminal cases in the history of her home state are well documented. What most people don't know about Payne is that her life was inexorably marked by tragedy when she was only a few weeks old. Her young parents were both employed by pharmaceutical giant Quarmark—Christian as the head of marketing and Shannon as a rising chemist. With their careers on track, their next goal was to settle down and have children. They found their dream home quickly—a two-story Tudor-style mansion in a small town named Callowhill. They got pregnant on the first try—with twins. "They were classic overachievers," Trinity relates, smiling.*

"Twins?" Josie muttered. She had no idea that Trinity had a twin. She had known that Trinity grew up in Callowhill. It was a small town a couple of hours away, on the other side of Bellewood. In fact, the county seat was just about equidistant from both Denton and Callowhill. Josie stood and hastily prepared a cup of coffee for herself, returning to her laptop.

While many first-time parents might have been intimidated by twins, Shannon Payne says she and her husband never once worried how they would handle two newborns. "The day our girls were born was one of the happiest days of our lives."

The day our girls were born. Something gnawed at the back of Josie's mind, but she couldn't put her finger on it.

She read on: *Tragedy struck just a few weeks after the twins were born when a house fire destroyed their four-bedroom home. Their nanny was home with the twins at the time, but was only able to save one of them—Trinity.*

"My God," Josie said.

She skimmed over the rest of it—how the Paynes had never truly recovered from the loss of Trinity's twin sister, and how Trinity was glad she didn't remember anything because it would be too painful. A shiver ran down Josie's spine. She didn't know how a person could ever recover from the loss of a child. There was no doubt in her mind that it was an open wound that Shannon and Christian Payne would take to their graves. Josie felt a wave of sympathy for Trinity, and yet, she couldn't help but wonder if Trinity would have turned out less mercenary had she had the influence of a sister. Now they would never know.

She skimmed the rest of the article, but the only other new piece of information was that Trinity had a much younger brother called Patrick, who was still in high school in Callowhill. There was no mention of any love interests. Trinity didn't strike Josie as the type who would have time for a boyfriend. Josie had what she needed though—the names of Trinity's immediate family members. She opened a new tab and searched for a phone number for the Payne family in Callowhill. It was unlisted. Of course, with a daughter as famous as Trinity, the Paynes wouldn't want their number so easily accessible to the public.

Josie had only been suspended for a few hours. It was quite possible that no one at Denton PD had revoked her access to the police databases. Logging in to one of them, Josie pumped her fist in the air as her credentials were accepted. She searched for Shannon Payne first, banking on the hope that the Paynes still had a landline because cell service was spotty in the more remote areas of Pennsylvania. Luck was with her today.

Josie punched the number into her cell phone and listened to it ring eight times before the call went to voicemail, a female voice that sounded similar to Trinity's urging her to leave a message. At the beep, Josie said, "This is Josie Quinn. I'm the chief of police in Denton. I'm calling about your daughter, Trinity. It is very important that you call me back as soon as you get this message." She then left her number and hung up.

As she went to close out the browser on her laptop, the last paragraph of the alumni magazine article caught Josie's eye. *When asked if the tragedy of her sister's death has influenced her as a journalist, Payne smiles bravely, and a faraway look creeps into her eyes. "I think never knowing what really happened—who set the fire—will haunt my family forever and has definitely made me more diligent in my reporting. I will never stop until I have all the answers. It's just something that's in me."*

Josie looked at her cell phone and, realizing she had nothing to do while she waited for the Paynes to call her back, she opened another tab, pulled up a search engine, and typed in *Payne Callowhill house fire.* There were results with *Payne* and *Callowhill* in them, and *Callowhill* and *house fire,* but none with all three terms. Of course, Josie knew that Trinity was around the same age as she was, and if the fire had taken place a few weeks after her birth, that meant it would have happened in the late '80s—before the internet was a staple of daily existence. Back then, if the fire had made the news, it would have been in one of the county newspapers.

She finished her coffee and set off for the library.

CHAPTER 65

The Denton Library was a two-floor stone building designed by a local architect in the early 1900s in neoclassical style, complete with a grand staircase and large Doric columns. Josie had always loved the building; she had spent many hours as a teenager tucked away among the shelves, studying in the reverent hush that presided over the massive collection of books. In the intervening years, much of the building had been modernized, upgrading from tables to computer stations and expanding into conference and activity rooms. Josie explained to one of the librarians what she was looking for, and the woman led her to a computer station on the second floor.

"Would it be on microfiche?" Josie asked.

"Oh no, dear. We moved all that old stuff onto this new database. It's all computerized now. You'll see. We've got the *Denton Tribune*, the *Bellewood Record*, and a couple of the other local papers from the county. When you put in your search terms, it will trawl all of those papers, or only the ones you designate." The librarian reached across Josie and maneuvered the mouse until an image of an old *Denton Tribune* cover popped up next to a login bar. She typed in her credentials and gave Josie a short tour, showing how to do a search and narrow down the parameters.

Once the librarian left her alone, Josie glanced at her cell before setting it on the desk next to her—still nothing from the Paynes. Getting to work, it only took a few minutes to find two results. One was from the *Denton Tribune* dated October 4, 1987. It was on the front page and offered no more than Trinity had disclosed in her alumni magazine interview. The Callowhill fire marshal was quoted as saying the cause of the fire was still under investigation. Josie saved it and moved on to the next article, which was dated December 17, 1987. This article was from the *Bellewood Record*, on page four, with a number of county items that weren't newsworthy enough to warrant space on the front page. The headline read: *Cause of Callowhill Fire Arson; Police Open Murder Investigation.*

Josie skimmed the article, learning that the nanny who had rescued Trinity had died of smoke inhalation after going back into the house to rescue the other twin, making the case a double homicide. There were no leads and no suspects. Only a few months after the fire, the case had grown cold. The article ended with a quote from Shannon Payne that punched a small barb of pain into Josie's heart. "From the day my girls were born, I never left them alone. That was the only time I ever left them alone with the nanny. I can't help thinking that if I had been there, we could have saved them both."

From the day my girls were born. The amorphous shadow in the back of Josie's mind shifted, making itself known but not becoming clear. With a sigh, Josie saved the second article and went in search of the librarian to gain access to a printer.

As the woman clicked on several drop-down menus and selected a nearby machine, Josie asked her, "Uh, do you have kids?"

"I certainly do," the librarian answered. "A girl and a boy. They're grown now, of course. Why do you ask?"

"Oh, you looked familiar," Josie lied. "I thought maybe I had gone to high school with your daughter at Denton East."

"Oh no, dear," the librarian said, smiling at Josie. "I only just moved here from Pittsburgh a few years back. Maybe I just have one of those faces. Do you have children?"

Josie was glad the woman was chatty, and she wouldn't have to work too hard to bring up the subject she was really aiming for. "Oh no," Josie answered. "I mean, maybe one day. The world is a scary

place these days. The thought of bringing a child into this chaos..."
She trailed off, and the woman picked up the thread immediately.

"Oh, every parent feels like that, dear. When my daughter was born, I was terrified. It seemed like the world was worse than it ever was. Then, a few years later, my son was born, and it seemed even worse. But life goes on, and you manage."

"Thanks," Josie said. A large printer across the room whirred noisily as it spat out several sheets of paper. The librarian bustled over to it and picked them up. Josie thanked her again before she was called away by another patron. Settling back at her computer station, Josie pulled up the newspaper database again and searched the words *baby* and *adopted* for the years 1982 and 1983.

The shadow at the back of her mind had fallen away as she spoke with the librarian, revealing what had been bothering her. When Shannon Payne talked about her twins, she talked about the day they were born. When the manager at the Eudora told Josie about his drug-addicted son, he used the same language: the day his son was born. When the librarian talked about her own children, she too used the word *born*.

But when Josie and her team interviewed Sophia Bowen, she had said that she stopped working in the summer of 1983 "when we brought our eldest son home." Something about the phrasing had stuck in the back of Josie's mind, needling her, begging to be examined further. Maybe she was reaching. She was no longer chief and didn't have a police department to run to keep herself busy. Maybe she was just making things up to keep herself distracted from the fact that her life had fallen apart, and neither she nor the Denton PD were any closer to finding Lila Jensen. Perhaps Sophia Bowen had merely been referring to the day they'd brought their eldest son home from the hospital.

It was a long shot. She knew that. Adoptions weren't the sort of thing that ended up in newspapers—not in the '80s, and not now. But if a prominent judge and his young bride adopted a baby, there was the tiniest possibility it would have been newsworthy on a slow day.

With time on her hands and a research database at her fingertips, Josie had nothing to lose.

Most of the results were articles having to do with changes to the adoption laws in the state, lawsuits, and adopted children searching for their birth parents. Her heart leapt as she found what she was looking for in an issue of the *Bellewood Record* from December of 1987—the same year as the fire that took the Paynes' daughter and their home. It was just a small piece buried on page eight of the paper next to the announcements of the schedules of various church services over the holidays.

Five Years Later, Alcott County's Manger Baby Plays Joseph in Live Nativity.

When he was only a few days old, little Andrew Bowen was the unwilling star of the Maplewood Baptist Church's outdoor nativity. Just before Christmas of 1982, someone left him swaddled in white cotton towels in the manger of the church's nativity scene. Residents of Alcott County were shocked by the discovery. The Manger Baby, as he became known after he was discovered, had been left in the freezing cold during an evening church service. Members of the congregation heard his cries as they left the service and called the police. Although the baby's parents were never found, he found a family with local judge Malcolm Bowen and his wife, Sophia.

The Manger Baby's case came across the judge's docket after he was placed in the foster care system. "As soon as I saw him, I fell in love," Judge Bowen recalls. "My wife and I were already trying for children, and I came home after seeing that baby for the first time and said, 'Sophia, what do you think about adoption?' Of course, she was on board immediately."

The Bowens were able to bring the Manger Baby home in the summer of 1983, when he was six months old. "It was the happiest day of my life," Sophia Bowen exclaimed. "I became a mother."

Five years later, young Andrew Bowen is thriving in his new home—he even has a little brother—and this year he will star as Joseph in the live nativity at the very same rural church where he was abandoned as an infant.

"We've made our peace with what Andrew's biological parents did to him. We've forgiven them, and we hope when Andrew grows up, he will too. We don't know what type of desperate situation the mother was in that she would give up such a precious little baby. What I know is that God gave us a gift," Sophia Bowen said. "Andrew made us parents for the first time. There is no greater gift than that."

Just in time for Christmas.

Knowing what she knew about Malcolm Bowen and Belinda Rose, the cheery, saccharine tone of the article made Josie's stomach turn. She thought of the photos of Andrew Bowen she'd seen in Sophia's home, and of the times she'd met him in his capacity as a criminal attorney in Denton. He was the spitting image of Malcolm Bowen, except blond. Was it possible that Malcolm Bowen had arranged to adopt his own son? Had Belinda left the baby in the manger?

Josie thought of the locket Belinda had returned with after she disappeared to give birth to her baby. It was one thing for her to go off and have the baby and then abandon him somewhere, but she had been gone for months, not days. Belinda Rose had had a plan. She had had somewhere to go. She had had help. Malcolm Bowen would have had enough power and influence to make sure that his own son ended up with him and Sophia.

On her phone, Josie googled Andrew Bowen's office number and called it. His secretary told her that he was in court. She left her cell phone number and asked that he call her when he was out. She was still reeling from her discovery about the Bowens when her phone rang in her hand. She recognized the number immediately and answered.

"Chief Quinn?"

"Mrs. Payne?" Josie said. "Shannon Payne?"

CHAPTER 66

Josie caught several glares from nearby library users and lowered her voice, pressing the phone to her ear, gathering up her printouts, and heading outside. "Thank you for calling me back, Mrs. Payne," she said.

A cool wind whipped up the steps of the library, so Josie moved behind one of the columns and out of the stream of people going in and out of the building.

Shannon Payne said, "I'm returning your call about my daughter. I talked to one of your detectives earlier. Is everything okay?" Josie heard her breath catch in her throat. "I guess it's not, or you wouldn't be calling—the chief of police. My God—"

"Mrs. Payne," Josie interjected before she became hysterical, "I'm sorry. I don't have any news. I was just calling to follow up and make sure that you, your husband, and your son are safe. I assure you that my team is doing everything they can to find Trinity."

She hated lying to Shannon, especially while she was under such stress and worried about her child, but trying to explain the current situation would take too long. Plus, Josie knew that it was true that Denton PD would do everything in their power to find Trinity—Gretchen and Noah were already several steps ahead of her if they'd already contacted the Paynes.

"Oh, thank you," Shannon said. "I certainly appreciate that. We're fine. I mean, we're not fine. We're worried about my daughter, but we're all accounted for and safe."

"Excellent," Josie said. "I just had a couple more questions, if you don't mind. Does Trinity have a boyfriend?"

Shannon laughed. "Oh no. She doesn't have time for that."

"Thought so," Josie said. "How about close friends? Anyone she would perhaps go and stay with if she needed to get away?"

Shannon was silent for a moment. Then she said, "I hate to say this, but Trinity doesn't really have time for friends either. That sounds terrible, but you have to understand, she's very career-driven."

Josie couldn't help but laugh. "Oh, I know, Mrs. Payne."

Shannon laughed as well, albeit a little nervously. "I guess you would. She's worked with you on a couple of cases, hasn't she?"

"Yes, she's been an invaluable resource."

"I gave Detective Palmer the names of all the people I could think of that she's friendly with in New York," Shannon said. "But really, if she needed to get away for a while, she'd come here."

"I understand," Josie said, throat tightening. If Trinity didn't have any friends, lovers, or other close associates she might run to in her time of need, then the likelihood that Lila was holding her against her will increased exponentially. Josie continued, "If you have any questions or you need anything at all, you can call Lieutenant Fraley or Detective Palmer. Of course, you're welcome to contact me as well, but they'll be actively working the case."

"Well, there was just one more thing," said Shannon. "Since I've got you on the phone."

"Oh? What's that?"

"Well, I don't know that it has anything to do with Trinity, but it's been bothering me." She stopped. For a moment, Josie thought the call had dropped. Then she added, "It's silly. I don't even know why I'm bringing it up."

"Go on," Josie said. "I'm listening."

A sigh. "Well, WYEP is running a story about a woman the Denton PD is trying to locate. They keep showing her picture and saying she is a person of interest in a number of local crimes. It's quite an old photo, though."

"Yes," Josie said, wondering where this was going. "Her name was Lila Jensen, but she used the alias Belinda Rose for many years."

"I knew her as Belinda."

Josie's heartbeat skipped twice. "What?"

"My husband thinks I'm crazy," she said, laughing nervously.

"That's men for you," Josie replied. "Go on."

"She used to work for the cleaning service that came out to our house. In the mid to late '80s."

"Handy Helpers?" Josie asked before remembering that Handy Helpers had closed in 1984 after the death of its owner.

"Oh, no. I think they were called AB Clean. There were a few girls who used to come out, and she was one of them. After she started, things began disappearing from our home. Mostly my jewelry. I reported her to her boss, and he fired her. Not even a week later, our home burned to the ground. My girls were home with the nanny. They were only a few weeks old. Only Trinity survived."

"I'm aware of the fire," Josie said. "Did the authorities ever check her alibi?"

"They did look into it, they claimed, and said she had an alibi for the day of the fire, but I've always thought…" She trailed off.

Josie filled in the end of her sentence: "You think Belinda had something to do with the fire?"

A heavy sigh. "I don't know. I've never even been able to say it out loud until very recently. Like I said, the police told us that she was nowhere near Callowhill when the fire started. But it always bothered me. She was…there was something about her, something…dark. That sounds terrible. Really, I should just shut up. None of this has anything to do with my daughter. I'm probably just trying to distract myself—bringing up this old stuff so I don't have to think about where my daughter might be or what's happening to her." Josie heard her sob, then suck in several deep breaths. Then she added, "I don't know if I'm even making sense."

Josie leaned against the column and closed her eyes, the phone still pressed to her ear. "You're making perfect sense."

Shannon took in several more breaths. "Anyway, I just saw her picture on the television, and it gave me a shock. It brought back all the memories from the fire. It just hit too close to home. Losing a child, and now with Trinity missing…"

It was too strange, too coincidental. Belinda getting fired from cleaning the Paynes' house and then the fire soon after. All of it taking place the year Josie was born.

"I understand," Josie said. "I do. Listen, if you don't mind my asking, where were the girls when the fire started?"

"They were sleeping in their playpen in the family room. The nanny—before she died—said they were both asleep, and she'd just nipped to the bathroom for a moment. When she came out, the downstairs was filled with smoke. She said she could hardly see. She ran to the family room to get the girls, but only Trinity was still in the playpen. She scooped Trinity up and ran her outside. One of our neighbors had come out by then. The nanny handed Trinity to her and went back in. When the fire department arrived, they found her searching the house and made her come out. The police were always very suspicious of her. They never believed her story that only one of the girls was in the playpen. If she hadn't died, I think they would have tried to pin the whole thing on her. But if she had started the fire, why would she rescue only one of the girls, and then go back into the house? It makes no sense. She was lucky she survived for the few days she did after the fire. The fire department said my daughter was—" Shannon's words halted, and a high-pitched cry penetrated Josie's ear. She took several moments to recover herself, and Josie could hear her quiet weeping like a hundred thorns piercing her heart. Clearing her throat, Shannon said, "The fire chief told us that she had been…incinerated in the fire. She was so tiny. We didn't even have any remains to bury."

Josie tried to speak—to say she was sorry, to utter some words of comfort or empathy. She wasn't a mother, but it had taken her only moments to bond with little baby Harris. Even though she saw him infrequently, she knew that if anything ever happened to him, she would never recover. And Misty would be utterly destroyed. Normal mothers—good mothers—loved their children. This was a fact Josie had always known intellectually, but never experienced.

"I'm sorry," Shannon said. "I shouldn't have brought it up. It's ridiculous. Like I said, I'm just deflecting or whatever psychologists call it so I don't have to think about the fact that my Trinity is missing."

"I'll find her," Josie said, her voice returning. This she could do. "I promise you, I'm going to find her."

CHAPTER 67

Lisette was in her usual spot in the cafeteria, sitting at a table working on a crossword puzzle as other residents drifted in and out. A pair of glasses sat low on the bridge of her nose, and her gray curls fell around her face as her head bent to the page in front of her. She looked up when Josie appeared beside her. "Sweetheart, how lovely to see you. In the middle of the day too." She craned her neck to look behind Josie. "Work again?"

Josie shook her head. Lisette must have seen from her expression that something was very wrong. Abandoning her puzzle, she stood and grasped both sides of her walker, pushing past Josie. "Come then, we'll talk in my room."

Lisette sat in her recliner while Josie perched across from her on the edge of her bed. "What's going on, Josie?" Lisette asked. "What's wrong?"

"Gram," Josie said, "I need to ask you some questions, and I need you to be honest. Promise me. If you do nothing else for me in this life, I need you to answer my questions truthfully."

Lisette gave a nervous chuckle. "Of course, dear."

"When I was born, was my dad there at the hospital?"

The faint smile on Lisette's face tightened into something strained. "No, he wasn't. Your mother—well, they'd been living together, and they got into some big fight. Your mother left. She was gone for months. Eli thought it was over. He never expected to see her again, honestly. He was about to move out of the trailer, had met another girl and gone on a few dates with her. Then one day he came home, and there was your mother sitting on his couch with you in the crook of her arm."

A band of pain wrapped itself around Josie's skull. Throbbing began in her temples. "She just showed up with a baby one day?"

"Not just a baby. You."

"Dad didn't question the paternity?"

"Of course not," Lisette scoffed. "What kind of man would do that? Belinda said that she found out she was a few months along after she left him, and that she wasn't going to even tell him about you, but that once you came the guilt was too much, so she came back. She gave him the option—to be involved, or not. Naturally, your father wanted to be involved. He loved you the very instant he saw you."

Josie knew that there weren't DNA tests back in 1987—not the kind that were readily available to anyone in the public. These days, you could order a paternity kit online, swab your cheek, and mail it to a lab. But in the late '80s, if you had suspicions, you'd have no way of proving whether or not a child was your own.

"Did she say what hospital I was born in?"

"Oh, she had a home birth. Actually, she hadn't even sent away for your birth certificate until after she brought you home to your father."

"How old?" Josie asked. "How old was I?"

"Three months. She brought you home sometime in December; it was the most wonderful Christmas present we'd ever received!"

Under normal circumstances, Josie would smile, basking in the love her grandmother had for her. But at the moment, every muscle in her face felt frozen. The suspicion that had started growing during her conversation with Shannon Payne was still shrouded in her mind. To tear away the veil would mean shattering everything she knew to be true. Not to mention the absurdity of what she now suspected about the Payne fire and her own origins. She couldn't bring herself to think it, let alone say it aloud.

"Josie, why are you asking me these questions? What's wrong?"

Josie's voice trembled. "Did you know right away that I was someone else's child?"

Lisette went very still, holding her posture like a granite statue. "What are you talking about?"

"I don't look like Dad," Josie said. "And I don't look like you."

"You got your mother's looks," Lisette said.

"No," Josie said. "Both of us having black hair doesn't mean much. Gram, you knew, didn't you? You had to have known, or at least suspected, that I was not a blood relation to you and my father."

Lisette's face flushed. "Does it matter? Does it really matter? You're mine. You've always been mine. I didn't need a blood test to prove that, and you shouldn't either. Who helped raise you, Josie? Who fought for you? I battled like hell to bring you home with me."

"The deck was stacked, Gram. The judge you went before, Malcolm Bowen? He knew my mother, knew she was using an assumed identity. I was always leaving with her, no matter what happened that day."

"You don't know that. Judge Bowen was a good man, a fair man. When your mother finally left, he put the custody order through quickly and painlessly. He helped me."

"Judge Bowen was *not* a good man. Sorry to shatter your illusions, Gram. If he helped you, it was only because—" She broke off as her brain worked through it.

It was only a theory that Judge Bowen had been involved in helping Josie's mother, but Josie was sure that she had it right. She was certain that her mother had gone to him after Lisette first filed for custody and had him handle the whole thing quietly, using private mediation. Lila had had something on him—probably the knowledge that he had been having an affair with the real Belinda Rose as a minor. He wouldn't have wanted her exposing that secret, so he would have helped her. The only way that he would then turn around and help Lisette four years later is if Lila allowed him to, and Lila wouldn't have allowed Lisette to have custody of Josie after fourteen years unless...

"Gram, what did you do?"

"Josie Quinn," Lisette began in a scolding tone.

"Judge Bowen was in league with my mother. They wouldn't have let you have me unless you did something. My mother never did anything for nothing. What did you give her? What did you promise her?"

Lisette's head hung. "My sweet Josie."

"Just tell me."

With a sigh, Lisette said, "Fifty thousand dollars."

"What?" Josie's voice came out high-pitched. "Where did you get that kind of money?"

"Your father had a life-insurance policy. I didn't touch it after he died. I knew he would want me to save it for you to use for college or to buy your first home. But after the fire in the trailer, your mother came to me. She said she wanted to work something out. I think the police were really looking at her for burning the trailer down and for what happened to that poor boy, Dexter. I didn't argue. I offered her twenty-five thousand, but she had to leave and never come back. She wanted more. I told her for fifty she had to give me full legal and physical custody and never set foot in your life again."

Josie stood and paced the room. "Jesus, Gram."

"I had to. It was my only chance. I know it was a lot of money, but it was worth it. I had to get you away from her. I'm just sorry I couldn't do it sooner. The damage she did—Josie, I hope you know how sorry I am."

Josie held up her hands. "Stop. Just stop. I can't—I can't talk about that. I just—I don't—Gram, you knew I didn't belong to you all along. You worked so hard to get me, but why did you keep me? Why didn't you say anything? Did it ever occur to you that some family out there was missing me?"

Lisette gave a dismissive laugh. "A family? Please. Maybe some drug-addled man that your mother took into her bed for one night. Don't you see? For all I knew, whoever had really fathered you might be even worse than your mother. It was hard enough getting you away from her, especially after your father died. We were supposed to fight for you together. He promised me we would petition the court for custody. We were not going to be intimidated by her. He was going to spend every last dime he had, and I was going to help him. I'll never understand why he gave up. It wasn't like him at all. But then he was gone, and you were alone with that…that monster. All I knew was that I had to get you away from her."

"You could have said something," Josie said. "Told someone you didn't believe I was hers. Raised hell. Talked to Judge Bowen. Sent up red flags. But you didn't."

Lisette's eyes flashed. She pointed a crooked finger at Josie. "You're not listening to me. What if I had done that and we somehow figured out who your real father was, and he was worse than your mother? Have you never thought of that?"

"Not my real father," Josie said. "My real family. Gram, I think she *took* me from another family entirely."

"Josie, what on earth are you talking about?"

Josie knelt before her grandmother and held both her hands. "Gram, what I'm about to tell you is going to sound crazy. Or maybe, knowing what you already know about my mother, it will sound exactly right."

CHAPTER 68

Josie returned home, trudging into her kitchen and making another pot of coffee, although the way she felt, she doubted it would help—her limbs felt like they were moving through molasses. She hadn't felt so drained since she pulled little baby Harris out of the Susquehanna River six months ago. The day had been filled with a series of shocking discoveries, but she was no closer to figuring out where Lila and Trinity were.

Josie was so deep in thought that when she heard three loud knocks on her front door, she nearly jumped out of her skin. Through the peephole she saw Noah standing on her front stoop, both hands in his jeans pockets, his gaze fixed firmly on his feet.

She opened the door and stared at him. "What are you doing here?" she asked. "Did you find Lila? Trinity?"

He shook his head, still not looking at her.

She hated this awkwardness between them, and the last thing she felt like doing was discussing what had—and hadn't—happened between them the night before. But he was here all the same. "Would you like to come in?"

He stepped past her into the foyer, and she pulled the door closed behind them and motioned toward the kitchen. "I made coffee."

Only when he was seated at her table did he look at her. "I'm sorry about this morning—about Tara," he said. "I wanted to call, to warn you, but Tara wouldn't let us go."

"I understand," she said.

She set the coffee mug in front of him, and as she turned away, he touched her arm. "I was trying to figure out the best way to protect you."

Josie sighed and took a seat next to him. "Noah," she said, "you can't protect me from this. No one can. This fight has been a long time coming, and I'm the only one who can do it."

"No you're not," Noah insisted, his hazel eyes earnest. Seeing something besides hurt and confusion in his face instantly made her feel better. "Gretchen and I are going to help you. We already convinced the mayor that it's not you on that tape. We just have to find Trinity. We'll get this sorted out."

"Are you interim chief of police now?" Josie asked hopefully.

"The mayor doesn't trust me or Gretchen to be unbiased, which is probably smart on her part. She has this guy coming in. He's semi-retired. Has his own security firm. Used to work as a high-ranking police officer in Pittsburgh before that. He'll be the interim chief until further notice."

It was no surprise to Josie that Tara had someone waiting in the wings to take Josie's job. "Right," Josie said.

"Well, hopefully this guy is more reasonable than Tara."

"Nothing on Trinity?" Josie asked, turning back to more pressing matters. "I know Gretchen went to the hotel. Did you get her phone unlocked?"

He raised a brow at her, but didn't ask questions. "There were texts between her and an unknown number—a prepaid burner phone. We're trying to see if we can track down its location now. Whoever it was said they had information about her sister. We called Shannon Payne though—that's her mother—and her sister died as an infant."

"Yeah, I heard that."

"The messages were very cryptic, and after they stopped, there were a few phone calls back and forth, including one from the unknown number to Trinity's cell just before she ran out of her room."

"It was Lila," Josie said.

"But why? Why go after Trinity? And who the hell is this Heinrich guy? I couldn't find any connection between him and

Belinda Rose or Lila Jensen. Although he's on the sex offender registry. Did you know that?"

Josie nodded. "Yes. He served almost ten years for molesting his thirteen-year-old niece."

"How do you know that?" Noah asked. "Was it one of your cases?"

"No, by the time I started at Denton PD, he was being released."

It had taken a long time for Josie to identify Heinrich as the man Lila had sold her to, and since nothing had actually occurred between them, there was nothing Josie could legally do to him. She'd worried that he would prey on more young girls once out of prison, but it had only taken a few days of surveillance to see that Heinrich was in no shape to assault anyone. Whatever had happened to him in prison had left him with a permanent limp and restricted range of motion in one of his arms. Most of the time he moved slowly, as though in great pain.

"I don't understand," Noah said.

The piercing pain in her temples was back. "There are some things I need to tell you right now."

The easy part was telling him what she had found out from Trinity's mother, and what her own grandmother had confirmed about Josie's birth—Josie's father hadn't been present when she was born. Lila had disappeared for months and then shown up unexpectedly one day with Josie. There was no actual proof that Lila had ever been pregnant or given birth, which meant there was a definite possibility that Lila had taken her from the Paynes.

Noah was on his second cup of coffee by the time she finished. His eyes had collected dark circles beneath them.

"I know it sounds insane," Josie said.

"No. I mean, yes. It does. Completely insane, but knowing everything we know now, I can see it. When all of this is over, you should take a DNA test. You can do them by mail now. Fast. My only question is why would Lila steal someone's baby?"

"Because it's the worst thing you can do to a woman."

"All because Shannon Payne got her fired?"

"Lila's reactions to things were never proportionate," Josie pointed out.

He downed the last of his coffee, and they sat in silence for a few moments. It pained her to bring up the last piece of the puzzle, but Josie knew she had to. Noah had supported her blindly in the face of the mayor's coup, and he was fiercely loyal to her—even after she had cut off their encounter so abruptly and clearly wounded him. He deserved to know everything, which meant telling him about Heinrich. "Noah," Josie said. "There's something else. Something I need to tell you. It's about Ted Heinrich."

He didn't say anything after she told him, and it didn't take long. The few words she could muster were inadequate to express the breadth and depth of what Lila had done to her and what was almost taken from her that day. Maybe that was okay, she thought. She had spent so many years pushing those feelings down and keeping them out of her consciousness, finally saying the words might make them lose a little of their power.

Josie watched the range of emotions pass over Noah's face as she spoke: shock, horror, pity, sadness, disgust, anger, and relief that Needle had intervened. She knew he was searching through the silence for something to say—anything.

She was relieved when Noah's cell phone rang. Slowly, without taking his eyes off her, he pulled it out and silenced it.

"Noah," she said softly. "You have to get that."

His eyes were intense, zeroed in on her with laser focus. "No," he said, "I don't."

They stared at one another. His phone rang again. Again, he silenced it. "Noah, it could be important."

He tapped his index finger on the table. "This is important. *You* are important."

She smiled. "Then help me. Answer your phone. It could be about Trinity. Or my mother."

"Lila," he said. "From now on she is Lila. She was not a mother to you."

"Lila, then."

His phone rang again, and he answered it, listening briefly and ending the call with, "I'll be there in ten."

Josie looked at him hopefully, but he shook his head. "Sorry. Nothing on Trinity. But Gretchen did pick up one of those teenagers working at the Spur Mobile store and got him to admit that a 'really weird old lady' gave him weed in exchange for giving out your new number, and that she 'did some other things' to get him to place the craigslist ads."

Josie stood up and walked him to the front door. "I knew it," she said. "I bet I know which one of those rotten little punks it was too. See what else you can get from him. If she came into the store, there might be video. Find out if she told him her name. Maybe we can figure out what alias she's using now."

Noah stood by the front door, smiling at her. "You got it, Boss," he said.

"Sorry," Josie replied. "It's a hard habit to break—bossing you around."

"I don't mind." He gave her a small smile, and her heart leapt.

CHAPTER 69

Josie's cell phone rang shortly after Noah left, breaking her thoughts. Those final moments with him had stirred up so many emotions within her, she was having a hard time keeping them down. She answered without looking at the number. A man's voice asked, "Is this Chief Quinn? Chief Josie Quinn?"

"Yes," Josie said. "This is Josie Quinn. Who is this?"

"Chief, this is Andrew Bowen returning your call—"

"Oh, yes. I called for two reasons. One is your mother—"

"Yes, my mother," he interjected. "She told me you called her and asked her to come in for a more formal interview. You should know that she's retained me as her attorney."

Josie suppressed a groan. "Let me guess, you have no intention of producing her for an interview because she's already told my detectives everything she knows. Does that sound right?"

He laughed. "Yep, that about covers it."

"And if that didn't work, you were going to cite her age and status in the community and argue that there is no reason to bring her into the police station like some kind of criminal."

More laughter. "Want to tell me how I'm going to handle my next trial too? I'd really like to know if I win or not."

"Sorry, I'm not psychic," Josie said. "Just used to dealing with criminal defense attorneys. So tell me, Mr. Bowen, if your mother hasn't done anything criminal and has nothing to hide, then why not bring her over for a cup of coffee to answer a few more questions?"

She heard what sounded like him taking a drink. Then he said, "Okay, Chief, what are you really hoping to get here? You questioned Mrs. Bowen about the murder of a girl she barely knew that happened over thirty years ago."

"I wouldn't say they barely knew one another," Josie said. "Several people we spoke to said they were quite close. Your mother even admitted that she became good friends with Belinda after your father took an interest in her. They felt sorry for her because she was a foster child."

"So what?" Andrew said. "Sure they were friends, but according to my mother—and this was confirmed when you and your detectives came to visit with her—Belinda Rose went missing in 1984. That was almost a year after my mother left the courthouse to be a full-time mom. What do you think she knows that she isn't telling you?"

A lot, Josie thought. She didn't believe for a second that Sophia didn't remember Lila, but she still couldn't figure out why she would lie about it. Josie could see her lying about her and her husband's relationship with Belinda Rose. Perhaps Sophia had found out that they were having an affair. Whether it was before or after they became friends was anyone's guess, but Sophia had stayed with her husband for decades, raised his children, and played the role of dutiful wife. Admitting that she had knowledge of her husband's affair with a minor over thirty years ago was probably not something she wanted to do. But why lie about knowing Lila?

"Look," Andrew was saying, drawing Josie out of her thoughts. "My mother is a good woman. She was a faithful wife and an excellent mother. She is active in her church and does a lot of community service and volunteer work. She's done a lot of charity work in this county to help local foster children. I just don't understand why you are dragging her into this investigation when she has nothing to do with it. You're going to have to help me digest that. Otherwise, I would definitely not recommend that she meet with you or any of your detectives again. Certainly not at the police station. Now, what was the other thing you called about? Is it a different case?"

For the moment, Josie abandoned the topic of the formal interview.

"It was a personal question," Josie said. "Nothing to do with a case."

There was a beat of silence. Then he said, "Okay, I guess. Can't promise I'll answer, but go for it."

"When you were growing up, did you ever have…extra teeth?"

"Supernumerary teeth?" he asked.

"Yes," she said. "Exactly."

"Err. Yeah, I did. My mom took me to have them removed as soon as they grew in. She was always worried I would grow more, but nothing ever came of it. We had to go to a special oral surgeon in Philadelphia. Apparently, it's pretty rare."

"I've heard that," Josie said.

"How on earth did you know about that? What's this about?"

"Wild guess," Josie said. "I'm sorry, Mr. Bowen. I've got to go. It's an emergency."

CHAPTER 70

Darkness was creeping in as Josie pulled up in front of Sophia Bowen's house. A single downstairs light glowed through one of the living room windows. Josie waited to see if anyone was coming or going, and when she was relatively sure that Sophia was home alone, she went to the front door and knocked. Sophia answered wearing a pair of tan slacks and a pink button-down blouse that flared at the waist. Her smile froze when she saw that it was Josie. She started to close the door, but Josie jammed a sneakered foot between the door and its frame. Sophia kept on pushing, but Josie pushed back harder.

"I know about Andrew," she said. "I know that he is Belinda Rose's son. She had an affair with your husband, and Andrew was the result."

Sophia's hands went slack against the door. Her gaze dropped to her feet as Josie pushed her way into the foyer and closed the door behind her. "Why did you lie?" Josie asked.

Sophia took a moment to collect herself and then lifted her chin and glared at Josie. "You have no right to come here, barging in and making such outlandish claims. I'd like you to leave now."

"Or what? You'll call the police? Listen, I don't care about your husband's affair. I don't even care that you lied to your son and told him he was adopted when he's not. What I care about is finding Lila Jensen. I know that you remember her. Hell, I know you've been in touch with her."

"I haven't—I haven't been—"

"Save it," Josie said. "Lila has been wreaking havoc on my life for the last month. She's done things it would be impossible to do without help. Sure, it was easy enough for her to find a couple of dumb teenage boys to carry out simplistic pranks or to rely on her old drug buddies for other things, but now she's moved on to more elaborate schemes. Schemes she would need a lot more help for—money, a place to stay, a place to hold someone. You live all alone in this big house. You have money to spare. You're the perfect target for someone like her. So tell me, what does she have on you that would make you help her?"

Sophia's face was ashen. She twisted her fingers together, her eyes darting around the room. "I didn't want to help her. I really didn't. She's not here, if that's what you're after. She wanted to stay here, but I told her absolutely not. I hadn't seen her in over thirty years, then a month ago she showed up on my doorstep wanting money, a car. I told her I couldn't do it, but she threatened me."

"She knew about your husband's affair with Belinda Rose," Josie said. "She was going to tell Andrew that he wasn't really adopted. That his father wasn't the saint everybody thought he was."

Sophia spread her palms in a helpless gesture. "What could I do? I didn't want her to destroy Malcolm's memory, his legacy. What does it matter if he slept with some girl thirty years ago? He did the right thing. He made sure that Andrew came to him and that he was a good father. Why destroy that now? And Andrew, he looked up to his father so much. He became a lawyer because Malcolm was a lawyer. It was just a little bit of money she wanted. That was all. What's a little bit of money compared to my son's memory of his father?"

"How much?" Josie asked.

Sophia folded her arms over her chest.

"How much?"

"Twenty thousand," Sophia muttered.

"Jesus," Josie said. "You gave her twenty thousand dollars?"

"It was a small price to pay."

"Why did she come back? Why is she here? Why now?"

Sophia said, "She wouldn't say, but I think she might be sick. She didn't look well. I asked her the same thing you're asking. All these years. I thought all of that was behind me. She said she had some scores to settle and she didn't have much time left. I said, 'Time for what?' and she said that wasn't my business."

"Where is she?" Josie asked. "Where is Lila now?"

Again, Sophia looked all around the room, refusing to settle her gaze on Josie. She was like a small child. If she didn't look directly at Josie, maybe Josie wouldn't acknowledge her.

"Tell me!" Josie snapped.

Finally, Sophia sighed. She walked over to a table near the back of the foyer and picked up a purse. "I'll take you to her."

"Just tell me," Josie said.

"It's pretty remote," Sophia said. "If she sees just you and not me, she's likely to bolt—or come after you."

Josie didn't want Sophia coming along, but she couldn't argue with that logic. If there was even the smallest chance of finding Lila and rescuing Trinity, Josie had to take it. "Fine," she said, "but I'm driving."

CHAPTER 71

They drove in silence, broken only by Sophia giving Josie directions to an old abandoned textile mill near the Susquehanna River. She parked the Camry along the access road and went to search the trunk for a flashlight. She made a show of riffling through the array of items that filled Sergeant Lamay's trunk while Sophia waited in the passenger seat so that she could fire off a quick text to Noah. If Lila and Trinity were there, she would need backup.

Textile mill with Bowen, she sent. He would figure it out.

The two of them walked along the old access road in darkness with only the moonlight to illuminate their way. If Lila was on one of the upper floors, Josie didn't want her to spot the bobbing flashlight beam. Sophia, in two-inch heels, kept stumbling along the cracked asphalt. "Slow down," she hissed at Josie.

"No," Josie said simply. "You keep up."

By the time they reached the southern entrance of the mill, Sophia was sweating and huffing out breaths. Josie stared up at the behemoth—five floors of old yellowing brick and smashed-out windows like empty eye sockets staring down at them. Josie felt a tickle along the back of her neck. "Where is she?" she asked Sophia.

"The third floor," Sophia answered. "That's all I know. This is where she said she was staying."

For twenty thousand dollars, Lila could have done a lot better, but not many places would let you keep a hostage on the premises. "You go first," Josie said, and she pushed Sophia through the creaky doors.

Once inside, she turned on the flashlight and swept it around the cavernous room. Broken glass, garbage, and other debris littered the floors. Old equipment sat abandoned like dilapidated sentries. A rat scurried just out of view as they walked through the place looking for the stairwell.

"Over here," Sophia said, pointing to a set of double doors to their left. Graffiti and rust marred the paint on the doors, and a blackish fluid leaked from the wall above, over the door handles, and onto the floor. "Open it," Josie said.

In the peripheral glow of the flashlight, Josie saw the look of disdain that Sophia gave her as she riffled in her purse. "We don't have time for this," Josie said.

A tissue appeared in her hand, and she used it to cover the doorknob before pulling it open. The door groaned behind them as they entered the stairwell. In the silence of the huge building, it sounded like the roar of a jet. The concrete steps crumbled beneath their feet, and Sophia stumbled again, grasping desperately for the railing. Josie kept the flashlight pointed ahead and her ears pricked for any sounds above them. They had gone up two flights of steps when Josie suddenly realized that she no longer heard Sophia's labored breath behind her.

Instinctively, her free hand reached for her gun, but of course it wasn't there. She curled both hands around the long handle of the flashlight, but it was too late. She was yanked back by her shoulder, down the steps, tumbling into darkness.

CHAPTER 72

Josie fell and fell until she stopped with a thud on the landing they'd just cleared. The back of her head ached, and her right wrist throbbed. Searching around her in the dark, she realized she'd lost the flashlight. It must have broken on impact, because not even its beam was in sight. Feeling her way along the wall, Josie found the railing and pulled herself to her feet. Pain shot through her left ankle, and she stopped for a moment to try and listen over her thundering heartbeat for Sophia. Then she felt the cold, steel circle of a gun barrel against her cheek, and Sophia's icy voice in her ear.

"Don't move."

Josie put her hands in the air even though she wasn't even sure that Sophia could see her. She blinked several times, trying to acclimate her eyes to the absolute darkness of the stairwell. High above them on one of the upper flights of stairs, a thin shaft of moonlight crept in through one of the broken windows.

"If this is about your secrets," Josie said, "no one is going to hear them from me. I'm only interested in stopping Lila."

"Oh, this is about my secrets all right, but not the ones you think."

Josie shifted her face fractionally, nudging the barrel of the gun back slightly toward her ear. She could just make out Sophia's angry glittering eyes in her periphery. "You sure you know how to use that gun?" she asked.

Sophia pushed the barrel hard into Josie's cheekbone. "A rich old lady, living alone? You're goddamn right I know how to use this."

Josie didn't doubt her. "What is Andrew going to think if his mother kills the chief of police?"

"He's going to think I had no choice. Don't you worry. I'll cover this up just like I covered up Belinda's murder. Except this time, the secrets will stay buried."

Josie felt a cold shock go through her. "What are you talking about? You killed Belinda?"

"Of course I did," Sophia spat. "She was a whore, pretending to be my friend while she screwed around with my husband."

Playing for time, Josie asked, "You said you left the courthouse long before she died. You had Andrew. Did you know then that he was Belinda's?"

"I didn't know anything. I was blissfully unaware of what a disgusting pervert my husband was. Did you know he screwed every young woman who came into that courthouse? I think he even had an affair with Lila, but I could never prove it. I had no idea what he was doing. Belinda and I were good friends. Great friends. I trusted her, and I believed him when he told me he was trying to be a father figure to her."

With each word, Sophia dug the barrel of the gun deeper into Josie's cheekbone. Josie lowered her hands slowly and tried to shift away from Sophia, but she clamped a hand down hard on Josie's shoulder. Josie had to keep her focused on her story and not on the gun she was holding to Josie's head.

"You really believed your husband was trying to help Belinda because she was a foster kid?" Josie asked.

Sophia humphed. "I was young and stupid. I loved my husband, and I wanted to believe him. Then Belinda disappeared for a few months, and when she came back, she started seeing that teacher, Mr. Todd. She was more reserved those days, but we were still friends, so she confided in me—every detail about her relationship with Todd. I didn't think there was anything to worry about between her and Malcolm."

"But then Andrew came along," Josie said. She tried to take a step, and Sophia, lost in tales of the past, moved with her.

"Yes, Malcolm came home and said he had seen a little boy who was up for adoption and fallen in love with him—would I adopt? We could do for this little boy what no one had done for my good friend, Belinda. Well, I met little Andrew, and I just fell in love with him. I was living the dream. A full-time mother. No more typing and getting coffee for these asshole judges and lawyers. Answering phones and filing. So tedious and boring."

"If you didn't know that Belinda was ever even pregnant, how did you find out about the affair?" Josie asked. The barrel of the gun had slid slightly, and she could feel Sophia's hand tire with the effort of holding it up for so long.

"It was Valentine's Day, 1984. Malcolm was working late. I put little Andrew into the stroller and walked him in the cold over to the courthouse. Pushed him right up to Malcolm's chambers' doors, and then I heard them. I heard them…screwing. I hid in the stairwell and looked through the window in the door, waiting to see who it was. Imagine my shock when Belinda walked out of Malcolm's office, looking rosy-cheeked and satisfied with her buttons done up wrong."

So Belinda had broken off her affair with Lloyd and Damon Todd's father to pick back up where she'd left off with Malcolm Bowen.

Sophia lowered the gun to Josie's waistline as she spoke, reducing the pressure and seemingly taking some pleasure from getting it all out at last. "I didn't confront them. What would be the point? I hustled the baby home, put dinner on the table, and tried to get on with my life. But I just couldn't forget." She paused for a moment, taking herself back. "A few weeks later, I visited the courthouse during regular hours and ran into Lila. She could tell something was wrong immediately, so we went outside for a smoke break, just like old times, and I told her that I had seen Malcolm and Belinda. She said that she suspected he was probably screwing her before she'd disappeared too. Two years he was carrying on with that girl. That nobody. We had only been married for three."

"So you decided to take matters into your own hands," Josie prompted as, distracted by her memories, Sophia let the gun fall to her side. Relief flooded through Josie at having the barrel of the gun finally pointed away from her. She dared not make a move and break the trance. Noah and the cavalry would be there any minute.

"It was Lila's idea," Sophia explained. "She came up with a plan to lure Belinda out to a playground on the outskirts of Bellewood. She thought I'd just confront her, maybe throw a few punches. But when I saw her there, I just lost it. Two years. Right under my nose. Malcolm probably only adopted Andrew so he could get me away from the courthouse and they could carry on more freely. I hit her."

"With what?" Josie thought she heard the sounds of cars over asphalt, but she couldn't be sure. "With what?" she repeated.

"It was a bar from one of the jungle gyms; there was some storm damage and one of them had broken down. Belinda kept going on about how Malcolm loved her more than me, and that it was only a matter of time before he got rid of me. She would be eighteen in six months—all she had to do was wait, and then he would divorce me, take the baby, and start a whole new happy family. I didn't even know that Andrew was *her* baby until that moment. The lies. My God, the lies. I picked up the bar and…I didn't mean to kill her."

"But you did. How did she get buried in Denton?"

"Lila took her. We put her in Lila's trunk, and she said she would help me cover it up if I helped her with something else."

"Helped her how?" Josie asked.

"She wanted money. She said her boss was…molesting her. She needed to get away. So I agreed. She took Belinda's body and the money, and I never heard from her again. Until last month."

"You didn't give her money," Josie said. "Your husband did. What did you tell him to get him to pay her off?"

"I told him everything. He had a choice: turn me in and become the judge whose wife murdered his underage mistress, or pay Lila and make the entire thing go away forever."

"He chose his reputation."

A loud bang sounded from below them, followed by shouts. In the moonlight, Sophia's eyes gleamed with anger. She raised the gun back to Josie's face. "What did you do? Who did you call?"

Josie didn't answer. Instead, she turned toward the gun, knocking it out of Sophia's hand and punching Sophia square in the face. Sophia stumbled backward, crying out as she fell. Josie dropped to her knees, searching frantically around the debris-strewn landing for the gun. One of Sophia's hands clamped around Josie's damaged ankle, making her cry out in pain. Josie kicked out, but Sophia had already pulled herself up and was looming over Josie. In her hand was the gun that Josie was searching for. She held it by the barrel, and before Josie had a chance to react, she brought it down hard onto Josie's head.

The stairwell tilted, and Sophia's shadowy form went out of focus. Josie tried to stand, but her legs wouldn't work. Next thing she knew, Sophia's hands were under her armpits, pulling her up the flight of steps she had just tumbled down. Josie willed her limbs to fight back, but there was no response.

She was dragged quickly through a side door, and the sounds of boots pounding along concrete and the shouts she had heard earlier faded. The moonlight was brighter on the third floor, but still, Josie couldn't seem to get her vision to clear. "Stop," she mumbled. But Sophia kept dragging her along; she was surprisingly strong. Finally she dropped her, and Josie rolled onto her back. A giant soft-flow dye machine loomed over her, a vast network of piping, nozzles, and pumps surrounding a massive cylinder so large that one would need a ladder to climb to the top of it. The tubular chamber had long since rusted, leaving a gash down the middle of it. Josie watched as Sophia slipped in and out of focus, poking her head into the jagged opening of the cylinder and turning back for Josie.

"No," Josie said, her heart hammering. "I can't…" she tried. "I can't go in there."

Sophia ignored her plea, dragging her closer and lifting and pushing her uncooperative body through the hole in the dye machine. The jagged metal edges of the hole scraped against Josie's back, pinching through her jacket and T-shirt and painfully scraping away skin. Her arms and legs tried again to fight Sophia off, but Sophia seemed to be everywhere at once inside the cylinder, pulling her deeper into the darkness.

"I can't..." Josie tried again.

Sophia laid her out flat on the cold rusted metal and lay down beside her. When Josie tried to speak again, Sophia clamped a hand over her mouth. "Now shut up," she told Josie, "'cause we're going to be here awhile."

Panic burned through every cell in Josie's body. She tried to get her bearings, to hold onto some piece of herself that understood that the darkness couldn't hurt her—just as Ray had always told her—but she couldn't. She was a young girl again, in the closet, spinning and falling through a dark abyss without end.

"I said shut up," Sophia hissed, pressing her palm more firmly over Josie's mouth. As Josie's breath came faster and faster, her hands reached up, trying to pry Sophia's hand away from her face. Sophia took her hand away momentarily, but all that came out of Josie's mouth was a high-pitched noise—she was hyperventilating. Josie felt her arms being tucked against her sides, then she felt Sophia straddle her, pinning her in place and settling her weight across Josie's middle. Sophia's hand was across Josie's mouth again. Josie's chest burned with the effort of trying to take something more than the short, shallow gasps of sheer panic. With each moment that passed, she took in less and less air.

Finally, mercifully, she passed out.

CHAPTER 73

Josie was awoken by the intense pounding in her head, like someone was driving spikes into her temples. She dared not open her eyes as her mind searched for some thread that would lead her back to reality. Where was she? How had she gotten there? Where was she last?

She focused on her senses. Her mouth was painfully dry, her lips pasted together. It seemed as though every inch of her body ached. It only took a small attempt at movement to realize she was hog-tied—hands tied behind her back and then bound to her feet, which bent behind her, her heels pressing into her buttocks. The air around her was warm though, and her cheek rested against something surprisingly soft.

Not the dye machine.

Then it came back to her: Sophia Bowen, the textile mill, her team breaching the doors on the first floor, the struggle in the stairwell, being stuffed into the bowels of the old machine. How many hours had Josie spent in there? The very thought brought bile to the back of Josie's throat, and she choked out a series of coughs. Her eyes snapped open. She was lying on a carpeted floor, her face next to what looked like a bed—the box spring set right onto the floor without a frame. Sunlight streamed from somewhere overhead, though she couldn't turn her body to see.

For just a moment, she was so grateful to be out of the dark hole Sophia had put her into, she thought she might cry. Taking several deep breaths, she tested her restraints again. She was stuck, everywhere except her head, which she lifted and turned in the

other direction, coming face to face with Trinity Payne, whose
swollen, bruised face lay inches from hers. Dried blood crusted at
the corner of her lips, her nose looked crooked and smashed, and
a wheezing sound came from her as she breathed.

Josie felt a surge of relief, despite their circumstances. If she was
breathing, Trinity was still alive. Josie called her name a few times,
but she didn't stir. Josie wiggled closer, trying to touch some part of
her face against Trinity's, but she could barely move. She puckered
her lips and blew air at Trinity's face. After the fourth or fifth try,
Trinity's mouth twisted, and her eyelids fluttered open as far as they
could. Trinity attempted to speak, but nothing came out. Licking
her lips, she tried again, her voice scratchy but audible this time.
"What are you doing here?"

"Where is here?" Josie asked.

"I don't know," Trinity said. "I'm not sure."

"I saw you on video at the body shop."

Josie thought she saw a tear leak from the corner of one of
Trinity's eyes. "I didn't want to do it. She made me."

"Lila?"

Trinity made an attempt at shaking her head but stopped immediately, wincing and sucking in a sharp breath. "Barbara Rhodes."

The name was familiar. Why did Josie know that name?

"How did she get you to do it?" Josie asked.

"First she called me and said she had a story for me—the fire
that killed my sister. She said she had proof of who'd really set
it—someone from the cleaning service my mom used—then she
hinted that my sister wasn't really dead."

"My God," Josie said.

"I didn't want to upset my mom in case it was bullshit, but she
knew things, details I only ever heard my parents talk about. She
made me meet her a few blocks away from the hotel. Said I had to
walk, no car, no bag—she was afraid I'd hide a weapon—and she
made me promise I wouldn't bring my phone. She said she didn't

want me recording her or sending information from my phone until she knew she could trust me. She said she would give me ten minutes, and if I wasn't there in time, she would be gone forever. I thought she might be dangerous, but when I showed up, she was just this fat old lady. She wasn't even armed, and she was so nice. I didn't think she was…"

Trinity broke off as a cough erupted from her body, spraying blood from her lips onto Josie's face. "Sorry," Trinity said as the coughing fit receded.

"It's okay," Josie said. "You didn't think Barbara was a threat?"

"Right," Trinity said. "I got in her car, and we started driving. She mentioned some diner, and I knew the one she was talking about, so I thought it was okay. When it became apparent that she wasn't taking me there, I confronted her. That's when she told me that if I wanted the story, I had to do something for her."

"You killed Ted Heinrich for a story?" Josie couldn't keep her voice from rising.

Trinity looked as though she was trying to shake her head. "Not a story—and I didn't kill anyone. When she told me what she wanted me to do, I told her she was crazy. I told her to pull over and let me out; I'd walk back to my hotel. She pulled over. I got out. But she came after me. We were on this quiet little mountain road. No one around. We had a fight. She won. I woke—I don't know where. Could have been here. Tied up. She told me I would do what she said, or my family would die. She had help, Josie. She was facetiming with some guy who was outside my parents' house. She told me if I didn't do exactly what she said, she would kill them all. My parents and my little brother."

"How old is your brother?"

"He's only sixteen. This guy was following him around. Taking photos of him. I don't know who he was, but I was terrified, so I did what she said. She drove for what seemed like hours and then parked a block away from the body shop. Some other guy pulled up in an Escape. She told me to get in, drive to the body shop, and go inside. As soon as they left me alone in it, I checked the glove compartment. It was your car. I knew then that whatever she was doing had something to do with hurting you. Then when I got inside the body shop, she was already there. She came in through another entrance—in the back. The owner was already tied up. He was in bad shape. She made me watch while she tortured him. She said if I tried to run away, that's what would happen to Patrick. She told me to drive back to her car, and her friend would take the Escape off my hands. He tied me back up, put me in her trunk, and left in your car. I was in there for hours just trying to figure out why they were involving you. Why both of us? Then I thought about why she'd contacted me in the first place—telling me my sister might still be alive. There's always been such a resemblance between us. Surely you've noticed it too?" There was a hopefulness to Trinity's voice.

"Yeah," Josie said. "I noticed."

"So then I thought maybe what she said was true—that someone from the cleaning service burned our house down and took my sister. And maybe my sister was really alive after all. And…and maybe it was you."

Only a DNA test would tell them for sure, but Josie felt in her heart and her gut that Trinity was right. They were sisters. "What's my…what's my real name?" Josie asked.

Something that looked like a smile stretched across Trinity's battered face. "Vanessa. Vanessa Anabelle Payne."

Josie groaned. "I like Josie better."

"Very funny."

It was still too much to wrap her head around. Her entire life was a lie. She'd been taken from her family and raised in poverty by a woman whose cruelty knew no bounds. All the while, her actual family was only two hours away in an affluent small town, mourning her loss. Every time she thought about it, the room seemed to spin.

She brought the subject back to Heinrich. "This woman—did she tell you why she was targeting the man in the body shop?"

"No. She just said I shouldn't feel sorry for him. I tried to stop her, but she said if anything happened to her, her friends would hurt Patrick. I should have tried harder. I should have tried to save that man." Tears leaked from Trinity's eyes. A bloody snot bubble popped in her nostril.

"It's okay," Josie said. "It's okay. You did the right thing."

"It was disgusting. The smell. She made me watch."

"Stop crying," Josie said as more liquid leaked from Trinity's nose. "You can barely breathe as it is. I need you to keep it together."

"I can't," Trinity blubbered.

"You can, and you will. We need to find a way out of this."

"Yeah, right. How are we going to get out of this?"

"Have you tried shouting for help?" Josie wondered.

"How do you think my face got like this?" Trinity replied.

Again, Josie tested her bindings, but there was little give. Already in the short time she had been awake, her shoulders and legs began to ache.

"She's not going to leave us here like this," Josie said. "At some point she's going to have to move us. That will be our chance."

"Not if she's got one of her friends with her."

Josie didn't respond. Somewhere nearby, a door banged open and closed. Muffled female voices traveled toward them, getting increasingly clearer.

"Don't ever summon me again." The sound of Lila's voice after so many years sent a shudder through Josie's body.

The second voice was Sophia's. "I had no choice. If it weren't for you, I wouldn't be in this damn mess. We had a deal, and you went back on it when you showed back up here, so I'll summon you whenever I please."

Josie heard what was most definitely a slap, then a gasp, and what sounded like a tussle—grunts and thuds and then glass breaking. So, Lila had come to the mill and helped Sophia transport her.

"…and I'll use it. Get away from me. Get back…" It was Sophia. The sounds of struggle had stilled. Josie imagined she must have pulled her gun. Sophia added, "Now, you'll clean up this mess you made, and you'll leave Denton once and for all."

"Not without my money," Lila said.

Josie expected Sophia to protest or threaten Lila some more, but all she said was, "Fine. Come see me after you've finished whatever this is you're doing."

"Oh, I've got a few more people to visit after this," Lila said.

"Why? Why are you doing this? Why can't you leave the past in the past?" Sophia cried.

"Because I ain't got much time left."

"What did these people ever do to you?" Sophia asked.

"They think they're better than me, that's what. I'm through being treated like dirt."

There was a heavy sigh. Then Sophia said, "You're paranoid. No one thinks they're better than you, and that's not a reason to ruin people's lives."

"Says the hoity-toity bitch who lied and paid me off to keep her and her husband's reputation clean," Lila shot back. "Now put that thing away."

There was a beat of silence. Then Sophia said, "Malcolm told me what was in your file before he destroyed it. He and Mrs. Ortiz had quite the shock over it."

Lila's voice was hard and menacing. "You better leave now before I change my mind about killing you."

CHAPTER 74

Josie waited for Lila to come into the room where she and Trinity were sandwiched between a bed and the wall, but she didn't come. Trinity fell back to sleep, her broken nose whistling. Josie racked her brain, trying to figure out where Lila would be keeping them, her mind still addled from the pistol-whipping Sophia had given her. She couldn't tell if hours or minutes were passing. She thought about calling out to Lila, but she didn't want to draw her attention until she had some kind of plan. She was just drifting off when the sound of a phone ringing came from another room. Again, she heard Lila's voice. "Hello? Yeah, this is Barbara. Okay, I'll be right over." Then there was the sound of a door slamming. Lila had gone out.

Again, Josie wondered why the name Barbara was so familiar to her. Then she remembered arriving at the trailer park the day the Price boys had found human remains. The neighbor who had been watching them, who had called 911, was named Barbara Rhodes. Josie hadn't met her because she'd already been interviewed and sent home by the time Josie got there.

Belinda Rose. Barbara Rhodes.

"Son of a bitch," Josie said. She wiggled closer to Trinity, rocking her body from side to side until one of her elbows nudged Trinity. "Wake up. Trinity, wake up!"

Had Lila been under Josie's nose all along, now posing as Barbara Rhodes? Noah had interviewed her the day they found the bones and not long after seen the sixteen-year-old photo of Lila Jensen that Dex had given her. Why hadn't Noah made the connection? Trinity had said Barbara was overweight and old. It had been sixteen years; perhaps Lila looked markedly different.

"Trinity," Josie said. "I think I know where we are. I think we're in the trailer park."

Trinity stirred with a soft moan but didn't wake up.

"Trinity. Wake. Up. Lila's out. We're in the trailer park. I think we should scream. Someone might hear us."

Josie thought of the little Price boys living next door with their mother. She took in a deep breath and started screaming at the top of her lungs. She screamed until her throat ached and her lungs could take no more, periodically falling silent to listen for anyone who might be coming. There was nothing.

Trinity's voice was barely audible. "No one will hear you. Don't waste your time."

Josie knew she was right. Josie had grown up in this very park, and no one had heard her screams then either. Or if they had, they hadn't come to her rescue. "If she hears you," Trinity added, "she'll hurt you."

"She's already hurt me," Josie said and filled her lungs to scream some more.

CHAPTER 75

She shouted until there was barely anything left of her voice. Next to her, Trinity wept. At long last, as her cries receded into helpless croaks, Josie heard a door open and close, and heavy footsteps approach. She heard another door swish open, and the air in the tiny room changed. Josie's heart paused, and then kicked back into motion. "Josie," Trinity whispered. "I think I wet myself."

"Shhh," Josie said. "I'm going to get us out of this."

Josie had to crane her neck to see a fat pair of ankles beneath the hem of a white cotton dress approach. She had just enough time to notice Lila's feet were crammed into a pair of ugly, black flats before she was yanked up by the bicep and tossed onto the bed. She fell on her back, her hands and feet crushing painfully beneath her. Lila's face loomed above her.

Josie saw immediately why Noah had not recognized her, how he couldn't possibly have recognized her as the woman in the photo Dex had given her. Now in her sixties, Lila Jensen's long, silky black hair had gone shock white. Gone was the sheen, replaced by a straggly mane of thick, dry strands that tumbled down her back. She had gained weight. A lot of weight. Her flesh spilled out from the shapeless white dress draped over her form. Her once smooth, youthful, pale skin was stretched taut from the added pounds, her cheeks so chubby they seemed to swallow her eyes. Sophia had said Lila was sick, and Lila herself had said she didn't have much time. Josie wondered with what. Cancer perhaps?

"Little JoJo," Lila said.

It was the eyes that gave her away, though. They narrowed as Lila smiled the smile that had filled Josie with unbridled terror for as long as she could possibly remember. The little girl inside of her recoiled, but the adult inside her—the chief of police—fought back.

"My name is Josie," she said.

Lila cackled. "No. It's not. That's not even your name." She kicked out a leg, and Josie heard Trinity grunt. "Hey princess, what's your little bitch sister's name again?"

There was only the sound of Trinity weeping.

"Why are you doing this?" Josie asked, trying to draw Lila's attention away from Trinity. "Why did you do it? You took away my life. Everything. My real mother thought I was dead. My whole family. Why?"

"Why not?" Lila said.

"You could have walked away," Josie said. "At any time."

Lila's face flushed, and her eyes glowed with anger. She pointed a pudgy finger to her chest. "You think I get to walk away from this life? Is that what you think? That I ever had a chance to walk away? All those godawful foster homes with their degenerate foster parents? What a joke. I wanted to walk away. I wanted to run, but I couldn't. Everyone else got two parents, money, loving homes. Bullshit. I got nothing. Even that slut, Belinda. She got to live in a nice foster home with a woman who loved and protected her girls. What did I get? Every shitty home I went to, someone hurt me, and no one did a damn thing about it. When I left the homes, it didn't stop. Why should other people get to live perfect lives while I get shit on over and over and over again?"

Josie watched in perfect stillness as spittle flew from Lila's mouth. She had a feeling that Lila had been waiting a very long time to unleash that particular tirade. When she finished, Josie asked, "But why *me*? Why did you take me?"

"Because I could. You were there. I kept waiting for the police to come for you, and they never did. Then I didn't know what the hell to do with you, so I came and found Eli. I knew he would take care of you if I told him you were his. Except he went and fell in love with you, didn't he?"

"He thought he was my father," Josie said. It hurt to say it out loud; Eli Matson was the only father she had ever known. Her memories were old and out of focus now, but what she remembered most about her father was how much he had loved her and how safe she had felt whenever she was with him.

"He was mine. He was supposed to love me more," Lila said. "After I gave him the baby he so desperately wanted, he turned against me, he hated me in return. How's that for sense?"

Josie remembered her father uttering those words in the hospital after her mother had taken a knife to her face: "I hate you." The battle for Josie had started a while before that, but that was the first time she'd ever heard him say those words. Other memories came flooding back to Josie. The conversation she had heard from her bedroom the night her father killed himself was eerily similar to the exchange she had heard earlier between Lila and Sophia when they had been arguing—suddenly Lila's tone changed completely, became calmer and a little nervous. Josie's skin prickled, goosebumps erupting all over her flesh. She might not have believed it before, but after what she had learned about Lila in the last few weeks, there was no doubt in her mind now that she was capable of something that unthinkable.

"Did you kill my father?" Josie asked quietly.

Lila laughed. "Took you long enough to figure that one out. A fine detective you are."

"Why?" Josie asked, incredulous. "You could have left me with him and gone away. Started over somewhere else. And my gram—" Here Josie's voice cracked, thinking of the grief and confusion that Lisette had carried around with her for decades, thinking Josie's father had given up on them.

"You're not listening to me, little JoJo," Lila said. "He got what he deserved. He betrayed me. He said he loved me, but he didn't.

I didn't mean to kill him. Not at first. But then we were walking out in the woods to 'work things out' after I showed him the gun I got from Zeke, and I just did it. I waited for the police to arrest me, but they believed me when I said it was a suicide."

"And you kept me because you didn't want Lisette to have me," Josie said.

"You were a little bitch, but you had your uses," she replied, smirking.

"Until my grandmother paid you to leave. Why did you come back? Why after all these years did you feel the need to ruin my life? And Trinity's?"

Lila glanced down to where Trinity lay at her feet. "Two years ago, I'm sitting in the waiting room of a doctor's office watching the TV. There the two of you were—being interviewed about all the 'good' you did up in those mountains. You're a famous police chief. The other one is a famous reporter. Then they call me back to the exam room and tell me I've got cancer. That's not how things were supposed to end." She kicked out again, and Josie heard Trinity yelp. "And this bitch. Every time I turned on the television, I saw her face. Your face. I couldn't go without making sure you knew what it felt like to be me. You don't get a happy ending while my insides rot to hell."

"Then why did you dig up Belinda?" Josie asked. "It was you, wasn't it? You got the boys to find her. That's why there were so many foxholes."

Lila nodded. "Took those little idiots a week. I didn't think they'd ever find her. I needed money."

"You squeezed Sophia Bowen for twenty thousand," Josie pointed out.

"Yeah, but there's this experimental treatment I could get if I had enough money. It might be my only chance. I can't get that much from Sophia. Maybe close to it, but it wouldn't be enough. I pulled every con I could think of, but I was running out of time.

Then I remembered Belinda kept saying she had a big payday—she just had to cash it in. She always said that. She begged for me to help her when Sophia was after her, and she said she would share it with me. I didn't pay her any mind back then. She was a stupid kid. But then I remembered that locket she always wore, and I thought, 'Holy shit, did I miss that?' Sophia always said it was cheap costume jewelry, but I got to wondering, what the hell was Belinda always talking about? Did she mean the locket? So yeah, I paid a couple of kids to dig her up."

"You have the locket," Josie said.

"I tried to sell it, but turned out Sophia was right. It was cheap costume jewelry. All it had inside was a lock of hair. Stupid bitch. All that for nothing."

It must have been Andrew Bowen's hair. Judge Bowen had given Belinda the locket and had obviously promised he would take care of Andrew. The "payday" Belinda had bragged about was what she could get by threatening to expose the judge.

"Anyway," Lila said, "I think I can get it from Sophia now, especially after that business in the mill the other night. I saved her ass again. I depleted my funds with these little projects of mine." At that, she laughed again and reached down, pulling Trinity upward. "The drug lackeys around here got expensive since I was here last."

Trinity cried out in pain as Lila dragged her toward the door. "What are you doing?" Josie asked, unable to keep the panic out of her voice. "Where are you taking her?"

Lila dropped her onto her side, and Trinity's body made a loud thud. Her strangled cries turned into an angry shout. "Leave me alone, you old twisted bitch!"

"What are you going to do with her?" Josie asked.

"You'll be joining her soon enough," Lila answered. She bent toward Trinity, eliciting more screams from her, and slowly untied her feet. She pulled Trinity upright, but she fell down immediately, her legs useless from having been tied in the same position for so many hours. "You better learn to walk real quick, princess," Lila told her. When Trinity's legs collapsed under her once more, Lila sighed, slid her arms under Trinity's armpits, and dragged her out of the room.

Josie's chest felt like it was being crushed. "Trinity!" she screamed.

"Josie!" came the answer.

There was a series of grunts and a couple of thumps, the front door opening and closing again, and then silence.

Lila was going to kill Trinity.

Josie opened her mouth and started bellowing at the top of her lungs once more.

CHAPTER 76

Josie had no sense of how much time had passed, but suddenly a face floated above her. Not Lila. A boy. It took her panicked brain a moment to process what she was seeing. She tried to remember which boy was which. The shaggy-haired one was older. Was he Troy or Kyle?

"Kyle?" she croaked.

He nodded. In his hands, he held a long gun with the words RED RYDER emblazoned on the stock. A BB gun. His simultaneous innocence and bravery brought tears to her eyes. "Can you untie me?"

He nodded again. Carefully he placed the gun onto the bed next to her and helped her turn onto her stomach so he could work at her bindings. He struggled for several minutes, until Josie could feel hot drops of sweat falling from his face and landing on her arms. "Go get a knife," she told him. "From the kitchen."

Wordlessly, he left and came back, then started gently sawing away at the ropes. Both of them kept silent, listening for Lila to return. Her hands came free first, allowing her to flip onto her back and stretch her legs out in agony and ecstasy. Kyle handed her the knife, and she quickly sawed through the ropes binding her feet. "Thank you," she told him.

He snatched the gun up from the mattress and motioned toward the door. Josie couldn't help but smile. He wanted to go in front of her, to protect her. "I'll go first," she said. Then she stood up and fell right to the floor. She hadn't been bound as long as Trinity, but her legs were numb and weak. Kyle helped her stand and tucked himself under her left arm. Together, they hobbled out to the living room of the trailer, where they found a kitchen table covered with fast food wrappers and prescription pill bottles. On the couch sat a laptop and two cell phones.

Outside it was dark, with only the golden glow of the exterior light over the Price trailer's front door. The air was cool, and after several deep breaths, Josie's head started to clear. Leaning on Kyle, she flexed and tested each leg until she could stand.

Kyle pointed to the dark wooded area across the street. "They went into the woods. Come on."

He took a few steps toward the forest and stopped, turning back to her. "Aren't you coming?"

Josie wanted to squeeze him, but instead she smiled again. "Kyle," she said. "Thank you for saving me, but I can take it from here. I do need your help with one more thing though. I need you to go inside, wake up your mom, and have her call 911. Tell them that your neighbor was holding two kidnapped women next door—a reporter and the chief of police—and tell them she took us into the woods. Can you do that?"

He nodded solemnly.

Josie laid a hand on his shoulder. "And then I need you to stay here and wait for the police, okay? So you can point them in the right direction."

"I can do it," he assured her.

"Thank you," Josie said. She waited until he was inside the trailer before she took off into the moonlit woods.

CHAPTER 77

Josie's muscle memory kicked in the moment her feet hit the trail. When she and Ray were teenagers, they had met in the woods during the night countless times. Her legs carried her into the heart of the forest without conscious thought. She was halfway to where they had found Belinda Rose's remains—where her father had been murdered—when she stopped, trying to steady her breathing and listen for the snap of twigs or the rustle of brush. All that came to her were crickets chirping and the low, mournful hoot of an owl. Her heart was pounding so hard it felt like it might jump right out of her body.

Once her eyes adjusted to the darkness, trees and rocks took shape around her. The moonlight was stronger here than it had been in the warehouse, filtering through the canopy of trees overhead. As quietly as possible, Josie found a nearby rock, hopped onto it, and swung her body up onto the low branch of a tree. Bear-hugging the branch, she used her vantage point to search the nearby forest. She thought she saw the flutter of crime-scene tape from where they had excavated Belinda Rose in the distance. To the left of it was movement, and then she heard what sounded like a wail. Trinity. She was still alive.

Josie lowered herself back down and ran in the direction of the crime scene, her stiff legs working more quickly now. The wail became louder as she approached the hole from which Dr. Feist had excavated Belinda's remains. She slowed to a halt.

Suddenly, pain streaked across the back of her shoulders, and she went tumbling forward into the black hole, landing face-first in a pile of loose dirt. As she rolled to her side, her arm brushed against something fleshy. Feeling around, she found one of Trinity's elbows. Josie's fingers scrabbled over Trinity's prone form, trying to get to her ties. "Trinity!" Josie whispered, clutching the hard knot of her shoulder. "Trinity, I'm here."

Above them, moonlight reflected off Lila's pale face, and the edge of a shovel gleamed in her hands. A pile of dirt hit Josie's face.

She was going to bury them alive.

Josie abandoned her efforts to untie Trinity and struggled to her feet, feeling around the edges of the hole, trying to find a foothold. Her fingers closed over a tree root protruding from the dirt wall, and she put a foot on it and hoisted herself up. Lila was there waiting, the shovel raised high above her head. She brought it down as hard as she could, but Josie rolled to one side, narrowly avoiding it. She stumbled forward, her foot catching on a rock and sending her flailing. She broke her fall with both hands and felt the end of the shovel whiz past her head. Josie scrambled to turn onto her backside as Lila swung the shovel again. Josie kept backing up as fast as she could, fear closing her throat, but the shovel caught her forearm this time, causing a sickening crack and a white-hot streak of pain through Josie's entire arm. Instant nausea rocked her body. Pulling her lifeless arm in close, she shuffled further backward, trying to put some distance between them again.

Lila raised the shovel one more time, laughing maniacally. "Come on, little JoJo. I've been waiting a long time for this. Stop running. Be a good girl."

A pop sounded, and Lila froze. The shovel fell to the ground as her hands flew to the side of her head. "What the hell?" she muttered.

Another pop burst through the night. Then another, and another. Each time, Lila jumped as though startled. Josie spun around, searching the woods for the source, her addled brain taking a moment to figure out what the popping noise was—Kyle Price's BB gun. Josie scrambled to her feet and picked up the

shovel with her good hand. She raced toward Lila and took a
wild swing that made contact with Lila's back—a solid kidney
shot. She fell to the ground. Josie pulled back and swung again
but missed. Lila reached out and wrapped a hand around Josie's
ankle, trying to pull her off balance. Josie brought the shovel
down again. It glanced off Lila's shoulder with just enough force
for her to release Josie's leg.

Josie turned and ran away from her, trying to make her way
back to Trinity.

"Stop, JoJo," Lila gasped. "I'm your mother, remember?"

"You're not my mother," Josie said over her shoulder. "You took
me away from my mother."

"I raised you."

"No, you hurt me, you abused me, you tried to sell me. You're
not a mother."

Lila's voice was getting closer. "I'm the only one you ever had."

"Are you out of your mind? You tried to ruin my life, and you
just tried to kill me."

Josie turned, and Lila was right there. She raised the shovel over
her head, but Lila grabbed it. As they fought over it, Lila changed
tactics, huffing, "I've got money. I'll give you money. Give me the
damn shovel. We'll bury the reporter together and go our separate
ways. No one has to know. Come on, I'm dying. I don't want to
do it in prison."

"I don't give a shit what you want," Josie told her. "It's over.
You're over. You're finished ruining lives. I'm going to make sure
you rot in prison every day for the rest of your shitty life."

Josie won the tug-of-war, sending Lila off balance. She stumbled
backward without falling, and Josie turned away to flee just as one
of Lila's arms shot out, pushing at the small of Josie's back. The
ground rushed toward Josie's face. She dropped the shovel and
tried to break her fall with her good hand. As soon as she hit, she
rolled. She lost sight of Lila, but she kept moving so Lila couldn't

zero in on her. Footsteps sounded close by, but then Josie heard the pop of the BB gun again.

"Knock it off!" Lila shouted.

Pop. Poppoppop.

Getting her bearings, Josie stood again. Lila was turned partially away from her, her eyes searching out the source of the BBs. The shovel hung loosely in one hand. Beyond her, Josie saw two sets of crime-scene tape around the other holes the Price brothers had dug. Holding her broken arm against her side, Josie planted her feet into a runner's starting position, tucked her chin, and bolted as fast as she could. She shoulder-tackled Lila's torso, and the two of them flew through the air into one of the empty holes, Lila's fleshy body cushioning Josie's fall. Josie heard her struggling for air, the wind knocked out of her. Sweat poured off Josie's brow as she struggled with one good arm to turn Lila's body over and push her face into the dirt. She sat on the backs of Lila's legs and screamed for Kyle to go get help.

Flashlight beams cut through the trees. Josie heard shouts and the sound of boots pounding along the forest floor, then Noah's voice, which brought tears to her eyes. "Josie!"

"Here!" she shouted back.

Her staff rushed in. What seemed like a half dozen of them stood over the hole, shining their flashlights down on her. "Trinity's over there," she said. "In the other hole. One of the other holes. She needs help."

"We'll get her," Noah said. Josie heard more boots pounding the ground. Shouting. The night was awash in flashlight beams. Two of her officers climbed into the hole with her and Lila. They secured Lila's hands behind her back and then lifted Josie up, out of the hole, and into Noah's arms.

CHAPTER 78

Josie dozed in a vinyl chair beside the bed they'd given Trinity in Denton's emergency room. Trinity was badly dehydrated, with wounds on her wrists and ankles where Lila had bound her. Her face was swollen and covered in various shades of blue and black and green. Her nose was broken, just as Josie had thought, and a CT scan of her head had revealed a small hematoma, but she wouldn't need surgery. A couple of her ribs were broken, and two of her fingers, but she would survive.

A hand touched her shoulder, and Josie bolted upright, an involuntary cry escaping her lips. "It's okay, Boss," Gretchen said softly. "I told them I'd come get you. You've got to go back for pre-ops now. Noah will be there with you."

Josie's arm was badly broken. She'd undergone a full exam and various x-rays on her arrival in the ER—she would need surgery. The nurses wanted her to wait in her own curtained-off area, but she'd refused, instead keeping vigil by Trinity's bedside. Josie glanced over at her sister and back at Gretchen. "When will her parents be here?"

"Soon," Gretchen said.

Josie stood up and let Gretchen hook an arm through hers, guiding her out into the hallway and off to another set of cold, bright, sterile rooms. Josie was numb and silent as she changed into a hospital gown and let the nursing staff take over. Hands probed her, taking her blood pressure and temperature, sliding in an IV, sending medication into her veins that made her feel relaxed and drowsy. She was grateful for the slow tranquility that overtook her. When Noah appeared by her bedside, she smiled broadly and reached for him with her good hand.

He took it and grinned back at her. "Well," he said, "I see whatever they're giving you is better than Wild Turkey."

She laughed. Or at least she thought she did.

Then they were wheeling her down a long hallway. They passed Trinity's room, and Josie saw Shannon Payne clutching her daughter and weeping into her matted hair. Even in her semi-stupor, Josie was struck by the resemblance between herself and Shannon Payne. How had Lila gotten away with it all those years, passing Josie off as hers? It didn't matter now. The worst was over. Lila was going to prison. Josie closed her eyes, her mind too tired to think.

When she opened them again, she was in a cavernous room filled with people rushing around. The air was freezing. A nurse with a skullcap pressed a vial of medicine into her IV. "I'm gonna ask you to count backward from ten in a minute, hon," she said. "Then you're gonna have the best sleep of your life."

Josie smiled at the nurse. That was exactly what she needed. She opened her mouth to say "ten," but sleep arrived first.

CHAPTER 79

TWO WEEKS LATER

Josie perched on the edge of the hard plastic chair the county jail had provided. The walls of a cubicle closed her in on both sides. Thick glass separated the visitor's room from the inmate room. It wasn't thick enough, Josie thought as Lila Jensen was marched up to the seat across from her. The guard left Lila cuffed and pushed her down into a chair. Lila shot him a dirty look as he said something Josie couldn't make out. He walked off, standing in the corner of the room, hands clasped together at his waist, eyeing Lila like she might jump up and attack someone at any moment. But there were only two other inmates with visitors, and each one of them were seated several slots away.

Lila's face was saggy and yellow. Josie couldn't tell if the jaundice was from the struggle in the woods or because her liver was failing her at last. She had refused to tell the doctors at Denton Memorial where she had been treated for her cancer or what her alias had been before she was Barbara Rhodes. A local oncologist was able to determine that she had ovarian cancer. She'd had at least one surgery, radiation, and chemotherapy, but the cancer had returned, spreading through her body. They gave her two months to live. Josie thought she was just mean enough that she would probably outlive that prognosis—maybe even by years. Josie still wasn't sure what would give her more pleasure—knowing Lila was dead, or knowing she was suffering in prison.

Lila smiled at Josie and picked up the phone receiver on her side of the glass.

Josie's right arm was casted and in a sling, so she used her left hand to pick up her own receiver and press it to her ear.

"Didn't think I'd see you again, JoJo. 'Cept on TV. I'm tired of seeing your face, to tell you the truth."

Josie was tired of seeing her own face on television as well, but it was unavoidable. Trinity was a correspondent for a national news show, and she now had the story of a lifetime. Rumor had it the network was working to find an anchor position for her, so hungry were they for her and Josie's story.

Josie got right to the point. "I want the names of your accomplices."

"What do you mean?" Lila asked.

"You know what I mean. Anyone who helped you with, what did you call it? Your 'projects.' Anyone you paid to place craigslist ads or break into my house or stalk Trinity or her family. Or move Trinity. Or take my car to Ted's Body Shop and then drive it back to where he found it."

Lila laughed, dark blue eyes glittering. "No," she said.

"I can make you more comfortable in here," Josie offered. She hated to do it, hated to even offer it, but what she hated more was the thought of nameless, faceless people all over Denton who had helped Lila carry out her twisted plans.

"Fuck you," Lila said. "You think I'm going to give you your happy ending, JoJo? No, you're not getting it. Not from me. You made a choice out there in those woods. You could have let me go."

"I made a choice?" Josie asked incredulously. "I never had a choice. Ever. You took that away from me when I was only a few weeks old."

"Oh, you want to play that game? Who had the worse childhood? You don't want to know what happened to me."

Josie leaned forward. "You're wrong. I do want to know. Your foster-care file was destroyed. There is nothing left. I don't even know where you came from."

Lila considered this for a moment. Then her hand tightened around the receiver. "I'll tell you what, JoJo. You're a detective, right? Big-time chief of police and all that. I'll give you a clue. You figure it out before I die, and I'll give you those names."

"What is it?" Josie said.

Lila hung up the phone and stood. Behind her, the guard startled, hand on his gun, and took a small step toward her. She leaned forward, opened her mouth wide, and breathed along the glass until it fogged. Then with one finger, she traced a series of letters and numbers into the spot she had made.

OY9555

Then she turned away and signaled to the guard. Josie watched the message fade as Lila Jensen was led back into the bowels of the jail.

CHAPTER 80

Josie dozed on Noah's couch, nestled in a blanket, the remote in her good hand. She was watching *Ally McBeal* reruns while she waited for her pain medication to dull the throbbing in her arm. She had been back to her own house, replaced the kitchen window, repainted her bedroom walls, replaced all the bedding that had been destroyed, and bought a new jewelry box. But she didn't feel right, not as safe as she did right now in Noah's home, where no hungry reporters waited outside, shouting and vying for photos and any comment she might make. At Noah's she felt hidden and out of harm's way. He had assured her that she could stay as long as she needed. He had tried to be there with her as much as possible, but there was so much work to be done to wrap up Lila's case that he was only home a couple of hours at a time.

The remote dropped from her hand when she heard the front door open and close. She blinked the fatigue away and smiled as Noah entered. He grinned back at her, placing the large wooden box in his hands on the coffee table and then planting a kiss on her forehead. "How do you feel?" he asked.

Josie lifted her cast. "Like someone broke my arm with a shovel."

"I'm sorry," Noah said.

Josie shrugged. "It'll heal."

"Did you figure out Lila's message yet?"

She shook her head. "I'll sleep on it. It'll come to me. What's that?"

Noah tapped a hand on the box. "We found this in Lila's trailer. I thought you might want a look at it."

Josie threw the blanket off her lap and lowered her legs to the floor, moving to the edge of the couch. "Silverware?" she asked. The box looked like an old box Lisette used to have where she kept her expensive silverware set. She'd given it to Josie and Ray when she'd moved into Rockview. Josie remembered because she and Ray had argued over it. Josie thought they should use the silverware, because what else would you do with it? Ray thought it was too fancy to use on a regular basis. The box was still sitting unused in Josie's garage.

"No," Noah said. "I mean, I think that's what used to be in here, but now it's—I don't know. You have a look."

Josie reached forward and lifted the lid. The inside was lined with dark-red velvet that was worn in many places. There were several pieces of jewelry, including jewelry that Needle had taken from Josie's home. She sifted through the pieces until she found what she was looking for. Tears filled her eyes as her fingers closed around her old engagement ring, then the pendant Ray had given her when they'd graduated from high school. On a normal day, the sight of them would have been like a spike in her heart, but now they filled her with joy. They were relics from the life she had made in spite of all that Lila had done to her. Symbols of the great loves of her life thus far.

She set them aside and sifted through various newspaper clippings, including one about the Payne house fire. There were also photos—of men, mostly, including Josie's father. There were other trinkets that had little meaning to Josie, whose import she couldn't guess. Belinda Rose's locket was there with the tiny piece of Andrew Bowen's hair inside. "You'll have to get this to Andrew Bowen," Josie said.

"Of course," Noah replied.

She picked up a long purple scarf wrapped around something soft and unraveled it. A gasp escaped her throat. "Oh my God."

In her hands, his small face covered with rust-colored blood stains, was Wolfie.

CHAPTER 81

Josie sat at a table in the back of Komorrah's Koffee, her black hair tied in a ponytail and covered with a baseball cap. She had managed to evade the press, even though she wasn't that far from the police station, where several reporters had taken up residence, hoping to catch someone coming or going who might have information about the sensational Lila Jensen case. It was going to take months for the fervor to die down.

Wind chimes positioned over the front door tinkled as Gretchen entered. Josie smiled and waved her over. Gretchen slid into the booth across from her and pulled a file from inside of her jacket.

"Did you get it?" Josie asked.

Gretchen pushed the file across the table. "Yeah, I got it. It's all there."

Josie's fingers brushed the edge of the folder. "Did you read it?"

"I did."

Josie flagged the waitress over and Gretchen ordered a large coffee. Josie had already purchased several pastries, and she pushed the plate across the table toward Gretchen, spinning it so that the pecan-crusted sweet roll was positioned just under Gretchen's nose. Gretchen eyed the pastry as though she were sizing up an enemy. "We're about to discuss toxic mothers," Josie said. "You're going to need it."

Gretchen laughed and picked it up, taking a hearty bite. A small piece of pecan hung from her bottom lip. "You better have one too, because Lila Jensen's mother is the mother of all toxic mothers."

Josie selected a cheese Danish and ate it in three bites. Gretchen savored her roll more slowly, appraising Josie as she ate. "Have you cried yet?"

Josie shook her head. She wiped her hands on a napkin and sipped her latte.

"You'll need to cry," Gretchen said matter-of-factly. "I mean, just do it. You've got to release some of that pressure."

Josie nodded.

"Did you meet with the Paynes?" Gretchen asked.

"Sort of. They came to the hospital. My grandmother suggested a dinner party. Them and my people. She thinks more of a party atmosphere will be easier for me."

Josie had barely been out of surgery when Shannon and Christian Payne, together with their son, Patrick, had burst into her room. Shannon had gathered Josie up into her arms, holding her, crying and whispering things Josie couldn't remember. Christian and Patrick had hung back, the teenager looking uncomfortable and awkward while his father stood stoically, silent tears streaming down his cheeks. Two days later, Trinity had shown up with a mail-in DNA test, and she and Josie had sat cross-legged on the hospital bed, spitting into tiny vials and laughing like teenagers.

Josie put a palm over the file. "Will you tell me what it says?"

"Of course," Gretchen said. She sipped her coffee and then folded her hands on the edge of the table. "You were right. The clue that Lila gave you was an inmate number. Lila Jensen's mother is serving five life terms in maximum security."

Josie's eyes widened. "Five life terms?"

"She's listed as Roe Hoyt, but that's just the name she was given after she was found."

"What are you talking about?"

"Roe Hoyt lived alone in a shack in the woods high up in Sullivan County. No electricity or running water. The land was technically owned by the state, so she wasn't living on any type of family land. They think the shack was an old game warden building—a place the wardens could stop and take shelter if they found themselves out that far. No one had been out there for years."

Josie asked, "Who found her?"

"Hunters," Gretchen said. "They were put off by her because she didn't talk much except to make noises—one of which was the word roe, which is how she got her name. She was wild-looking, dirty, unkempt. They might have left her alone except she had a little girl."

Josie felt a sinking feeling in her belly. "Lila."

Gretchen nodded. "The hunters said she looked to be about five years old. She was running around the woods buck naked like a feral animal. They tried to take her with them, but she attacked them. So did Roe. So they went back to civilization and got the authorities. Police came and took them both into custody. When they searched the shack, they found the remains of five infants."

"Jesus," Josie said.

"Lila went into foster care. Her first foster mother named her Lila and gave her their last name—Jensen. She was delayed, had a lot of behavioral problems. The Jensens couldn't handle her, so she was shuffled from foster home to foster home. This isn't in that file. I got this from Alona Ortiz. She read Lila's foster-care file before Malcolm Bowen destroyed it."

"She told you?"

"The DA isn't interested in prosecuting Ortiz. She made a deal to tell everything she knows and testify against Lila and Sophia. She was the one who helped Belinda, by the way, the first time she ran away from Maggie Lane's house to have her baby. Bowen paid her off to give Belinda a place to stay until the baby came. Then he made arrangements for Andrew to go into the foster-care system and greased some more palms so he could adopt him. Anyway, everything bad you can imagine happening in a foster home happened to Lila Jensen."

"My God," Josie said.

She tried to picture Lila as a small child. Feral, forced into a world she didn't understand filled with people she couldn't trust. Had she even had a chance?

Gretchen tapped the file. "You can keep this. One day, you'll be ready to open it."

They each sampled another pastry, and the waitress refilled their coffees. Changing the subject, Gretchen asked, "Did Tara talk to you?"

"Yeah. She took me off leave and said that I could return to my post as chief when my medical leave was finished. I told her no."

Gretchen choked on the Danish she'd just stuffed into her mouth. She coughed and spit into a napkin. "What?"

"I don't want to be chief," Josie said. "I never did. Tara only wants me back now so she doesn't look bad for firing me after I found out my whole life is a lie. I told her to appoint another detective position, and I'll go back to doing what I was doing before Chief Harris died."

"What did she say?"

"I don't know," Josie said. "I stopped listening after 'you've got some nerve.'"

Gretchen laughed. "She'll come around."

CHAPTER 82

ONE MONTH LATER

The smells of pasta sauce and garlic bread filled Josie's house. From her place on the living room couch, she could hear the sounds of dishes clinking and the kitchen faucet running. She could hear Ray's mother and Misty talking and laughing, although she couldn't make out what they were saying. Harris was fast asleep on Josie's chest, his head turned toward Lisette, who sat next to Josie on the side of her casted arm, stroking Harris's fine blond hair.

"Smells good," Lisette commented. "Mrs. Quinn said Misty made the pasta herself. Homemade pasta! Who knew the stripper could cook?"

"Gram!" Josie admonished.

Lisette laughed, one arthritic finger stroking Harris's rosy cheek. "You're strange bedfellows, you two."

"I'm just helping her out," Josie said. "She's not so bad. I get to spend lots of time with little Harris here."

A blast of cool air announced Noah's arrival. He closed the front door behind him and looked around, his eyes landing on Josie. He grinned. In his arms was a large bag. "I got three different kinds of wine," he said from the foyer. "I wasn't sure what kind of wine went with meeting your long-lost daughter you thought was dead after thirty years."

"The answer is all of the wine," Josie said.

Noah laughed and headed off to the kitchen. Lisette elbowed Josie, her eyes sparkling. "You're getting to spend a lot of time with that handsome fellow too, aren't you?"

"Slow your roll, Gram, we're still work colleagues."

"So? You don't outrank him anymore, right? You and Ray were married, and you both worked for the Denton PD. It's not an impossible situation."

"Not now, Gram," Josie said, but she couldn't keep the smile off her face. Harris stirred, and Lisette lifted him from Josie's chest, cradling him in her arms. Josie stood and peeked out the windows.

"Don't be nervous," Lisette said.

Josie turned from the window. Not being nervous wasn't an option. It wasn't possible. There were no guidebooks or tutorials for this scenario. She didn't know if spending more time with her blood relatives excited her or terrified her—a little of both, really.

Josie sat back down beside Lisette. "Gram, are you okay with this? Really? I don't have to pursue this."

Lisette raised a brow. "Nonsense. You can't walk away from your family."

"But you—"

Lisette squeezed Josie's knee. "I'll always be your grandmother. You'll always belong to me. But now you'll also be theirs, and that's okay. Truth be told, I'm happy you've found this out."

"Happy?"

Lisette nodded. "I'm not getting any younger, dear."

"Gram."

"One day I'll be gone. That day will be sooner rather than later. I feel at peace knowing you've got people to look after you."

Josie leaned her head against Lisette's shoulder. "Thanks, Gram."

A moment later, the doorbell rang. Josie hopped up and walked into the foyer. She looked back toward the kitchen. Noah, Misty, and Ray's mom stood in the doorway, offering smiles of encouragement.

Josie took a deep breath and opened the door.

A LETTER FROM LISA REGAN

Thank you so much for choosing to read *Her Mother's Grave*. If you enjoyed it, and want to keep up-to-date with all my latest releases, just sign up at the following link. Your email address will never be shared, and you can unsubscribe at any time.

https://lisaregan.com/

Thank you so much for returning to the fictional Pennsylvania city of Denton to follow Josie Quinn on her latest adventure! I hope you'll stick around for more as Josie returns to her position as detective and takes on more exciting cases.

I love hearing from readers. You can get in touch with me through any of the social media outlets below, including my website and Goodreads page. Also, if you are up for it, I'd really appreciate it if you'd leave a review and perhaps recommend *Her Mother's Grave* to other readers. Reviews and word-of-mouth recommendations go a long way in helping readers discover my books for the first time. As always, thank you so much for your support. It means the world to me. I can't wait to hear from you, and I hope to see you next time!

Thanks,
Lisa Regan

LisaRegan.com
Facebook.com/LisaReganCrimeAuthor
Twitter @LisaLRegan

ACKNOWLEDGMENTS

First and foremost, I must thank my amazing readers and faithful fans! Thank you so much for your enthusiasm and passion, and for sticking with me on this wonderful journey. Thank you to my husband, Fred, and daughter, Morgan, for your infinite patience and unending encouragement. Thank you to Nancy S. Thompson, Dana Mason, and Katie Mettner—my first readers and some of the best writing friends an author could ever ask for! Thank you to my parents—William Regan, Donna House, Rusty House, Joyce Regan, and Julie House—for your constant support. Thank you to the following "usual suspects"—people in my life who support and encourage me, spread the word about my books, and generally keep me going: Carrie Butler, Ava McKittrick, Melissia McKittrick, Torese Hummel, Christine & Kevin Brock, Laura Aiello, Helen Conlen, Jean & Dennis Regan, Marilyn House, Tracy Dauphin, Michael Infinito Jr., Jeff O'Handley, Susan Sole, the Funk family, the Tralies family, the Conlen family, the Regan family, the House family, the McDowells, and the Kays. Thank you to Lilly Billarrial for the goody-goody line. Thank you to the lovely people at Table 25 for including me, encouraging me, and teaching me. You know who you are. I'd also like to thank all the lovely bloggers and reviewers who read the first two Josie Quinn books for taking a chance on my work and spreading the word!

Thank you so very much to Sgt. Jason Jay for answering all my law-enforcement questions so quickly and in such great detail that I can get things as close to authentic as fiction will allow.

As always, I must thank Jessie Botterill for her continued brilliance, patience, and faith in me, as well as the entire team at Bookouture. You are miracle workers, all of you, and I feel so blessed and grateful to be working with you.

I'd like to thank the incredible team at Grand Central Publishing for their hard work and everything they've done to bring this series to so many new readers. In particular, thank you to Kirsiah McNamara, Alli Rosenthal, and Ivy Cheng. It's been a dream working with all of you!

ABOUT THE AUTHOR

Lisa Regan is the *USA Today* and *Wall Street Journal* bestselling author of the Detective Josie Quinn series as well as several other crime fiction titles. She has a bachelor's degree in English and a master of education degree from Bloomsburg University. She is a member of Sisters in Crime, International Thriller Writers, and Mystery Writers of America. She lives in Philadelphia with her husband, daughter, and a Boston Terrier named Mr. Phillip.

LisaRegan.com
Facebook.com/LisaReganCrimeAuthor
Twitter @LisaLRegan